Coven

A Soulmark Series

Rebecca Main

www.RebeccaMain.com

www.ViaGraphia.com

TABLE OF CONTENTS

BEGIN AGAIN

- Chapter 1 -

"Congratulations!" I'm swept up into a hug before I can react, though my smile widens nonetheless at Ben's enthusiasm. My laughter joins his as he sets me down and kisses me sweetly on the lips.

"Thank you," I murmur, tucking away a stray curl of dark chocolate hair. It springs back into its wayward place almost immediately, earning a quick chuckle from my boyfriend.

"My superstar graduate!" he exclaims loudly, drawing amused looks from the other families congregated around us.

"Ben!" I try for something akin to a scold but find another giggle escaping instead, as he places another kiss on my lips. This one borders on PG-13.

"Now, now," comes a much sterner voice, "none of that nonsense." I pull back sheepishly, a blush heating me from neck to cheeks as I turn to face Gran. Her silver hair is kept neatly in its natural state, creating a halo around her face. "My baby," she coos, her arms opening to welcome me into her embrace. "I'm so proud of you," she whispers fiercely into my ear, pulling back and gazing at me with her all-knowing gaze. "Family is watching down on you right this very moment, Zoelle Renee Baudelaire. You haven't just made me proud. You've made them proud. I can feel it in the air. Their spirits are surrounding us. Their love reaching out to touch you—feel it, Zoelle. Close your eyes and feel their love, darling."

So I do, and for the most wonderful second, I think I do feel it. Three light pressures were reaching out to touch me and fill me with warmth and love. It's gone all too soon, but tears deign to come regardless of the fleeting feeling. Normally I don't agree with Gran and her notions, our bickering and teasing over our beliefs having softened in the most recent years, but today... today, it means something.

"How long has it been again, Zoey?" Ben asks politely, his tone gentle as he navigates his way into the conversation. I let out the breath I've been holding and dab none too discreetly at my eyes with a weak laugh.

"Fourteen years?"

"Fourteen years." Gran nods resolutely. "But enough of this talk. They're happy for you, and so am I!" she exclaims, instantly brightening the mood as she raises her hands with a lavish wave, her many bracelets tinkling happily along. "My granddaughter, a college graduate of the culinary arts! You've worked so hard for this day. I'm so proud of you."

Her nostalgic look almost has me tearing up again. "Gran." I warn with a laugh and let Ben tug me into his side. Pride shines through her eyes, and I stand a bit taller under her regard. Today I feel unbeatable, and beautiful to boot. Underneath my maroon graduation robe is a delicate white-lace dress that falls just above my knees. One I know will turn Ben's head with its open back and the way it pops against my deep brown skin. Like Gran, I wear my hair in its natural state. The springy curls have an

2

extra bounce today from the black three-inch heels I sport.

"So, what's the game plan? How are we going to celebrate? It's not every day you get to celebrate a summer graduation and enjoy this kind of weather."

"You two," Gran says, her tone once again nonnegotiable, "go out. Have fun."

"But—"

"No buts! Go out and have fun I said. Tomorrow I'll give you your gift." I share a knowing smile with Gran. I'm a sucker for her presents. Well, presents in general.

"All right."

"*All right,*" Ben suggestively whispers as he places a kiss on my temple.

"I'll see you tomorrow, Gran." She raises her eyebrow to my burning cheeks, but a smirk tugs at the corner of her lips regardless.

"Tomorrow."

+++

The thing about Ben is... well, the thing about Ben and me is—that is to say; the thing with me is that I don't know how to love him.

A fact I acknowledge is both odd and pathetic. Though, it doesn't change it. Ben is my safe spot. He's my comfort zone. Yet, I can't seem to plunge past hesitations and fears and doubts. Even if Ben is more than eager for me to do so. He doesn't push me knowing my last relationship ended on a sour note.

Initially, I resisted Ben's courtship. I wasn't willing to put my heart back on the market. Yet, Ben's genuine interest in me thawed my cold-shoulder treatment. His pursuit was laughable most of the time, but the cute coffee dates and study sessions were endearing. In the end, it was his understanding of my feelings and patience that stole past my defenses. Ben

3

seems to know inherently what I need. Someone steady and reliable in my life. Someone I don't have to worry about leaving me.

A tightness develops in my throat. Feelings I've tried to escape dredging up.

Somewhere along the way as our relationship grew, so did my feelings for the beautiful man. And man, is Ben beautiful. He keeps his thick, warm-brown hair short. It's just enough for a girl to run her hands through while looking into his misty hazel eyes. A dreamy sigh escapes me. His fair skin is a lovely contrast to my chocolate brown. At least *I* think it is. Ben is... perfect. A little too perfect sometimes. But I'm not interested in getting hurt anymore. I'm not willing to risk it all on anything less than a sure thing. Not yet anyway. Maybe not ever.

There's not a thing wrong with Ben. He's handsome, kind, and has a wry sense of humor. And he respects the odd distance I try to keep between us. Though I suspect he's been holding off a more full-hearted pursuit until I finished school. A thought, I admit, that makes my stomach curl unpleasantly.

I gaze at Ben from across the table. His soft smile soothes my nonsensical train of thought. He's taken me to a nice Italian restaurant for our private celebration. An empty bottle of champagne and breadcrumbs spot the table, the rest having been cleared to prepare for our dessert. My lips tilt upward in reciprocation, and I reach for my champagne flute. I'm unprepared for Ben's cool hand to capture mine midtask. My eyes widen as I stare at him in silent wonder.

"I love you," Ben tells me earnestly, squeezing my hand for effect. My stomach drops.

"Oh!"

"*Oh?*"

"Oh." I give a gentle smile in return. "Ben..." The words fall flat on my tongue as I try to regain my

4

equilibrium. I feel my lips quiver uncertainly as they hold their shape.

He ducks his head and releases me to rub at the back of his neck. "Well, that isn't the reaction a guy hopes for," he says with a forced laugh, his eyes darting upward to capture my reaction.

"You're wonderful, Ben," I say, daring to meet his eyes, which are both hopeful and restrained. "It's just...."

"I know," he says with a slight cringe, sitting back in his chair and fiddling with his napkin. "Between what happened with Jamie and all the history with your family."

The thing with Jamie being that after three years of being together, I found out the last eight months of our "relationship" he had cheated on me. The thing with my family being that they are *dead*. They've been dead for the past fourteen years. I lost both parents and my older sister to an awful car accident when I was ten. I was the sole survivor.

Talk about trust and abandonment issues, I think with bitter humor.

"Yes," I finally say, trying to hide the uncertainty and sadness I feel. "I just—I don't want to rush anything. I hadn't planned on being with anyone for a while and then—"

"I swept you off your feet?" Ben's charm comes back in full force, his dimples winking at me, his hazel eyes shining. "Dazzled you with my wit and intellect?"

"By sweeping me off my feet do you mean...?" Ben groans, head tilting back as he shakes his head with exasperation.

"I knock into you one time—"

"And knock me flat on my ass in the process."

"I'll never live it down." I shake my head, giggling as he leans forward across the table to steal a kiss, all awkwardness swept to the wayside. "Fine," he says, sitting back as a slice of chocolate cake is set between

5

us along with a fork and spoon. We stare at the utensils and then at one another, the moment lingering a tad too long before our hands collide as we each reach for the fork. Laughter erupts between us, even as Ben holds the fork triumphantly.

"Ha!"

"That's not fair!" I say with a pout, "I'm the graduate, I should get the fork."

Ben rolls his eyes but relinquishes the fork to me and takes the spoon reluctantly, eyeing it with distrust. "Aw man, it's dirty. What kind of service is this anyway?" He looks cross, and rightly so, but the cake won't eat itself.

My fork breaks through the dessert with little effort. I can immediately tell it will be incredible. Something to savor and enjoy. I close my eyes as my lips wrap around the morsel, letting the flavor of it sink into my taste buds. The thin layer of fudge is what grabs my notice first, melting quickly against my tongue before the rest follows. I chew slowly, letting the bittersweet chocolate overwhelm my mouth. It's still warm, and so delicate and perfectly moist.

"Oh my God," I murmur, lazily peeking one eye open to see Ben staring at me with a mixture of frustration and amusement running across his face. "It's so good."

"I couldn't tell," he says dryly, frantically searching for the missing waitress. I take another piece, cutting the cake quickly and holding out the fork to Ben who looks at me in pure excitement.

"You're welcome. This is heaven. I am presenting you with one of the best bites of cake ever, and I expect your full appreciation later." He leans forward, mouth open and ready. "Seriously," I tell him, "you are about to enter the most serene state of mind as this chocolate hits you." He glares and opens his mouth wider. "*Seriously*," I repeat. My lip twitches upward.

"Zoey." Gone is his amusement as he sends me a hard glare. I smile brightly in response. "*Feed. Me.*"

"Say please," I tease, inching ever forward.

"Ple—*oh my God.*" His face scrunches and pulls in delight as he chews. I can't help but laugh and scoop another piece into my mouth quickly. "I don't know how you do that," he says, stealing the fork before I can protest.

"Do what?"

He takes a bite, fingering the fork thoughtfully. "You say some of the most bizarre things about food sometimes, how it tastes, how it makes you feel. Just now, before I even ate my food, everything you said perfectly described what I tasted and felt. I was fucking Zen that first bite." He takes another helping, passing me back the fork with a smirk.

"What can I say?" I spare Ben a dainty shrug while taking my turn.

"Whenever you decide to open up your restaurant—"

"Patisserie," I correct quickly.

"Patisserie," he amends, "I will gain at least 50 pounds." We laugh. I'm all too grateful for the break in our previous conversation and the delicious dessert before us. Ben, ever the gracious one, allows me the last couple of bites, his eyes focusing on me with a building heat. By the time I finish off the last bite, he can see the eagerness in my eyes.

"Check!"

+++

Ben drops me off with a kiss and wave in front of Gran's house, persuading me to leave the box of donuts we picked up along the way with him for his drive back to Missoula. The drive is roughly an hour from Deer Lodge where Gran and I reside. Even though it's still early in the morning, I'll need a considerable amount of luck to sneak past Gran to change out of yesterday's dress.

I take a moment before I enter our little home, closing my eyes to enjoy the breeze as it brushes against my calves and the back of my neck. The scent of lilacs is in the air. With a sigh, I feel my entire body relax at the soothing and familiar scent.

I did it. I'm a proud University of Montana graduate.

Even with starting a year late at nineteen, it's taken me six years to graduate as a half-time student. No more papers or tests. No more chopping and dicing my way to *A*s. No more cramming study sessions between jobs. Only the terrifying prospect of trying to find a job.

"Child, get inside!" Gran calls from somewhere in the house, breaking my reverie. With a wry grin, I enter. The door gives its telltale creak as soon as it swings inward. My boxes litter the front room, and I cringe in apprehension at the task of unpacking my things. Living in a shack of an apartment for the better part of the last six years, I'm surprised I accumulated so much. Yet, proof stands before me, blocking my way.

"Hi, Gran," I call as I hurry to my room to change. When I find her minutes later in the kitchen, she is preoccupied with a batch of french toast.

"Come on, this food won't eat itself," she tells me, one brow raised in a superior manner. I hesitate in the kitchen's entryway, surprised to see even more boxes fill the room. "I didn't realize I had this much," I say with some unease.

"Oh, these aren't yours, sweetheart," she tells me with a snort, passing back a look to me. "Go on and eat. You don't want that food getting too cold on you."

"We ate on the drive over," I tell her, even as my hands move of their own accord to fill the empty plate in front of me. Bacon, eggs, and of course, one of

Gran's mini blueberry muffins. She's working the pan to finish the french toast as I continue to dissect the room. When Gran takes a seat across from me, I level her with my most probing glare.

"Gran...?" She hums in response, avoiding my look effortlessly. *As usual*, I think with exasperation. "*Gran*," I say more sternly, sliding the plate that holds the bacon out of her reach. She gives me a dry look in return. "Gran!"

"Oh, what?"

"What's with these boxes?" I ask in exasperation. "If they aren't mine, whose are they? Are they yours?"

"Of course they're mine. If they aren't yours, sweetheart, whose do you think they would be?" she responds tartly, snatching the plate of bacon back into her possession.

"Yours?"

"Yes. Mine," she tells me with a pointed look. "I'm moving."

"You're what!" In my surprise, I falter, somehow knocking my glass of juice down across the generous spread of food. Gran and I both let out surprised squeaks before groaning in despair.

"Now look what you've done," she says, her voice a gentle tease as we try to salvage my mess. "You've gone and ruined your graduation breakfast extraordinaire!"

"Was this my present?" I ask, instantly feeling even more remorseful. The blueberry muffins, much to my chagrin, are tinged an orangish yellow at their bottoms. They are the fatal victims of my impromptu spill.

"No," she says with a shake of her head, "this was." She moves quickly to and from the fridge, snagging a rectangular piece of paper. She presses it into my hand before I can protest.

"Gran—"

"Honey, you've given it your all these past few years. This is just a little something I've been saving for you. Use it for whatever you want. Go on a vacation! Buy yourself something nice for once. Enjoy yourself!"

I throw my gaze to the ceiling, blinking back the tears that surface as I take in all of the new information. "You're moving?" I finally say, looking her in the eye, just like she taught me when I was younger. Always look people in the eyes when talking to them. It doesn't just show respect, it conveys a person's strength and power.

"Yes, sweetheart, and I want to invite you along with me."

"But, Gran, I don't understand. Why? Why are you moving?"

"Oh Lord, now isn't that a question! Come on and help me finish cleaning this all up, then we'll have ourselves a nice talk."

We quickly clean off the kitchen table and take stock of breakfast's survivor: the bacon. Thank goodness. By the look Gran passes me, I can tell she's thinking the same. Her hand darts forward to grab one of the crispier pieces as I lay into one of the fatter ones.

"So...?"

Gran doesn't look pleased, but there is a resolute air about her. "I'm needed back home" she says finally.

"Back home? As in the Falls? Barns Falls?"

"Branson Falls."

I give a short shrug at my error.

"I've—sweetheart, when the accident happened, I knew Branson Falls wasn't the place to raise you," she says with graveness I'm unused to hearing.

"Was it not safe?" I hedge a guess.

"At the time, Branson Falls had been undergoing a lot of change in the makeup of its residents. We were growing. And not everyone appreciated that. We were

10

a close-knit town and liked things just the way they were. It wasn't that I was so opposed to the change, but with all that negativity in the air." She scowls, then gives a grimace for good measure as if she remembers exactly the way it felt. "All that negativity, it bites at your skin. Makes a person uncomfortable, even in their home. There was no way on this green earth I would have raised you in such a place. It was out of the question, but I left a lot of unfinished business when we came here. Now, now. I see that look. And I don't regret my decision one bit."

"Oh, Gran, I didn't realize," I say, my words softly spoken.

"Well of course not, dear"—she reassures me with a slow smile—"and you weren't ever meant to, sweetheart. But the facts haven't changed, and now, now, it's time for me to go home. I'm needed."

"Are you going to go back to your job at the practice? Be the town's doctor again?"

"Yes."

"But can't they get a new one?"

"No."

I give a little groan of frustration at her petulant tone, snagging one of the crispier pieces of bacon off the plate in spite. It tastes like coal in my mouth. The flavor a bitter reflection of my feelings. Sometimes Gran gets this way, so obstinate, so stubborn. I know I picked up this trait from her, and on my worse days, I wield it like a flaming sword, but I never enjoy it. Not too much at least. "Why?" I grind out. I know how to play the game at least, readying myself to pry the answer from her.

"Because."

"Gran," I finish my bacon with a few quick chomps. "Why can't the town just get a new doctor? Why does it have to be you? You haven't been in practice for years now! Besides, you're retired. Retired people don't have to work, you know?" I withhold my smirk, knowing my last remarks will have her answering my questions.

"Zoelle, that town is a part of me. I owe it to the people I left behind to return now that you're grown." My bitterness dissipates. "I know the timing seems off to you, abrupt even. But it's been on my mind since you began your last semester at school. I've already contacted a realtor. As soon as this place sells, I'll be leaving. The only question is will you be coming with me?

"I don't know what the job market is like out there, but you know you can always work alongside me. I've always wanted to teach you things. Things every woman in our family should know," she tells me passionately, holding out her hands to accept my own. They are worn and warm, and a comfort to me instantly.

A shiver tracks up my spine as her fingers tighten around mine. Gran's impassioned words sparks something inside me—a flare of hope, perhaps? A hope for something greater, something far past my wildest dreams. My teeth sink gently into my bottom lip as I stare into her expressive eyes. They hold me captive, as if attempting with just a look to convince me to come with her. I release my bottom lip, eyes tearing away from her gaze to trail over her face. A multitude of fine wrinkles gracefully trace around her eyes and mouth. A tiny stack of deep red stones dangle from her ears. They stand out starkly against her silver hair, even though it's kept back with a thick black headband.

"I'll understand if you want to go off with that boy of yours, or try living on your own once more. But I think we both know *I* would prefer the latter." An underlying amusement paints her tone, but I know she's serious despite it.

"I—"

"Just you think about it, sweetheart. I've already got a place lined up in Branson Falls. Everything is in order."

She gives my hands another squeeze and her eyes never leave my own. I feel a wave of uncertainty fill me as soon as she leaves the room, the kitchen having been cleared and cleaned. My hand goes to the necklace around my neck, fingering the long chain till I find its charm, a pearl-shaped piece of jade caged in gold. It was a gift, among a pile of others, from my parents on my last birthday with them. For some reason, I like to think it brings me clarity as it always makes me feel better in low times.

It doesn't take long for me to make my decision.

+++

"Thank you for helping," I say, my feet kicking at the ground as Ben walks past, a heavy looking box filling his arms. "Gran just has so much stuff, but she doesn't trust paying anyone around here to move her things."

"Does that mean I have her seal of approval?" He throws me a wink over his shoulder.

"Maybe." I smile and emit a light laugh.

He maneuvers the remaining boxes around to accommodate the new one, its contents tinkling in mild protest. His good mood, I know, is a fabrication. He is not pleased with my decision to go with Gran, my half-hearted reasoning falling on deaf ears. He hoped, or so he told me, that we could move in together. His face fell at my rather immediate, startled look and the following attempt to hide my dismay.

Ben and I had only been dating for a few months. We certainly hadn't been together long enough to consider moving in together. Well, at least not for *me* to consider. Maybe I should have seen it coming after

13

his profession, or rather his confession, of love. But Gran's moving is merely a kinder excuse than to tell him no outright. At least that's what I convince myself.

Maybe with time, my feelings could develop for Ben into something more. But three months? Well, that's asking too much of me.

"Benjamin, there's still a few more things in here, if you don't mind."

Ben tries and fails to cover his annoyed glance at our former home. It has taken only a few weeks to sell, and once the papers were signed, Gran rushed to pack up the place.

"I still can't believe she got the place to sell so fast." With his hands in his pockets, he shuffles his feet as he walks toward me. His head turns toward the house, a frown cutting between his brow before turning his full attention to me.

I meet him halfway, wrapping my arms around his waist and resting my head against his chest. "She said the people who bought it found it charming. Utterly charming." I dip myself backward to emphasize Gran's superior tone.

"Ben!"

He rights me and spares me a quick kiss before trotting into the house. I know he doesn't want to be here loading up the huge truck. Let alone drive the aforementioned beast all the way up to Branson Falls with us. It's a mighty task, and places me farther away from him. *From us.* I know he does it though because it will make me happy.

"Zoelle, come on, then, girl! We need your muscle on this one."

I hesitate.

My thoughts are suddenly racing around a million miles a minute in my head. I think about Ben and our relationship. What it is and could be. Of Gran and her big decision. Of me and my future. Of Branson Falls, and why, for the life of me, I feel like the town is going to turn my life upside down. My fingers glance over the jade between my breasts; oh yes, this move most certainly is going to turn my life upside down.

+++

Branson Falls is about a three-hour drive away. We make the trip without incident, but the butterflies in my stomach triple as we pass the See You Again sign exiting Branson Falls. Lucky for me, Gran trusts the people of the town enough to hire movers to help us unload. We see them awaiting our arrival as we pull up to the house.

"Gran, is this your old house?"

"Well, of course, sweetheart." Her eyebrow rises in an aloof manner. "Where else would I live?"

My eyebrows contract as my lips form the shape of an O. "I thought you sold it." *Like any other rational person.* "Have you been paying for two houses this entire time?"

"Oh please," she snorts. "It's been taken care of in my absence. You remember my friends Diana and Maureen." My eyebrows remain contracted as I slowly shake my head.

"You usually came to visit us, Gran. I've only been to your house a couple of times when I was younger... But those names are familiar." I soften my features, eyeing the house quizzically. "You talk to them on the phone a lot, don't you?"

Gran nods, satisfaction curling her lips. "I do. They've been watching over the house since I left, knowing one day I'd return."

I can tell upon closer inspection that what she says is true. They have taken care of it. The house sports a fresh coat of paint, and the yard looks well maintained. So, who exactly has been taking care of the house while Gran was away? I cast a curious look

15

at the front door, and my heart gives a nervous flutter. It opens half a second later with a clatter; two older women push against one another to hurdle through the door toward us.

"Diana!" one cries, the faster of the two. Her hair is a pearly white and runs long past her breasts. Her icy-colored tresses and alabaster skin is quite contrary to her vibrant dress, which is full of purples and blues and greens. Her larger-than-life presence takes me slightly aback. The older woman quickly gains ground. Her collection of bracelets produce pretty jingles and chimes with each stride.

Gran goes to meet them, her arms outstretched and ready to embrace them. The second woman, still trailing a step or so behind, has skin the color of dark cocoa and keeps her greying hair back in a severe bun. She is outfitted in all black and dons more jewelry than both Gran and the first woman combined. Her fingers hold at least one ring each. Some small, others bulky, but none so gaudy they make her appearance or accessories unappealing.

"My Mo!" Gran gushes, pulling back and planting two firm kisses on either side of Mo's face (the woman with the pearly pale hair). "Lydia!" she cries as the second woman weaves her way into Gran's arms, a giant smile glued on her face.

"Right," I mutter to myself, "definitely not left unattended."

"Zoelle Renee, get your butt over here."

I walk toward them, my hesitant smile growing more genuine by the second as they open their arms to embrace me. It's impossible not to let out a laugh when they squeeze me tight and stare so lovingly at me. As if I am their grandchild, and not Gran's. Their love and joy at seeing Gran and me outweighs any feelings of awkwardness or unrest I might have.

"Maureen Clybourne. Lydia Stein. Meet my daughter's daughter, Zoelle Renee Baudelaire." The women smile relentlessly.

"It's nice to meet you both."

"It's wonderful to meet you too, my dear. It's truly a sorrow and shame what happened to your family. Thank the Lord she had you, Diana." Lydia reaches out and cups the side of my face, her green, cat-like eyes taking in the details of my face. "A Baudelaire, through and through!" Her exclamation garners a joyful laugh from Maureen, who bobs her head in agreement.

"Yes, yes! Now, come on, then. The boys should be here in another hour or so, so why don't we all just head inside. I'll make some tea and we can chitchat for a while," Mo offers, already walking back up to the house. I follow at a slower pace. They must have been the reason Gran had been persuaded to come back.

I'm stunned to a standstill for a second time once I step inside the house. What weak memories I possess come rushing back. Everything is the same. Of course, some new trinkets and photos decorate the front hall entryway, but from what I remember, it's all the same. My feet lead me forward to the old secretary desk that holds all manner of things: mail and magazines, notes and knickknacks. The picture of my family and Gran picnicking in the park one Fourth of July still stands in the right corner of it all, the stained-glass lamp sitting directly behind it. My fingers grace its edges before peeling back. Why is everything still here? How long has Gran been planning to come back?

Laughter sounds and I follow it to the back, knowing if I want answers from Gran, I need to play it smart. Hopefully, Gran's girlfriends will find themselves in a good enough mood to spill the beans if she doesn't.

17

"Zoelle, I must ask, what do you prefer? Zoe or Zoey?" Lydia stresses the hard "e" for the former and a silky "y" for the latter pronunciation.

I hesitate a moment, my eyes glancing away for a second before I answer. "Zoe." I tell them with a slightly forced smile as I enter the kitchen. "Wow, this kitchen has certainly changed... unlike the rest of this house." Good, that sounded casual yet inquisitive enough.

"Oh yes," Lydia says with a serene nod. "There was some water damage, and it needed to be fixed along with the bathroom up above. So, we thought, why not give it a little update. But everything else is just the way Diana left it. We knew one day she'd come back to us and wouldn't want a thing changed, but some things just couldn't be helped."

"I like it." The smile on my face grows. "Actually, I kind of love it." The women and Gran laugh along with me.

"You be sure to call us your aunties, all right, dear?" I nod my head in happy acquiescence.

The kitchen is alive with lovely green cabinets and white countertops. But my attention is stolen by a wall completely lined with plants. Jasmine, lavender, sage, mint, on and on the herbs and flora scent the room with their earthy notes. They bring me peace as I take a deep breath.

My chef's eye takes in the rest of the details of the kitchen. An informal table and mismatched chairs fit snugly near the bay window at the far end of the room. To my left, the wall is made up of three distinct sections. The first and nearest to me is filled with cookbooks. In the middle section, a wood burning stove, even though a perfectly modern stove sits snugly between fridge and sink to my right. Past the stove is a collection of photographs. Some bearing the face of myself and my family.

A wistful sigh slips past my lips even as a pang of sadness hits my heart. I avert my gaze back towards the plant wall near the dining nook. All that greenery spilling forth from the wall... it's like a hidden valley or distant meadow has chosen to grace the kitchen with its presence. *A hidden valley I can use for fresh ingredients, I think greedily.* "Love it," I say once more under my breath, coming to sit by them. "So, tell me more about what has and hasn't changed.

REBECCA MAIN

THE INQUISITION
- Chapter 2 -

August is ending, and I'm feeling... flustered—and
that is the nice way of putting it. Job hunting is
fruitless so far, my brightest prospect, a barista. And
even that has tight competition. I knew finding a job
would be difficult after college, but I had hoped for
something a little more promising than a barista.
Until a job came through, I turned my concentration
to unpacking. Somehow, the task was even more
daunting than the former.

My eyes scan the mess I've made, critically
sweeping the open boxes. Where had I put my books?
Pushing off my knees with a sigh of frustration, I lap
the room. My confusion grows as the cookbooks I
search for remain out of sight. I enjoy the silence of
the house as I wander downstairs to continue my
pursuits. It's nice to have the house to myself for a
change. It's proven difficult to find a moment alone,
when everyone in town is determined to drop by to say
hello. The constant flow of people doesn't bother me as
much as the abrupt ending of conversations whenever

20

I enter a room. Or the knowing looks my dear new aunties gave me. It's weird. *Really weird.* And unsettling. *Very unsettling.* I make my way into my haven, the kitchen. I've fallen in love with its wood burning oven and large cooking range, the stashes of fresh herbs, and the insane amount of tea hoarded in one of the tall cupboards. It's perfect. "Zoe! How lovely to see you! I'm just running through—got to grab a few things!"

"Hi, Aunt Mo." She zips through the kitchen toward the tea cupboard. A woman on a mission. "What are you looking for? It wouldn't happen to be my box of cookbooks, would it?"

"Oh no, sweetheart, I'm looking for some tea." She studies its contents, leaning back and forth with her glasses pitched halfway down her nose as she decidedly scoops out almost half its contents into the folds of her dress. "As for your books," she says with a pointed, sidelong glance. "I believe they're in the study."

Of course. "Thanks. I'll be sure to check in there."

"Good." She twirls around the room in her exaggerated way, smiling serenely at me as she goes for her mortar and pestle, spilling various containers of tea leaves onto the island as she does so.

"What are you up to?" I ask, roped in by her smile and wild eyes.

"I'm creating," she says with a flourish of her wrist. Her bangles and bracelets jingle merrily.

"Creating what?"

"Magic," she says with a laugh. "I know just the remedy to get Mrs. Clark's daughter to sleep through the night, allergies or not."

"Magic?" I ask with a laugh.

"Oh yes, I dare say even you can cook up a little magic in the kitchen," she says, reaching over to pat my hand.

21

"It's nice that everyone here seems to be so… friendly," I offer.

"Oh yes, we're all quite close around these parts. We like to support one another, and we make it our business to see this town thrives. It's how all communities should be. I don't know what your old neighborhood was like, but around here, we like to keep our noses in each other's business, if you know what I mean." She gives me a sly grin. "That way we can offer our help, even if you don't want it. It's just what we do."

"I see," I say, watching as she grinds down on the dried leaves. "It must be nice living in a town like this, then, with everyone so *cozy* with one another."

"It's certainly something, although it wasn't always like this. Oh no, in fact, it was just around the time that you and your grandmother left that things around here got a little, turned upside down."

"Oh?"

"Mmhm," she says pouring her medley into a few pouches. "When you two left, a new family had just come to town. Wasn't too long after their arrival that a whole lot of their friends and family started to crop up and make themselves at home here too. And I mean a lot. Mind you, that wasn't too troubling. What stirred things up was them trying to get their people on the town council and police force."

"Wait," I say, as she bustles around me to put things away. "Are you trying to tell me they were trying to take over the town?"

"They were trying to do something," she says. Her keen gaze sinks into mine, and I fight the urge to squirm under her intense regard. "But we have a lot of strong-willed people in this town, who weren't about to stand for their antics. We weren't about to let some stray dogs"—she snorts, shaking her head—"come wandering into our town and piss all over it."

"Right," I say slowly, accentuating my vowel. "So, did you get them to leave? Are they still here? Have I met them?" My questions come out like bullets, one after another. Curiosity fully peaked. I play with my necklace, leaning more fully onto the kitchen island as I watch Aunt Mo finish her clean up. The small piece of jade is cool and reassuring between my fingers. I don't wear much jewelry, but this necklace... I never take it off if I can help it.

"No, we didn't." Her words ride on an exaggerated sigh. "Though many would have liked it to be that way. There's a large subdivision up north, near where the forest begins to encroach on the town. Almost all the newcomers live round there."

"Woof," I say. My reaction is better received than anticipated. Aunt Mo laughs for a full two minutes before we can continue.

"Oh my, you are a treat, Zoe. Hmm, now, where was I? Oh yes. They still live here, but I doubt you've met any of them. We ended up coming up with a truce of sorts. We keep to ourselves. They keep to themselves."

"I don't suppose any of them are hiring?" I ask.

"Ha! Don't go wasting your talents on them. They wouldn't know gourmet food from dog food."

"All right, all right! I can take a hint."

"Good," she says, letting her glasses tip downward again, giving me her signature look. "I'll see you later, sweetheart." With that, she departs, leaving me to mull over the only interesting piece of gossip about this town.

+++

Ben is here for dinner tonight. He's meeting the aunts.

It's the first time he's been to the house, our other *rendezvous* occurring in middle ground towns. I didn't

23

realize until the day before his arrival that I'm
nervous about the meeting. Ben meeting the aunts is
important to me and I desperately want their
approval. They have quickly become family over the
past few weeks. Almost seamlessly winding
themselves into Gran and I's daily life.

My entire body feels flush, as if I'm running a
fever, and my eyes dart anxiously to the dining room.
Ben's face turns a deeper shade of red every time I
cast a glance their way. My anxiety grows as I take in
the aunts' somber façade and Ben's none-to-subtle
glance for help. I let my shoulders sag in response.
He'll need to protect himself until I finish dinner. I
grimace and turn my attention back to my task.

"Oh, honey," Gran says with a snort, "if he can't
hold up to them, then..." She sips her wine—*her
third*—and gives a not so discreet glance toward them
before turning her knowing gaze on me.

"I thought you liked Ben."

"I do, I'm only saying—"

"Well, you don't need to say anymore," I tell her,
squeezing my eyes tightly shut. "Let's just eat. Will
you take the potatoes in?" When I open my eyes, Gran
is halfway to the table with the potatoes, and I take
one last moment to collect myself.

The lamb with its salt crust removed lies on the
silver serving plate with juices seeping delightfully
from it.

The homemade dressing drips artfully over the
salad.

The *second* wine bottle sits empty upon the table,
begging for its replacement.

I'm as prepared as I can be, but Ben isn't. I should
have prepped him more on Mo's eccentric behavior
and Lydia's dry humor. I should have prepared him
for the worst possible scenarios. Yet Ben laughed off
my concerns, assuring me it would all be fine.

Except it isn't.

Ben is clearly flustered and so am I. My cocoa skin radiates heat from head to toe, whether from the heat of the kitchen or secondhand embarrassment I'm not sure. I know deep down it isn't just the aunts' approval I want, it's validation of this relationship. My eyes slip closed again with a plaintive sigh. *Tonight will go well, it will,* I reassure myself. The dinner is cooked to perfection and the third bottle of wine will alleviate whatever tension has built up.

"Here you are, honey." Gran gives me a long, slow pour of the Bordeaux as I walk into the dining room. I set the salad between the olive oil potatoes and the hearty lamb.

"It looks wonderful," Ben says. "*You* look wonderful."

The wine runs down my throat smoothly as I melt back into my seat, shooting Ben a sincere smile once I finish my lengthy sip. "Thank you."

"Who'll be cutting the meat, then?" Aunt Lydia asks, taking the carving knife and serving fork in her hands.

"Why Ben will, of course," replies Aunt Mo.

"That's all right, I can do it," I try to insist, but Aunt Lydia has already pressed the utensils firmly into Ben's hand.

"He's a big boy, darling, and after all that hard work you did in the kitchen, it's the least he can do," she adds with a laugh. Ben gives me a small shrug and a smile, standing and pulling the plate of lamb nearer to him.

My faces bears my chagrin, forehead crinkling as my lips gently purse. The knife she holds isn't the best for cutting the lamb, but it's clear I'm the only one who knows.

"Actually," I say, cringing as Ben stabs the lamb with the fork, "it should be cut with an electric knife. And *thinly*! I'll just take it back into the kitchen." I stand as well, much more hastily than Ben and jerk the plate backward. Ben almost topples forward, staring at me aghast. "Why don't you help me in the kitchen, Ben?"

"You should have just kept it in here to carve it in the first place," he tells me once we are safely in the kitchen. I search the cabinets until I come up gold with the electric knife kit.

"I didn't want to keep you in there any longer than necessary. Also, have I told you they can basically smell fear?" A nervous laugh rattles from my throat over the soft buzz of the electric knife. "Just remember the basics. No talking about politics and religion, and you should be fine. Oh no." My hand stops its sawing motion as my eyes dart to Ben's. "You didn't try telling your accounting jokes, did you?"

Ben's guilty look draws a pained whine from my lips. His frantic look in response doing little to ease my worry.

"It's fine. Save the jokes and answer every question politely, okay? Maureen can be a little much, and Lydia comes off a tad severe, but they're just putting you through the ringer, you know? They want to make sure you're going to treat me with respect." Ben nods and I continue my dissection of the meat. The lamb holds a delicious pink all throughout its center and I let pleased smile curl my lips. Until Ben snatches a piece, letting out an exaggerated moan as he chews and swallows. "Ben," I hiss as he goes for another bite, "I am going to cut off your fingers if you do not stop this instant."

He quirks a grin in my direction. "That's nothing compared to the threats your aunts have been making."

"What?" I gasp, nearly digging the knife into the delicate meat.

"Well, not threats, but—"

"They really do mean well," I say with a cringe. "I think. I don't know. I didn't expect them to act like this. They're usually much better behaved."

"Sure," he says sarcastically, though not cruelly, and swipes another piece of meat. He moans more softly this time.

"They just have this thing about outsiders—not that you are. You are not an outsider because you are my boyfriend and you love me, and they can't just ignore that. Right?" I can feel Ben's heavy gaze on me, my words continuing after a quick breath. "It's just there are these people who moved to the town not long ago and left an awful impression on them, so now their trust is all sorts of compromised and—"

"Zoey, it's fine. I can handle being put through the ringer. You're worth it." I stop cutting and grasp his face gently, pulling him into a sweet kiss.

"You are so wonderful, Ben, much more so than I deserve." Out of the corner of my eye, I see his fingers inch toward the lamb. "But if you try to steal another piece of this meat, I will tell them the most embarrassing stories about you, and you will not make it through this dinner in one piece."

He folds his hands quickly behind him, his grin turning impish as he maneuvers around the island. When I finish, he takes the plate and walks back to the table with me, presenting the lamb with a flourish. Gran is the only one to crack a smile, though she does so behind her glass of wine.

"Zoe, this meal is just perfect," Lydia comments after everyone has covered their plates with the fine food and taken their first bites. I smile in thanks, chewing happily on the potatoes, enjoying their savory quality.

"Every meal Zoey makes is perfect," Ben adds enthusiastically, taking a large bite of lamb. "I don't know how I lived without her or her cooking."

27

Aunt Lydia casts Aunt Mo a sly glance, to which Aunt Mo whispers something under her breath in return before fetching another bottle of wine. When she returns she fills Ben's glass and the room returns to its silence.

"Do you often cook, Ben?" Aunt Mo finally asks.

"Hardly ever," he replies oddly truthful. His wide-eyed expression implies his disbelief and shock at his honesty, but he laughs it off good-naturedly. "I could hardly compete with Zoey in the kitchen. Plus, I like to think I'm her best test subject when it comes to trying new dishes."

Gran nods her head, "I don't know about that Benjamin. I've had my fair share of Zoelle's crazy ideas." As she speaks she spoons another helping of salad onto my plate. I roll my eyes at her antics, but I'm pleased with her teasing.

"Surely you can do something of use in the kitchen, so she's not left with all the work," Aunt Lydia says once I have a fatty piece of lamb past my lips. I frown and immediately try to catch her eye. *Why are the aunts set on conducting an inquisition?*

Ben laughs, his neck shading red while he takes a quick sip of wine. "I can make toast," he offers, looking at me for some kind of help as I try to chew faster. "Zoey is a natural in the kitchen. I'm completely out of my element there, so I find the best practice is just to let her cook and reap the benefits, so to speak."

"Did your mother cook your meals growing up?" Aunt Mo asks.

"Uh, why, yes. She did."

"And Zoe cooks all of your meals now?" Aunt Lydia asks.

"Well, not all of my meals."

Aunt Mo shares another pointed look with Aunt Lydia, "A natural in the kitchen, he said Lydia. Tell me, Ben, is that where you think women are most

28

comfortable. Where it's natural to find a woman… in the kitchen?"

"Aunt Mo," I scold behind my hand as I force the meat down my throat.

"Maureen." A warning settles firmly in Gran's tone. "Settle down now."

"I—" Ben's face has turned splotchy, a painful mixture of white and red. "I don't think that is a natural place to find a woman." He pleads. "I think *Zoey's* natural place is in the kitchen." He elaborates to both his horror and mine.

"Ben," my voice takes on a squawking quality as I say his name.

"No, no, no!" he practically shouts, waving his hands in surrender. "I didn't mean it like that—I meant—"

"That her natural place is in the kitchen?" Aunt Mo offers dryly.

"No—"

"Like her rightful place is to cook and serve you your meals like your mama did?" Aunt Lydia asks.

"No!" his voice raises, face now completely red. "Zoey is… is *magic!* Anything she makes is out of this world. I couldn't imagine her doing anything else in this life other than cooking. It makes her happy, and I'm just the lucky guy who gets to benefit from her undeniable talent. A talent that I *encourage*."

"Is that so?" Ben nods sharply to Aunt Lydia's question. "Did your mother cook the meals in your family?" Ben nods reluctantly, his body held taut and ready for the next attack. "Interesting."

The room goes silent, and a small wave of relief rushes through me as the table remains that way. The inquisition is over. Thank—

"And do you see your future wife doing the same? Staying home to cook the family meals and tend to the house?"

29

All eyes fall to Ben, who, in an odd turn of events, loses all color. I feel myself do the same, eyes pleading with Ben not to answer. *Why did he keep answering?*

"Of course."

The answer slips from him, coated in remorse, and once more the room goes silent. Aunt Mo's pointed *"Hmph"* keeping all lips sealed shut. *This is too much to bear.* I feel ashamed and horrified as I look at the scene before me. This is not the reception I wanted Ben to receive. This is not the way I wanted the aunts to react. This is not the way *Ben* is supposed to act. For a pained moment, the wine rushes to my head. I stand, startling the table and nearly spilling the other glasses of wine that sit atop it.

"I've lost my appetite," I finally manage to say, picking up my plate as well as the bowl of potatoes. "Ben?" He stands and follows me into the kitchen. "I am so sorry," I whisper to him harshly, barely holding back the angry tears assaulting my eyes.

"It's all right," he says cautiously.

"No, it isn't," I correct him. Depositing the items by the kitchen sink, I stride back into the dining room and snatch up the salad and lamb as well, the aunts coolly assessing me as I do. Their regard fuels the rising well of anger in my stomach. *How could they?* Never, not in a million years, did I imagine tonight going so terribly. It's clear as crystal the aunts don't approve of Ben, and now I doubt Gran's feelings as well. After all, how many times did she truly try to intervene? Why didn't she mediate the discussion between the aunts and Ben when he arrived?

When I return to the kitchen, Ben is on the phone. He shoots me an apologetic look, but I only nod stiffly in return. He passes me a small smile and steps to the small kitchen table nestled near the bay windows. His face pulling into a frown as he nods wordlessly at the conversation that plays in his ear.

I methodically wash the accumulated dishes. The sound of the aunts and Gran's sudden laughter grating on my last nerves. Before I lose myself to my growing anger, Ben's presence appears behind me. The warmth of his body pressing along the length of my back, and he tugs me away from the dishes.

"Are you all right?" he asks. I turn around in his arms, my eyes wide in confusion as I stare at him. Ben pulls me more tightly into the circle of his arms, dropping his face to my collarbone to kiss it lightly, or rather the birthmark that rests a couple of inches beneath it.

Why couldn't the aunts have asked normal questions? Like what Ben liked most about me? What his favorite food was?

Ben pulls back, waiting patiently for my answer. "I'm so sorry," I rush to tell him, "I had no idea they would act like that."

"Well, it wasn't exactly what I expected either, I guess." He scratches absently at the back of his neck, cheeks turning pink. "I wasn't exactly a delight either, and while I hate to end the night on this note, I have to go. Abby needs me in the office early tomorrow, and the drive back is a killer."

"Oh."

He frowns, "I really need this job. It could lead to bigger things for me."

"I know, I know," I say feeling a swell of disappointment in my gut. I swallow it down and duck my head. "I guess that means you won't be staying the night?"

"No."

"When do you need to leave? The cake should be done soon." I cast my eyes upward to watch his reaction.

He shoots a longing look at the oven, but the furtive glance he spares the dining room tells me my answer. "Next time you come, we'll have dinner just

31

the two of us," I whisper. Ben envelops me in a bear hug, his lips placing themselves firmly to my brow.

"Next time," he whispers back, "you come to me." His smirk teases, but there is a seriousness to his tone that cannot be mistaken.

"Deal." Cupping my face, he presses another kiss to my brow before moving to my lips.

"I love you." His words trail on the back of a hum, almost too soft to hear, even with our close proximity. A strange rush of emotion tumbles forth at his sweet declaration. But not love.

"I—"

"Ben." We both groan quietly at Gran's ill-timed intrusion. "Will you be staying for dessert?"

"Unfortunately, not."

"That's a shame. I was hoping to hear more about your work. We hardly got to talk, just you and me, this evening." She ushers him to the door as I follow at her heels. "I'll let you two say goodbye. Drive home safely, Ben."

"Have a pleasant night yourself," he tells her departing back, giving me a wide-eyed look at Gran's unusual behavior. "Before I go, I just need to know… did I do something wrong tonight?"

"Of course not" I exclaim quickly, though we both know that's not entirely true based on what he shared at the dinner table. A curl of despair tightens around my gut, but I plaster on a smile. "It must have been all the wine. But next time—"

"You come to me." I nod my head feverishly, and we kiss our goodbye. I close the door behind him with regret, desperately wishing the night hadn't gone so terribly. When a sudden bark of laughter bursts from the kitchen I feel my anger return.

I want so badly to go in and confront them. Yell and shout at how unfairly they treated both of us, but such heated conversations always end in tears, at least on my part, and I have no intention of letting

32

them see me cry. *A run will clear my head*, I think deftly. I take the stairs two at a time, ignoring the timer on the oven going off in the kitchen. *Someone else will take the cake out,* I think bitterly. I rummage through my mostly sorted belongings and put together a suitable outfit to run on the cool autumn night.

As I make my way back down the stairs and toward the back door located off the kitchen, I steel myself. With a deep breath, I stride through the room, noting somewhat savagely that once again all conversation dies upon my entrance.

"We'll talk when I get back," I tell them with hardly a glance over my shoulder.

"Where are you going at this hour?" Gran asks, her voice harsher than I expect it to be. I halt, the door opened halfway and primed for my exit.

"For a run." My voice sounds back in a perfect mimic of her tone.

"It's late."

I scoff. "It's barely after seven. The sun won't set for at least another hour."

"Stay out of the forest, Zoelle. It's no place to be at night." Gran tells me sternly. I look back, struck by her flinty demeanor.

"I'll be fine," I respond tersely.

"I mean it, Zoelle, stay out of the forest. It's a full moon tonight and—"

"Seriously." I huff and jerk the door open wider. "It's a full moon tonight, Zoelle," I parrot, pushing past the hard lump in my throat. "Beware the creatures of the night for their beastly natures do arise."

A look of hurt flashes across Gran's face at my bitter words. "Yes," is her only reply as she sits down next to the aunts stiffly. "It's practically nightfall and running alone in those woods is just plain stupid. And we both know you're not that, sweetheart."

33

"Well," I respond with a brittle smile, "with any luck the moon will be bright enough to light my way. I'll be fine."

"Zoe—"

"I'll be back in a while. Don't wait up for me."

"Stay out of the woods!" Gran's words fall on deaf ears, the door shutting with more force than I intend as I scamper off away from the house and those who inhabit it.

+++

Gran's house is on the east side of town, and conveniently close to the forest that curls around the city. Out of spite and laziness, I ran straight to it. I don't anticipate running into any wild animals because I don't plan to stay in the forest long after dark.

My thoughts drift back to the short-lived dinner. The wine, which I naively assumed would create an atmosphere of ease, escalated the situation. Then there was the food, something I had been sure would bring everyone comfort once I finally settled on it. I thought Gran would help me cook, maybe the aunts and Ben as well, as all of us gathered around the kitchen island laughing.... Instead, the entire task of cooking rested on my shoulders, and between my anxiousness over Ben being comfortable and worrying over the aunts making fools out of themselves—let alone Ben—my food lacked the attention I normally gave it.

I still find myself stunned over the aunts' presumptuous and hostile questioning. Never have I seen them act that way around anyone, especially not in their home. I'm as disappointed as I am angry.

Tears cloud my vision. I blink them back forcefully. Why didn't Gran intervene? She's supposed to be my secret weapon; the one I can rely on to smooth anything over with a well-placed look or well-timed joke. Instead, she just watched. She did nothing! Nothing except drink her wine and let my dinner go to waste.

When my lungs begin to burn, I slow to a jog, veering left to avoid the fallen branches and debris that block the trail I've happened upon and check my phone's clock. I almost stumble as I register the time, brow crinkling in confusion as I stare at the numbers on my phone's screen. Had I really been running for almost 40 minutes?

I scan my surroundings, focusing on calming my breath and note with some dread that the forest seems to have grown thicker around me. The trees and bushes fit more snugly against the trail, and more and more debris seems to litter the ground. I turn in a circle. It's darker too.

Colder and darker, I think. Time to go home and face the music. Turning sharply, I'm rewarded with a sharp stinging sensation that raps against my shin.

"Ouch!" I plummet forward. "*Shit.*" The word is released in a hiss as I crash to the ground, hands shooting forward to catch my fall.

Bad idea. Bits of earth and rock dig painfully into my palms as I pull my knee snug against my chest to examine my shin more closely. "Just fucking great," I groan. Little rivulets of red stream down my leg past bits of bark and dirt.

I hold both hands to the wound, hissing at the immediate pain, but giving a small sigh of relief as the throbbing sensation dulls. I'll need to wash up once I get home to avoid any type of infection. Gran and the aunts will be head over heels with worry if they see me like this. Which will go along nicely with a side of 'I told you so' ready on their lips. *Ugh.* Sitting up, and feeling worse for wear, I let out a pathetic sigh. The thought of limping home in the dark is completely unappealing. I look up and gaze at the full moon peeking out from beneath a maze of branches. It is especially bright tonight and beautiful.

Then, it sounds.

A low growl that reverberates off the forest floor. Something deep and primal. *Something wild.* And it's coming from behind me.

My pulse skips a beat as I slowly flatten myself on the ground, eyes darting along the forest floor fearfully. "Shit," I rasp, spotting something large and gray some thirty feet away. To my horror, the animal in question stiffens and turns its head in my direction. *Oh, God. It's a wolf.* A very large—*very terrifying*—wolf. *Oh fuck. Fuck!* I flatten further, horrified when I see it sniff the air deeply. A slow snarl tumbles from its mouth as it takes a step in my direction.

Well, limping home isn't on the table any longer, I think morosely. Maybe I can force myself into a sprint? Ignore the pain and just *go.*

I weigh my options as the second one appears. A sandy colored wolf barrels into the side of the first, and they tumble over the ground. Loud yips and playful barks ensue as they roughhouse, and a surge of hope sprouts inside of me. This might be just the distraction I need to get away.

With speed I hardly know I possess, I manage to stand and dodge behind the nearest tree to conceal my presence. The scuffling of the wolves still rings clearly throughout the trees, letting me know they're still near and distracted. I'll need to choose my next move wisely. Wait them out? Or run for it?

Building my courage, I ready myself to push away from the tree trunk. I just need to time it right. Run while they're still distracted with each other. I'm just about to bolt, when I hear a bout of laughter ring through the forest. The sound stills my heart, holding it hostage as I tremble in fear. *What on earth is going on?*

36

"There's nothing like a new moon, is there, brother!" cries a jubilant male voice.

"I'm not your brother," a gravelly voice responds. *Oh God,* I think, my heart's going into overdrive as I take in a rattling breath. *How many are there?*

"Come now, Keenan. We're all pack. Therefore"— the voice trails off, laced with condescension—"we are *all* family. Now, why don't you change?" *Why were these men out gallivanting in the forest with wolves?*

Slowly, I sink into a crouch and peek around the tree trunk. It's a weak view, but it's enough. The two wolves sit idly by the men, their tongues hanging out as they lightly pant. They seem... large. Much larger than what I imagined a real wolf to look like. I swallow, eyes drifting to the men.

The first, a man no more than twenty-five, stands tall and lean. His black hair is fashionably styled and his clothes are tailored to fit. There's no denying his handsome looks. His clean-cut jawline and the wicked smirk he wears, tells me he knows it too. I swallow with some difficulty. The 25-year-old stands with his arms crossed over his chest and a cavalier air about him in front of the other, older male. Though I can't presume to know why he looks so confident against the larger man. *Much larger,* I think fretfully.

The second, slightly older man is intimidating, to say the least. Tattoos cover the length of his arms, some crawling up over his stout neck. He seems the direct opposite of the other. His clothing plain, a T-shirt and worn blue jeans, and his hair military short. *He's older as well,* I think, *maybe in his early thirties.* When the larger man grunts and begins to strip I almost faint away.

I suck in a sharp breath, realizing belatedly that I've forgotten to breathe. *Of all the things to do,* I think in a stupor, unable to tear my eyes away from the scene. The younger, cockier man watches without

37

comment. His smirk only growing as the older man continues to strip.

What the *fuck*?

I'm more than prepared to look away, cheeks flaming hot in response to the flesh made bare to me, when a ghastly crack resounds from the now naked male. He lets out a snarl so terrible he begins to shake. Then he falls to his hands and knees, a shout of pure agony drawn from his lips. His body twists and bends. It *breaks*, transforming into some kind of monster or beast. *Or wolf.* A wolf with fur as dark as night. The new canine lets out an ear-shattering howl. One loud enough to make me gasp aloud as I clasp my hands over my ears.

What. The. Fuck?

Hot tears spill over my cheeks. Too terrified to wipe them away, my hands shake as they brace themselves against the tree trunk. The two original wolves pounce on their new acquaintance and begin to scuffle once more, while the remaining male laughs at the display. His hands drag his shirt up over his sculpted abs, and by chance, his eyes catch mine. Several emotions flit across his face. Shock. Sharp anger. He takes a calculating step forward and lets his shirt fall back into place, his head tilting to the side. A more inquisitive look falls upon his brow, and then a grin. One full of sharp white teeth.

"Hello there," he says smoothly.

The wolves around him still and come to attention. My heart gives a strange rattle in my chest as I gasp once more. His grin widens, the moment between us hanging precariously before I finally snap into action, turning and sprinting away as fast as I can. I ignore the terrible spiking pain running across my leg and cast a fearful look over my shoulder. If by some miracle I make it home, Gran is going to kill me.

SEALED

- Chapter 3 -

It's a shame time travel isn't a real thing.
Although, if people can turn into wolves, I'll wager a
guess time travel isn't *completely* off the table. If it is,
now would be the perfect time to wield it. Then I
wouldn't be in my current predicament. My heart is
ready to burst out of my chest, hyperaware of the
damp and suffocating forest air, and of course, the
threat of wolves and strange men that surround me.
  Not that I can see any of them.
  Once caught by that devilish man, I am quickly
restrained, my clothing adjusted and straightened,
and blindfolded. I wiggle my hands uncomfortably in
front of me. They are roped together with the pretty
boy's belt, and it digs unpleasantly into my skin.
Thankfully my legs are left unrestrained. Not that
that helps me. Any chance of outrunning the men and
wolves are comically slim, and we all know it. I stifle a
groan as the metal buckle sinks itself deeper into my
flesh. It hurts like a *sonofabitch*. More than it
reasonably should. Both of my arms ache painfully the

39

longer I am made to wait for their next move. An ache that travels throughout the rest of my body, and slowly but surely, begins to make me feel faint.

I try to keep my anger and energy in reserve, hustling both to the distant corner of my heart where they shiver and quake in anticipation. Stupid legs. Stupid wolves. Stupid aunts and Gran. If it weren't for them this entire night would have played out much, much differently.

Bzzz bzzzt; bzzz bzzzt; bzzz bzzzt; bzzz bzzzt.

"Ah yes, let me just—" Leaves crunch under foreign footfall, and then hands are quickly unfastening my phone from my arm.

Bzzz bzzzt; bzzz bzzzt; bzzz bzzzt.

"It seems as though you have a missed a call from your... grandmother. Adorable," pretty boy says. I want to ring his neck, for he chased me down and caught me. He had pinned me easily enough, but just when I thought he would go in for the kill, he stopped.

And now—well, now I'm getting impatient.

"If you're going to kill me, just do it." My voice hardly quivers. *Good.* I need to show a strong front. I refuse to die a coward.

His laughter sounds close by, with hints of malice tainting the undertone of his delivery. "Fear not. I have no such plans for you tonight." I want to sigh in relief or cry, but his fingers brush along my collarbone like a phantom. I flinch, pitching myself back against the tree I'm made to stand before. "Ah, ah, ah," he scolds mockingly. "Do calm down, and keep any notions of running away out of that pretty little head of yours, will you? It will only excite them more. And I'd hate to have them ruin the surprise I have in store for my brother. And you will be a *marvelous* surprise."

The wolves that surround me let off a chorus of subdued snarls that makes my skin prickle uncomfortably. They might not kill me, but there are worse things than dying. I grit my teeth and

40

experience something coiled and stinging hot inside of me begin to crack at the seams. A primal, but foreign cry to take a stand. One we all possess. I take a deep breath, trying valiantly to still my shaking nerves. *There's no way I'm going down without a fight.*

"Playing with your food again, Ryatt? I thought we had spoken about this, brother." I straighten at the new voice. It's... different. Strong and heavy. His tone leaves nothing to the imagination. This man expects to be obeyed. His words roll over the forest like a heavy shroud, calling not just me, but everyone and everything to attention.

Hope swells inside my chest. Maybe he can talk some sense into these strange men. I will swear to forget this night and return home without a scratch. Well, without a scratch from *them*.

No one responds. It stalls my breath, and in the falling silence, I hear it all. The wolves stop their pacing. The insects and birds cease their chatter. Even the breeze seems to fade. And it's all for him. With every step he takes, I feel my resolve crumble. My hope diminishes. That coil inside me sizzles and pulls away as a sob threatens to sound from my trembling lips.

Maybe Ryatt and his merry band of wolves are just saving me for *him*.

"We have!" Ryatt exclaims boisterously after another long beat of silence. "I was merely out to teach these pups how to hunt when we bumped into our new friend here. You see, she saw a bit too much and tried running off. I chased her down—she's remarkably quick—but when I caught her, I saw something very peculiar. A way back into your good graces, brother."

"Enough, Ryatt. Kill the girl and be done with it," he replies gruffly. "Make it clean." Fear strikes at my heart.

"What!" I cry, "No! *No way*. This is absurd! You can't just go around kidnapping and killing random

41

joggers. This was all just a misunderstanding. I was just—*mmph!*"

A warm hand firmly plants itself over my mouth, cutting off my frantic plea.

"I'm afraid I must side with the young woman here, Aleksandr. You'd be very unhappy with me if I did. She bares a soulmark, one of the pack's... your soulmark, specifically." The smugness in Ryatt's voice is grating, and the forest waits with bated breath for his brother to respond. As do I. The hand slips from my face, and a shuffling of feet sounds.

The blindfold, a ratty T-shirt, is pulled from my eyes and tossed to the ground a second later. I jerk to the side, crowding up against the tree for balance as I stare around wide-eyed.

The newcomer stands close to me, his eyes a mossy green against caramel skin. His hair is in disarray, his dark curls falling in waves carelessly in front of his eyes. He rakes back the long fringe without a thought, his muscles rippling in response to the casual action: abs, chest, arms. He's shirtless, *of-fucking-course*, and my eyes are helpless to resist trailing downward. Dark hair twines together over his muscled chest and down, down, *down*. I inhale sharply and quickly avert my eyes.

Bastard.

Kidnappers do not get to look so—*so sexy*. They definitely aren't supposed to have been allotted sinful abs or hair that trails down from chest to naval to... well.... He reaches out to touch me, running his fingers along the underside of my chin almost reverently. *Almost*. By the smug look he sports, one eerily similar to Ryatt's, I close my mouth with a snap and level him with my best glare.

"Don't touch me," I snarl, feet itching to take me further back. But going back isn't an option. Not with the tree pressing so snugly against me now. I side step again, hardly gaining ground, but it's something. His

42

wolfish grin dips deeper for just a second and a dimple appears. I hold my breath, heart beating painfully against my chest as I watch both grin and dimple disappear behind his stoic facade once more.

"Well, then, let's see it."

"It's just below her collarbone. You'll have to adjust her shirt to see it," Ryatt tells him cheerily. The green-eyed nods resolutely and crowds closer. Startled, I awkwardly attempt to side step, but he is swift to counter and traps me. One brawny arm bars either side of my head. His eyes sweep over my form, lingering on the belt that binds my wrists. "Iron?" The man tilts a look at his brother, who watches intently from the sidelines.

"But of course. Don't you recognize her, brother? It's Diana's granddaughter, the littlest witch—"

"Excuse me?" I utter impulsively. "What did you just call me?" The brothers share a look I almost miss, fleeting confusion, before the man's gaze returns to my chest. "Hey!" I shriek, "Eyes up here, asshole!"

Ryatt laughs as his brother flushes from my reprimand. But then his eyes harden, and one warm hand trails down my side to my waist, straightening and tugging down my shirt a few inches. Something akin to a growl rolls deeply through his throat. I can't help the cold fear striking at my belly, nor the way it quickly spreads.

Tears swim at the edge of my vision before he shushes me absentmindedly. He stares at my birthmark, now revealed. The little, curved sliver of pale-pink skin resembles a crescent moon. Green eyes meet brown, and he gives a smile that seemingly is meant to be reassuring but does quite the opposite.

This man is the real danger of the night. The one Gran had warned about.

His other arm drops as he leans forward, fingers caressing the bruises and welts that cradle the belt wrapped round my wrists. "Iron," he tells me, smile

43

slanting just enough to become patronizing, "and witches do not mix well."

"I'm not a witch," I whisper back, ensnared by his intense gaze.

"I'd beg to differ."

Our glares collide in a standoff. Just as I prepare to defend my claim, he concedes, dropping his eyes to my wrists once more. His fingers quickly undo my binds, letting the belt fall to the forest floor with a soft thud. I groan in relief, eyes drifting shut in a semblance of peace as the ache in my bones begins to recede.

Manners ingrained in me long ago beg me to thank my captor, but common sense points out the obvious; *my captor* will receive no thanks from me.

When his fingers languidly intertwine with my own, I buckle in shock and stare at him in astonishment. Words lost to his casual demeanor. The move is intentional, no doubt to stun me, and he takes advantage of my bewilderment slipping one steel-banded arm around my waist and pressing against me. I suck in a harried breath.

"This might be... unpleasant for you." He tells me, eyes half-mast as his gaze focuses steadily on my birthmark. "They say the sealing of a soulmark can be quite... intense. But what kind of pleasure is without its own pain? Hmm?" He releases my hand to scorch a trail upward and across my breast.

"Please." My voice cracks pathetically as his fingers inch toward my birthmark. "You're wrong. It's just a birthmark." My heart continues its erratic dance, but queerer still is the wild pulse now coming from my birthmark. "Don't!" But it's too late.

The point of his middle finger brushes against the mark, and I am gasping. Reeling. Hurtling toward darkness.

And then everything is gone.

Only he and I remain among the stars and trees and earth and air. A crushing wave of emotion and energy surges inside me. Finds every nook and cranny left unattended and takes root. *Rocks my fucking world.* Nothing has ever made me feel so... alive. It is as if my body is reclaiming some lost part of myself, and the soul-searing experience takes my breath away. All that's left in its wake is a sudden and all-consuming burning. A need. *A hunger.* I gasp, feel lightning strike at my very core, and watch helplessly as my entire world is turned and flipped. Wind whips around me. Rushes through me. Fills me so completely, I feel I might burst.

"Let it be known that thee are found," he whispers roughly, his head tipping to rest against mine as his hand presses flush against the birthmark, "and my soul awakened. The stars incline us"—we share a shuddering breath, eyes boldly meeting one another— "and so we are sealed." I stagger forward. Choke on the rush of power and heat as they barrel into me. Mercilessly. His scent and touch flood my senses. I feel him. Everywhere. Inside and out.

I push away from his embrace, breaking the blazing contact that is his hand to my heart. No. Not heart. Birthmark. The bark scrapes against my skin, reminding me of reality, but all I can hear is my blood as it pumps through my veins—screaming at me to move closer to this man. He leans forward. I cringe back.

"Don't," comes my hoarse reply. My breath sounds harshly against the night air as beads of sweat drip down my back. "What did you do?" He takes a step away from me, releasing me completely from his hold and my knees buckle comically in response. He remains near as I try to collect myself. As I try to douse the fire raging inside of me. Fill my lungs with air. Let my bones tremble in relief as the onslaught desists. But the blood that courses through my veins

45

remains on fire. And the birthmark yearns for his touch.

I raise my eyes to his, and all I see is me. Right at their very center.

Faintly I feel my birthmark pulse with two beats instead of one. Somehow, I know—without a doubt— that the other beat belongs to him. Tears burst forth before I can stop them, and I hardly notice the way his hands find their way back to me in my distress. He inhales deeply, nostrils flaring as he watches me, a thousand emotions swirling behind his green eyes.

"What did you do?" I whisper roughly as I slump toward the ground, my energy leaving me in one fell swoop. My words are greeted with a frown and downward flick of his mouth. Before I drift into unconsciousness, his words sound a soft echo in my mind.

"I've got you."

+++

I never suffered a migraine before, but there is a very solid chance I am experiencing one now. Tiny hammers pound relentlessly against the back of my eyes. Scratch that, big hammers, and ones that mean business with bitsy little skulls imprinted on their sides in red. My brain is also attempting to tear itself loose from my skull and damn near succeeding.

Nausea rests at the back of my throat as I stare dumbly around my new surroundings. The room I'm in is not my own, but the bed is achingly soft, and I whimper from the small comfort it provides.

"You're awake." Oh, God. Not him. I find him easily, sitting in a chair at the opposite end of the room. His head is slightly bent, those mossy green eyes staring at me through half-mast lids. His dark shaggy hair casts shadows over his Roman nose and full lips.

"You're a kidnapper," I murmur, cringing at the sound of my voice, raspy and rough.

"There's tea just there. It should help."

I pull myself upright, battling down the bile threatening to rise, and lean weakly back against the pillows and headboard behind me. The tea to my right lazily billows steam. The smell is familiar—surprisingly so—and I take hold of it with both hands. A cautious sniff and delicate sip bring a pleased hum to my lips. It is familiar; it's one of the aunt's creations. I ignore the way it scalds my tongue and throat on the way down and relax into the almost instant relief it provides against the pounding in my head.

He's still staring at me. "Better?"

I clear my throat, setting down the cup. "I'll be better once I'm home."

He gives me a wry smile, "I'm afraid we need to have a small chat before you can see your grandmother. I hope that's not too much to ask?"

I hesitate to reply. I want desperately to refuse him but know that I'm not the one with the upper hand. With chagrin, I find I cannot read his body language. Everything about him reads false, with his put upon casual demeanor and smooth confidence. My fingers itch to reach for my necklace and draw comfort and strength from it, but I hold still.

Green eyes darken in my continued silence, and he stands, walking over to the end of the bed. When he smiles his dimples appear once more, yet still his expression is unreadable. "Xander."

He says it like an offering, waiting expectantly for me to respond in kind. We stay that way for some time until a cramp begins to form in my lower back. I adjust my seating, grimacing at the soreness that seems to pulse from my bones. Speaking of sore... my eyes flit down to my chest. The crescent moon birthmark seems much darker than before, more

47

pronounced. I catch his expression as his eyes dip toward the mark as well, then back to my face. He seems... anxious.

"Zoelle, but everyone calls me Zoe."

"You bear my mark." Xander's voice is quiet but steady, and I find my hand traveling to just above my heart to shield the birthmark that lies there.

"It's just a birthmark," I tell him neutrally.

He snorts. His face is the picture of tired amusement. "It's my mark."

"*No, it isn't.*"

He responds by roughly tugging his shirt over his head and baring his back to me. Sitting inconspicuously on his left shoulder blade is a dark mark in the shape of a crescent. My heart gives a sudden and painful lurch. The mere sight of my mark's twin makes my mouth turn dry. It has absolutely nothing to do with the way his muscles rippled and contracted in the dim lighting. "That's... just a coincidence. Loads of people are bound to have birthmarks like ours." He turns around to face me.

"And how would you explain what happened in the forest?" His regard is wicked when combined with the thick timber of his voice, and I turn my gaze defiantly away. He doesn't have to sound so smug. "Well?" he inquires. I take another sip of the tea. Stalling shamelessly as my heart begins to race slowly. I can't explain it, and he and I both know it. "My brother only kept you alive because he caught sight of your soulmark, Zoelle. Because he knew it matched mine. All lycans have soulmarks, but not all find their match. If they do... well, it's quite like finding your soul mate. Only better. Everything is so much *more.*"

He smiles. Something real and genuine for once, and I find myself listening aptly, my gaze tentatively returning to his. "Bound soulmarks strengthen the pack because they are the heart of the pack. They are the reason we fight. They are our courage and strength. And you, Zoelle Baudelaire, are my greatest strength and weakness because of this. Yet, without you, I am weaker still."

"How do you know my last name?" I whisper, face surely turning ashen as a million reasons run through my mind. None of them good.

"Your phone," he says simply. "Your grandmother is Diana Baudelaire, is she not?" I nod reluctantly but feel the urge to slap the arrogant smile he shoots me.

I digest his earlier words, confusion and self-righteous anger rising forth as my migraine recedes. I lick my lips nervously. "Soul mates?" It comes out part scoff, part taunt. "You're joking, right?" I have been chased, captured, taken to some stranger's house with no remorse, and he has the nerve to spin me some bullshit story about love and soul mates?

"No, *soulmark*. Hasn't your grandmother taught you anything?" he inquires, seeming truly curious despite my hostile response.

Apparently not, I think furiously. "Kindly leave my grandmother out of this and let me go. I'm sure everything can be forgotten, and charges won't need to be pressed—"

"No," he says calmly, cutting me off. His jaw ticks as he scowls down at me. "You don't seem to understand. You bare my mark, and I yours. We belong together. The first step has already been completed. We are sealed."

A shiver darts up my spine at the memory. The lingering sensations send goose bumps across my flesh. I begin to disagree, but he is at my side in an instant. *How could he possibly move so fast?* "I felt you. I felt your breath fill me, and suddenly you were everywhere: in my gut, in my lungs, in my throat. I touched your skin, and you rose up around me. Filled every part of me. You embraced me, Baudelaire.

"I've dreamt of finding my soulmark all my life. I waited and waited until one day I placed all thoughts

49

of you to the far recesses of my heart. And now you're here." His eyes hold mine captive, a fire burning behind them to go along with his emblazoned words. "And you felt it too, I saw it. I saw it in your eyes. The way it consumed you, body and... soul. It may not be tonight, or tomorrow, or the day after that"—he laughs humorlessly—"but soon I'll be your every thought and dream as well. I promise you that."

A panicky feeling itches at my insides. Screams at me to leave. But I'm frozen in place. I take a deep breath, then breathe it out slowly and purposefully. "No," I say firmly. "If what you're saying is..." I pause unsteadily, let out a sharp bark of laughter, eyes widening as the panic crawls up the back of my throat. "... that we're—no. Just, no! There are no such things as soul mates. No lycans. No witches."

He raises an eyebrow at my show of hysterics. I glower in return. "You're still adamant that you're not a witch?"

"Of course, I'm not!" My hands jut upward and land in a flop at my side. "Are you crazy? I'm not a—a witch."

"I'm not letting you go, Zoelle."

"I'm not yours to do anything with, Xander. Your stupid seal be damned." I hiss back. He growls. Literally, *growls*. A deep guttural sound of frustration and intimidation. I shrink back, and he immediately softens.

"While this isn't how I planned our first encounter going," he tells me through gritted teeth, "there's no changing what has occurred. Maybe a chat with your grandmother will make you see sense, and afterward, we can talk again."

I sneer back at him before turning my hostile gaze toward the wall, but Xander growls once more. Taking me by the chin, he forces my face toward him once more. "Don't turn away from me, Zoelle. And don't show me your neck until you're fully ready to make that commitment—do you understand?" His fingers pinch painfully into my skin until I utter my compliance, and then they move, faster than lightning, to graze the length of my neck. I jerk backward and eye him distastefully. Taking in my expression, I note the flash of hurt that crosses his features, but it goes just as it quickly as it came. He exits the room without another word.

I'm shaking and crying when Gran comes in, my knees curled into my chest and my arms locked around as much of my body as I can.

"Oh, Zoelle." Her expression is downtrodden as she comes to sit by me.

"Gran, what is happening? What's going on? I don't understand. That... that man thinks I'm his soul mate! And there were wolves in the woods, Gran! Men who turned into wolves right before my very eyes. Oh God—" I let out a pathetic moan. "—and he keeps calling me a witch. A *witch*!" She pulls me into her arms, holding me tightly while I regain my breath.

"This is not the way I wanted you to find out," she whispers sadly in my ear. My entire body stiffens in response as she eases me away.

"What?"

"Sweetheart, what exactly has he told you so far?" I stare at her flabbergasted before detailing our conversation. Tears threaten to gush again with each passing word. She sighs once more, something laden and forlorn, before straightening her back. "You saw those men shift from man to beast? Transform?" I nod. Gran rolls her shoulders back, straightening before me. "It's true, Zoelle," she tells me, her voice unwavering.

"But, Gran—"

"Zoelle, you *are* a witch. All of those things that man told you... they are true. There's a whole other world hidden right before your eyes, but it seems I can't shield you from it any longer."

A thousand stones land at the bottom of my stomach at once. I blanch. My nausea comes back full force for one terrible moment before subsiding. It can't be true. Things like this don't happen! Witches and werewolves don't exist!

Except I saw with my own eyes the transformation of man to wolf.

"Gran... this can't...."

"My darling girl, the women of our family all carry magic inside of them. Me, your sister, and mother included." My mouth falls open in wonder. "Aunt Mo and Lydia, too."

"Witches?" I whisper weakly. Gran nods.

"Our family is blessed. In each generation, at least two women are born: one to cast, and one to brew. The elder and younger respectively."

"I'm a brewer? What does that even mean?"

Gran sends me a wry grin. "Why sweetheart you brew just about every day, don't you? You cook. You impart your emotions into every dish, letting your diners experience what you want. It's a particular kind of influence that—"

"Wait." I hold up a hand and screw my eyes tightly shut for a second. "My feelings go into my *food*?"

"Yes, sweetheart. Your sister was a caster, as was your mother. They follow in my footsteps, but I've learned a thing or two about brewing with my age."

"And did you know about...." My fingers graze near my collarbone. Gran shakes her head.

"I promise you, darling, *I didn't*. I only knew that I didn't want you to be a part of this world. Not until I felt you were ready. There's so much more to tell you—" A knock sounds at the door before Ryatt pokes his head inside. His dark hair is styled in messy spikes and he sports an annoyingly crooked smirk as he steps into the room. He gives a moment's pause before placing a hand mockingly over his heart. His blue eyes are startling blue, a fact I'm surprised I missed before.

"What a touching scene."

"What do you want, *dog?*" Gran asks coldly. He pouts.

"My brother asked me to fetch you. Won't you follow me?" His hand sweeps out in front of him and waits for us to stand before exiting. We follow stiffly.

We walk down a long hallway. The walls painted a creamy white, decorated with large art pieces full of abstract colors to catch the eye. I try to lose myself in the work and detail of each color I pass, doing my best to choke down my thumping heart. Gran walks ahead of me, only a foot behind Ryatt, head held high. God, I still feel like I'm going to throw up. If only I had Gran's confidence.

We walk into a formal room, the walls a vibrant royal blue with white crown molding and gold accents. The room is fit for a king with furniture that looks much too nice to sit on, let alone discuss supernatural politics. Xander stands near a drink cart, pouring himself a glass of liquid amber. Near him, a woman sits in a high-backed chair. Her hair is dark and reaches well past her small bust. She eyes us without a hint of a smile. Ryatt makes himself comfortable in the other available high-backed chair, gesturing for Gran and me to take our seats on the small settee.

"You've spoken, then?" Xander asks, coming to stand near the woman in the seat. Glass clutched tightly in his grasp.

"Barely," Gran retorts. "Ten minutes is hardly enough time to explain the situation we find ourselves in."

"I assume you were able to cover the basics," he says unmoved, "the mark and what it means. I suggest we begin discussion immediately on the forthcoming nuptials to occur between me and your granddaughter."

"Whoa!" I cry, "Nuptials? Let's all calm down for a moment, all right? A wedding? That hardly seems necessary."

"Of course, it's necessary." The woman sneers, her pert nose stuck permanently in the air. "Honestly." She tut-tuts.

"Irina," Xander growls in warning. They must be siblings. Their eyes are the same intense green and chins so similarly cleft. Not to mention their glossy dark hair, a trait all three have in common. Her lips form a pout.

"Your impatience has certainly done you no favors, brother," she remarks, glaring at Xander with a beautiful scowl. *Scorn has never looked so good on the woman*, I think mildly envious.

"You are here to observe and stand witness, Irina, not for your unamusing commentary." Irina releases a low-pitched growl; her lip beginning to curl when Ryatt barks out a laugh.

"These two are always at the ready to put on a show," he comments. "You'll get used to it."

Oh no, I will not.

"I'm sure some compromise can be found," Gran volunteers stoically. "Unfortunately, as circumstances stand, Zoelle has only recently been informed of her birthright and heritage. She cannot be expected to complete the bonding without all available knowledge presented to her. Nor will I force her into a marriage without her express consent."

Xander glares at Gran while the room stands silently at her statement. "How... unorthodox," Irina chimes after a minute. "Surely the standard courting procedure will do. The soulmark has already been sealed. It's only a matter of time before the marking and binding will be completed. Zoelle should live under our roof while terms of a treaty can be negotiated between our families."

I stare in a stupor at Irina, well aware that I am under her brother's scrutiny. "No deal." My firm response quiets the group. "If we're witches, can't we just undo this? With a spell or potion? Something?" I toss a helpless look at Gran whose face pulls into a frown.

"You cannot erase what is born, nor can we ignore the triggering of the seal," Gran tells me softly. "But you do have a choice in this, Zoelle. It is not unheard of for a soulmark to be rejected, but it will be uncomfortable to ignore."

"It will be impossible to ignore if I have anything to say about it." Xander all but barks.

"You will not force this upon my granddaughter," Gran retorts heatedly. "I'll be damned before allowing that to happen. And don't think for a moment the Trinity Coven will rally behind this union. Not if Zoelle doesn't want it. Remember wolf, if she does not wish to be found, we can make it so. Your soulmark be damned." The three siblings growl menacingly at the threat, but Gran doesn't back down.

"Surely an agreement can be reached. There's no reason for these two lovebirds to face the pain they are sure to endure by ignoring the mark," Ryatt finally says, all traces of joviality gone. "Think of the possibilities their union could bring—this town would need never know fear with our families and priorities aligned. Furthermore, why deny your granddaughter her soul mate? We both know she will find no other—"

"I have a boyfriend," I blurt out, face turning bright red as all eyes crash into me. "I... have a boyfriend. Who I love." My eyes find Xander's, pleading with this mysterious man to understand. "I'm sorry, but I just don't think this will work. Maybe we can be... friends?"

Irina snorts, her heading shaking in disdain. "In love," she mutters, "what you have now with your little boyfriend will pale in comparison to what you will have with my brother. Maybe you should be allowed more time to speak with your grandmother on the topic before she departs. Then we shall reconvene tomorrow to discuss the particulars?"

"I'm not staying here," I say after processing Irina's words. "I'm going home with Gran, and there will be no more—"

"We will speak on the matter more tomorrow, but I must agree with Zoelle. She will not be staying here."

Irina bristles. "Don't be ridiculous. It's customary for those who bear the mark to reside with the male's family. It's understandable that one might think these unusual circumstances might grant an exception, but I assure you, they do not." Gran stands slowly, eyeing Irina with disdain and her fingers begin to let off sparks.

I stare wide-eyed as the room holds its breath, the atmosphere charged with unrelenting energy just waiting to snap. Xander lets out a huff of annoyance, snarling sharply at his sister, who reluctantly tilts her gaze downward toward the floor, exposing her throat ever so slightly to her brother.

"Zoelle may leave with you for the night," he finally speaks, voice low and hard, "but I must insist on settling the terms of agreement on the morrow."

"Xander," Irina cries in distress, "you can't—"

"That's final," he snaps.

"You'll both suffer for it. You esp—"

"I said that's final, and I meant it." The room goes quiet once more as I stand quickly from the couch, hovering by Gran's side uneasily.

"You're aware of the consequences your actions may have if no... reasonable, compromise can be reached?" Ryatt asks pointedly of Gran, his voice ominous and face somber. Gran takes me by the hand and leads me out of the room, and out of the house, our answer clear.

My head spins in a daze the entire way home, my heart in my throat and feelings a blur as they cascade through me. Witches, werewolves, and soulmarks? What have I gotten myself into?

The Art of Negotiation
- Chapter 4 -

"So, let me see if I have this all understood. First and foremost, we are a family of witches." The words come out of my mouth without a trace of the bitterness I feel inside, and I mentally clap myself on the back. Considering I've been *lied* to my entire life, I feel I'm displaying a great deal of composure. "They are werewolves, whoops—*lycans*, who moved to town because of a dispute with another pack, and now the town is split into two territories, the witches and the wolves. Soulmarks are basically 'soul mates' but with matching birthmarks. And, I can cook up all my emotions into either fabulous or disastrous meals? I'm assuming I could *brew* up a mean potion or two as well."

"Correct," Gran responds into the silence that follows my rant.

"Show me." Gran holds her body still, but her eyes move pointedly to the kitchen windows. With a graceful flick of her wrist, the windows fly open.

Every. Single. One. *Holy shit.* "Thanks," I murmur in awe.

The aunts were shooed away earlier so Gran and I could chat, and I couldn't help but be thankful. I'm tired and sore. Leaden veins slow my movements and cause aches, which reverberate through my body. The fingers of the clock tick past one, and I know if our conversation continues—as it had for the past few hours—I'll never sleep.

"And," I say warily, "I might find myself in physical pain from not completing the soulmark bond—I mean, soul binding? Can you explain that bit again?"

Gran sips her tea before starting. "As you so aptly put, a soulmark indicates a person's one, true other half, or soul mate, as you like to say. It means your soul is split in half, with one half residing in you and the other in him." I nod my head along, feeling numb from her words. Words she has repeated a dozen times now. "To merge the souls into one, three steps must be completed: the sealing, marking, and binding. All happen in a similar fashion. Ancient spellbound words are spoken, and the mark touched by the other half. With each step, the souls are tied closer together. The bond between the two individuals growing deeper."

"I thought something different happened with each step?" I ask, voice quizzical as my brows pull together.

"The sealing happens with only the spellbound words spoken and mark touched. The marking involves an offering of blood, and the binding a reciprocation of words."

"And he sealed me?" Gran wears a troubled frown, before strumming up the nerve to confirm the horrid truth. My throat bobs traitorously. "What kind of pain happens if I don't complete the process? Cramps? Blistering headaches? Fevers? Maybe I should chance it."

"Fever, yes. Some hallucinations. An ache in your bones. A hunger for... more."

A shiver brings goose bumps to my arms and the nape of my neck. "And there isn't any helpful potion I could brew to avoid that is there?"

Gran looks contemplative, her silent reverie going on a bit too long for comfort. "It might be possible to conjure something, though there is no guarantee. Just know that—"

"Whatever I decide you will stand beside."

"As will the coven," she informs me.

"Gran, I'm so confused. How is it that I've never felt my so-called powers before? And if we're so magical, then why couldn't Clara and Mom save themselves when the crash happened? Shouldn't our magic have protected all of us?"

The questions tumble out before I can stop them. The want for answers is a deep pain inside me. "The necklace you wear was once your great-grandmother's. Did you know that?" I nod. "It's your talisman. Your mother wasn't wearing hers the day of the accident; it acts as a barrier of protection. Why she wasn't wearing it... well, she didn't want to be a part of the family business, so to speak."

"Then, why pass down the necklaces to us if she didn't want us to be involved in it?"

"Because, my dear, given the right opportunity you would have been told and left to make the decision yourselves. Regardless, the talisman was a sure-fire way to offer you two protection from harm."

"And Clara?"

Gran's sorrow shows on her face. "The paramedics either took it off of her or it broke off during the accident. Yours was kept on long enough while the paramedics and doctors stabilized you. By the time they removed it for your surgery it had done its job."

My fingers curl protectively around the jade stone. The urge to cry bubbles up—undeniable, but I hardly

60

have any left to spare. My head throbs with all the tears I've shed, and Gran seems to understand, ushering me from the formal sitting room near the entryway and into the kitchen. She ignites a fire under the kettle with a flick of her wrist while she rummages through the tea cupboard. I stare in unabashed shock.

"Can I do that?"

Gran turns around back to me, a jar of pink, green, and white tea leaves cupped in her hands. "Of course, you can."

"Seriously?"

"Yes," she says, kind amusement lacing her words. "Which leads me to your other inquiry and why you haven't felt the magic within you. You see this cabinet here?" She pats the door of the tea cupboard. "These teas all cater to a specific purpose. The one you're about to consume will allow you to sleep without dreams and cloud your mind. Some in here will grant you foresight or luck. Others produce lust or rage. There's even one to... suppress certain feelings or urges or...."

The furrow in my brow deepens, "My green tea mix has been suppressing my magic?"

"Your *herbal* tea has been." She corrects.

"But... it's not like I drank it every day."

"As long as you consume the tea at least once a week it does its job, sweetheart. I'm sorry to have kept it from you, Zoelle."

"That's all right, Gran," I say, followed by a sigh, "It was probably for the best." I give her a weak smile. "You don't suppose there's a spell to turn back time, do you?"

"Time is not ours to meddle with," Gran says while pouring our drinks. The front door opens and shuts. The aunts have returned. Their footsteps tread tentatively toward the kitchen entrance before Aunt Mo peeks her head in.

"Diana, is there enough water in there for two more cups?" Gran looks to me. My mind follows slowly behind.

"There is," I say finally, holding my mug with both hands and leaning into the kitchen island. The aunts bring their mindless chitchat with them, briefly explaining their outing to see Rebecca Germaine on Fourth Street who's trying to pawn off some of her bathtub gin.

"We brought back a bottle," Aunt Mo says.

"We brought back two." Aunt Lydia corrects. "One for each of us."

"That good?" Aunt Lydia snorts, raising an eyebrow impressively high.

"We'll be able to sterilize anything with them."

The room tapers off into calm silence, though I sense a small trace of tension in the air. I haven't felt this tired—this exhausted—since the accident. A wariness sinks down onto my shoulders, bending me to its will.

"Zoelle." Gran and the aunts look at me with varying degrees of concern, and finally, I see the peace offering. The chocolate bar in front of Aunt Mo, glides across the island counter without aide. My breath catches at the action and my eyes widen. The numbness I feel waivers as I pick up the treat and enjoy its rich, smooth taste.

"Thank you," I mumble past splayed fingers, still chewing.

"You've certainly gotten yourself into a pickle," Aunt Lydia finally says.

I groan. "I know."

"Have you told her about Melissa, Diana?" Aunt Lydia asks. Gran shakes her head, eyes hardening.

"The choice to move forward should be her own decision."

"Her decision should be made with all the facts present," Aunt Mo scolds, and for a brief moment, Gran looks away, ashamed.

"What is it?" I ask. My grip tightens around the steaming mug as my heart jumps a beat. Gran and Aunt Mo share a look before Gran lowers her eyes and gives her short nod of consent.

Aunt Lydia takes a deep breath. "It was a waxing crescent moon when it occurred. Melissa and her father were out collecting the violet oleander that grows wild near the Elder Creek when they happened across a young man. He said he followed a scent on the wind that led him to the pair. Once he saw Melissa, he knew without seeing her mark that she was his. Of course, Bart intervened, Melissa's father, and the mark was not sealed. This caused tension, and understandably so, between the coven and pack. Lines were drawn, the coven supporting Melissa's family in her refusal and the wolves pushing for completion of the mark.

"The coven ended up hiding Melissa. We kept her away from the boy whose name was Martin, Marcel—"

"Malcolm." Aunt Mo provides.

"Yes, Malcolm. But you see, the family held no love for the wolf pack. After all, it was only years before they lost a member of their family to a wolf pack in Troy. A town north of here. The very same town and pack the Adolphus pack came from. As you might imagine, the issue of the soulmark was always going to be contentious. Melissa held no desire to be bound to a lycan. But Malcolm grew... obsessed. Crazed. One day he was able to seal the mark, but the feelings it brought only scared the poor girl. The family refused to acknowledge it. Melissa refused to leave home. Refused to eat after a time."

"It was quite a shame. She had such potential. Such promise," Gran voices, her tea held close to her

63

chest. "She would have made a fine healer, but it was not meant to be."

Aunt Mo nods, a gentle tilting of her head. "Indeed she would have. Malcolm did not take the rejection well either. He became easily enraged. Distraught. Manic some might say. As your grandmother may have told you, past a certain point after the sealing is complete the two individuals need to maintain a certain amount of physical proximity and contact. Lest either endure some form of heartache. It disrupts the physical well-being of both parties in the long run, but wolves are so volatile to begin with that they are by far, worse off."

Aunt Lydia takes a long drag of her tea, rolling her shoulders back as she leans against the sink. With a small sigh, she cradles the tea in front of her breast, holding it close while the small spoon resting inside of it twirls lazily in a circle. My eyes trace the movement, mesmerized by the effortless use of magic the aunts possess. And Gran, for that matter. When I catch Aunt Lydia's eye, she is staring serenely back at me, a faraway look in her eye.

Aunt Lydia's voice takes on an odd, unaffected tone. One that reaches miles away. "In the end, Bart killed Malcolm, though he lost his own life as well. The whole event was awful. Malcolm was practically stalking the poor girl. Had driven himself mad in his pursuit. The pack was constantly trying to negotiate some agreement but to no avail. In the end, neither family won."

"What about Melissa?" I ask tentatively.

"She's not the same woman she once was. And after the deaths, the most peculiar thing happened."

"What?" I sit up straighter in my seat, more alert than ever at the harrowing story.

"She moved in with the Adolphus family. Her mother was destroyed, so she left to go live with her sister in Vermont. Nobody ever found out why."

"Oh my God." Hums of agreement sound from all three.

"Drink the rest of your tea before it gets cold, Zoelle," Gran reminds me gently. I knock back the lukewarm liquid feeling an almost instant wave of sleepiness hit me. The aunts can see the effect it has and take my mug away. "Go to bed, Zoelle. Tomorrow we'll... we'll figure something out." I nod.

The motion is minuscule as my eyelids grow steadily heavier. I slip up to my room quietly. Ignoring the murmur of voices from the kitchen, I find myself asleep before my head touches my pillow.

+++

My thoughts torment me. All morning and afternoon, I skulk in my room until Aunt Lydia is brave enough to coax me out with a well-placed and all-knowing glare. There's no use in trying to avoid it because the situation can't possibly be ignored. I must make a decision. Tonight. But with so much information to process, I've only managed to work up a nasty headache. When I finally decide to eat something and join everyone in the kitchen, I'm greeted with sympathetic and pitying gazes. It makes my throat tighten uncomfortably.

"How are you, sweetheart?" Gran asks once I sit down with a bowl of cereal to quench my hunger.

"Tired. Confused. Kind of miserable and—" I take a large bite of my cereal, finding some pleasure in the satisfying crunch that resounds. "—scared out of my mind." I cover my mouth as I speak, my words coming out garbled, but understandable.

"And have you reached a decision?" Aunt Mo probes with all her subtlety. She has her long white hair braided like a crown around her head, with gaudy earrings tinkling with each minute movement she makes. I slowly nod my head, avoid eye contact, and give my cereal the attention it deserves. "And?"

"And I've made it," I snap back. A flush draws at the bottom of my neck. Heat rises on my tawny brown skin. Aunt Mo seems more put in her place than offended, a fact I'm grateful for.

"Well, I'm glad you've made it." Aunt Lydia chimes in. "Because Aleksandr will be over in a few hours to discuss the situation with you further."

I frantically find Gran's unwilling gaze. "*What?*"

"We made the agreement yesterday, or have you forgotten already?" she asks me rather harshly as I slump back in my seat. "Unfortunately, I will not be able to attend—"

"What? But you have to! I can't do this alone, Gran. Please"—my voice cracks on the word—"I need you there."

"Don't worry, dear. We'll be there to chaperon. Mr. Adolphus will conduct himself in a manner that we see fit," Aunt Mo says. With a flick of her wrist, red sparks ignite briefly from her fingertips, a smug smile playing on her lips. "No shenanigans."

Aunt Lydia nods her agreement, a similar smile etching its way across her face. "No *lying*." The tilt of her lips changes, slanting in such a way that sends a little shiver down my spine. With grace and confidence, she raises her palm upward, a sphere of crackling blue flame appearing, then disappearing, with ease.

No shenanigans or lying, check, I gulp and nod along, my regard skirting back to Gran.

"Why won't you be there?" Gran turns her attention elsewhere.

"Business." Her response is the epitome of nonchalance and my back goes straight.

"What *business?*"

"The important kind."

"What's more important than your granddaughter practically being forced into some crazy, supernatural marriage?"

The air stills, but Gran does not answer. My heart plummets to the bottom of my chest, and I release a shaky breath. Standing, I grab my bowl and place it calmly in the sink before exiting the room and sulking back to my own.

The hours pass slowly as I wait for the clock to chime nine. During the excruciating hours, I grapple with my decision. Yes or no. Run or hide. Live or survive. I'm conflicted at every new thought that graces my mind until I'm reduced to a cool numbness.

Ten minutes before the fateful hour, the doorbell echoes throughout the house. A cruel shiver surges across my skin as anticipation and fear merge into one. I hear a pair of feet make their way upstairs. The old wood creaks with each step as they tread reluctantly toward my door. Would it be Aunt Lydia or Aunt Mo to get me? I shift in my seat, gently twisting a piece of paper in my hand before a gentle knock sounds at my door. I stiffen, my breathe suddenly switches to short, little bursts. The paper in my hand crunches in my painful grasp.

Am I making the right decision? The thought haunts me. I want desperately to run and hide from this situation. Avoid making any kind of decision until I calm down. Until I find my footing. And even then... I don't want the pressure of making such a huge choice. One that will affect my future irrevocably.

"Your guest has arrived." Gran's voice lilts. I stare at the door in astonishment, quickly rising and crossing the threshold to answer the door.

"You're still here," I say in one breath. Gran looks grimly back at me.

"Only long enough to set some ground rules. Come, dear." I follow behind her silently, dread beginning to push away all other feelings. The time is now, no matter how much I wish it had never come.

They're seated in the formal sitting room. Aunt Lydia and Aunt Mo sitting opposite one another in the matching set of floral armchairs, the ones too stiff for my liking, and Xander sits rigidly on the more comfortable loveseat. I eye the very clearly presented empty spot next to him with disdain.

"Now," Gran says, chin lifting as she eyes Xander from his seated position, "tonight will go as I instruct. Zoelle has questions. You will answer them. Honestly." She nods to the tea set before him. "After her questioning, you may present your case to Zoelle. After which she will provide you with her decision. Whatever it may be, the coven will support."

"Because that worked out so well the last time," he mutters, eyeing me with thinly veiled interest. "I'm sure we can work something out that is amicable to both parties."

Gran nods and turns to me, her hand squeezing my arm comfortingly. "Trust your gut, honey. We're all behind you, no matter what you decide."

I swallow and manage a nod in return, watching dispassionately, and not without a little heartache, as she leaves. The door closes with a quiet click, and I'm forced to look back toward the scene I am left with. Xander's eyes drift meaningfully to the seat beside him and then back to me with a look that clearly says, "Come now."

He has his hair styled back tonight. The dark locks held in place by some hair product that smells faintly of cedar. His strong jaw is clean-shaven, and eyes are still a piercing green. He's dressed rather formally. A crisp white button-down tucked into dark pants, sleeves rolled to the elbows. Everyone watches my slow inspection, waiting patiently for my next move. Just for spite, and a dash of curiosity, I let my gaze linger over the swell of his biceps and well-shaped shoulders. It's obvious Xander takes care of his body, a characteristic I like in men usually, but not this one.

Swallowing my nerves, I look Xander in the eye before turning and walking purposefully to the kitchen, returning a moment later with a stool. I place it near the staircase in case a hasty retreat is required. Xander frowns. The aunts can barely contain their glee.

I can do this, I think to myself. I am a strong, beautiful, independent woman. My hands fiddle with the red headband I wear, as I take my seat. It takes all of my strength not to fidget with any other aspect of my appearance, though I am acutely aware of Xander's probing gaze.

Seated, I carefully straighten the crumpled paper I've been holding onto like a lifeline. It contains my *questions*. All three of them. "So," I clear my throat, "Aleksandr—"

"Xander. Call me Xander." Summer-field eyes cut through me. How can a person make one's tone soft, yet so firm? My eyes fall inexcusable to his lips, watching as his tongue quickly darts out to wet them.

"Xander." His name falls cautiously off my tongue. My honey-brown eyes lock with his as he leans forward. All of his attention rests on me. With more force than should be necessary, I look back down at the crumpled paper. "Are you sure that I'm—that is to say, uh,"—*just breathe*—"are you sure you're right?" I blurt out, eyes immediately darting upward to see his reaction.

His lips purse before delivering a curt nod.

"Don't forget your drink, Adolphus." Aunt Lydia reminds him sternly. He heaves a sigh, irritation radiating off him as he drinks what is in front of him.

"Yes," he says firmly. "I'm positive."

My eyes linger on the tea questioningly. "What exactly is in the tea?"

"A little something to ensure the truth is told. *Lunaria*," Aunt Mo explains casually. "Your Ben knows its effects well."

Ben knows it well? As in, Ben was dealt the same magical truth serum the other night? Anger simmers my blood, then stops cold in its tracks. *It means what Ben said was true.* When I turn an inquisitive gaze to Aunt Mo my anger returns. She looks anywhere but at my eyes, despite my growing glare. Knowing I can't stay in this standoff forever, I reluctantly push aside my hurt and anger. This isn't the time for *that* conversation.

"Tell me about yourself. Your likes and dislikes. Anything." An unsteady exhalation escapes after my words. Question number two: check.

Xander cocks his head a small fraction to the left before leaning back into the couch. His eyes still heavy in their assessment of me. I fight a blush under his regard, feeling needlessly self-conscious over my looks. Maybe I should have put on more makeup? Or worn a different outfit. One that didn't fit so snuggly, showing off my curvy hips and slender waist. *Damn, athleisure wear for being so comfortable.* Xander's eyes flick down the length of my body, then back to my eyes, a façade of cool nonchalance drifting over his demeanor.

"I'm the eldest of three and alpha of my pack," he begins smoothly, and then pauses, as if reconsidering his words. "I assume your coven has informed you of when we first came to Branson Falls, but perhaps not the reason why.

"We come from up north, originally, and belonged to a much larger pack. The Wselfwulf pack. They hold very traditionalist values. A large portion of us found the traditional ways outdated and unseemly. When no change was made from our requests, my father led us in leaving the pack. Acting as my father's beta, I helped with the transition. For the most part, it seemed the split would be... amicable. We were wrong.

With little warning the Wselfwulf pack's alpha demanded repentance for our slight." His lips curl at the word. Xander's feelings of loathing made clear. "And killed my father."

"That's awful," I whisper aghast.

"One day we will have our revenge," he tells me confidently. His chest expands as he sits straighter, straining the crisp white button-down against his pectorals. "Our pack is growing with those who defect from the Wselfwulf pack, births, and of course, soulmarks found and bound. Each strengthens my pack and me."

"Right." The word falls from my lips low and long as I process the information. When silence proceeds, the occupants of the room shift uncomfortably. I keep my eyes steadfast on my paper, a frown developing over my brow before I look at Xander again. "And, that's it? That's all you have to say about yourself?"

Xander's eyes widen in some confusion. He looks to both aunts uncertainly before returning his gaze to me. "Pardon?"

"I mean... I sort of knew most of that already. I was hoping more for—I don't know—what you do for a living, hobbies, maybe your favorite sports team?"

A light, melodious laugh emerges from him. It sends shivers down my spine and curls my toes. Suddenly he oozes confidence and certainty. Xander leans back into his seat as if he holds all the assurance in the world. As if he's already won this game. His deep-set gaze lingers in their perusal of me. I swallow and shift under the acute scrutiny, unable to control the flush that creeps up my neck.

He's going to be disappointed with my decision tonight.

"I work as a data analyst. It allows me to work remotely and create my own hours. I enjoy the outdoors: hiking, swimming, *hunting*." He says the word like it's some kind of secret, the word spoken

71

with a languid air and an infinity of unspoken promises behind it. "I don't follow sports. I much prefer to be active and part of the action than sitting around and watching it happen."

"Oh." Xander loses some of his luster at my dismayed response. "Anything else?" I ask hopefully.

Shouldn't there be more to say to someone you're trying to win over? A little originality? Or is this bond between us just a means to an end for him to achieve more power? Am I just some possession to acquire and throw away later, when the newness of it all wears off? A wave of uncertainty turns my stomach. It urges me to flee to my room and lock the door behind me. *But I can't*, I think disheartened. There is no reprise for me. I shake the sullen thoughts from my head, tired of running through them over and over again.

"I—" Xander's mouth opens and closes rhythmically, but no sound comes to pass. "What else do you want to know?" Anything. Something. A crumb that maybe, just maybe, there is something we share in common. A connection. Something other than this damnable mark. *Anything but this*.

"What do you want?" My words heavy with desperation. The question has him leaning forward again. Gone is his confident attitude, replaced instead with determination.

"You," Xander says calmly, his words smooth and controlled. "Your heart, your body, your soul. Everything you're willing to give me and more. I'll take it all and offer you everything in return if you would just consider...." It's all said with such gravity, and yet, his words have a lilting touch to them that enthrall me. Tempt me. "Jewels for your body, silks for your skin, a crown to place upon your brow. You would be an alpha. A queen with an army of wolves at your feet willing to serve your every command if you'll be mine. Bind yourself to me. Let me mark you as my queen. My alpha. My match."

72

The soulmark throbs between heart and collarbone, presuming once more to be in possession of its own will at his heady offer. With dismay, I realize that I too lean forward, my body unconsciously curling toward him. Dark lashes sweep down to cover my eyes, brushing tenderly against my burning cheeks. When I open them, he is still there. Along with his persistent gaze. He looks ready to leap across the distance between us and sweep me off my feet. *Goodness*. The beat of my heart will surely leave a bruise.

His offer is... too much. His entire presence is too oppressing and consuming. Everything. From the way he speaks to the way in which he postures himself is set to entice. A neat trap to pull me to his side without fuss, to come to heel, to lose myself to his will. Something inside me screams and shouts. Alarms sound off inside my head. Giving in now will surely be the end of me; the force of his will almost too painful to resist. But I haven't come this far in life to succumb to the will of some man.

"Zoe, your questions have been asked. Xander, your offer made. What say you, Zoe?" Aunt Mo asks, breaking the stillness with her declaration.

The words get stuck in my throat. The paper torn and crumpled in my now-closed grasp. It's now or never. "I think it's best if we remain... friends."

Xander snarls. His lips pulling back in disfavor as his eyes alight with renewed fever. "*No.*"

"*Yes,*" I respond immediately, sitting up straight and staring him in the eyes. "I have a *life*. I have a *boyfriend*."

"Then end it," he roars, standing. I slip from my seat as well, hands balled at my waist.

"No."

"Tell her," he demands of the aunts. "This is not acceptable."

"Oh, I think it's by far more than you could have hoped or asked for," Aunt Lydia drawls. Her eyes gleam with soft alertness. The lights flicker, a tinkling and small surging of energy pulsing through the room as Xander and I remain in our standoff.

Just breathe. "Friendship is all that I can offer you."

He rubs a hand over his face, raking his hand through his neatly kept hair as he lets out an indignant huff. "I would offer you the world, and it would not be enough? Is that what I am to believe?"

"I don't want—"

"You think your boyfriend will satisfy you more than I could? Is that it?"

I go stiff. "I love him."

Xander barely contains his scoff. "And you'll learn to love me, in time. And when that time comes, what then of your precious boyfriend?" I remain silent, jaw clenched tightly shut. "The forces that bind us together cannot be ignored, and I will *not* let you ignore them."

"I'm trying to be fair, all right?" I finally yell, "What do you expect me to do? Follow you obediently around like some lovesick puppy? I have a life, and just because you've suddenly found yourself inserted into it doesn't mean you get to walk all over it. You don't get to push everything I care about to the wayside!"

"I wouldn't—"

"You would!" I shout over him and take a step forward. "You ask for everything, and I can't give you that." My earnest plea seems to cut through him, his shoulders dropping as his righteous anger fades. "I can give you friendship. That's... that's it."

He seats himself, his mouth narrowing to resemble something akin to a gash across his perfect face. "Friendship," he says tersely. "I accept."

"You do?" I cannot hide my surprise, the well of outrage suddenly tapped dry. "*Seriously?*"

He nods resolutely, "Yes." The room remains silent for a time, the aunts passing between them an unreadable look as Xander stares contemplatively down at the table in front of him. "And what are the terms of this friendship you offer?"

Uh...

"I don't know," I tread cautiously. *Terms of friendship?* "Um, just what normal friendships are?" I don't mean for it to sound so much like a question, but I can't help my uncertainty. This isn't what I expected to happen. I haven't prepared for this.

"So, the terms of the friendship are negotiable?"

Eyes turn to me expectantly as I weigh his words. Maybe having set terms to the friendship won't be such a bad thing. With ground rules in place, maybe things will play out more smoothly. "Okay," I finally say, taking my seat again, "Did you have anything in mind?"

He flashes me a grin, his dimple winking at me as he eyes me with renewed interest. "Only one, you must see me every day. As you know, going prolonged periods of time without contact can cause discomfort. For both parties."

"I'm sure we can manage a few days in between seeing each other."

"But at what cost to our sanity?" he counters quickly.

"Oh, I think I'll manage just fine," I respond.

"You think you'll be immune to the bonds ill-effects?"

"I think I'll handle it better than you." We both know the words to be true. I have an arsenal of teas and other magical medleys to help me get on. Surely some of them can offer me comfort. Xander swallows.

"Six days a week then."

"Three."

75

He scoffs, a frown deeply embedded between his brow. "Three days? You're being ridiculous." He all but snarls.

"Well, I'd hardly say that." Aunt Mo scolds lightly. His frown only cuts deeper.

"You were right when you said you would be able to handle our absence better than I," he concedes. "Knowing that, you may expect my attentions to be more zealous on the days we do agree to meet and spend time together. Bare that in mind, Zoelle." I frown at his use of my given name but let it pass. "If I am allowed to only be in your presence for three days, then I shall have you for the entirety of those day. It will be the only way to sate my sanity."

I worry the paper between my fingers, "Four days, and we'll spend afternoons together."

"Five and we spend the evenings together." I gape and a gasp escapes at his rebuttal. "Not overnight, Baudelaire, just the evenings. From five till ten I think should do. We can spend time together over meals and good wine."

"Six until ten. Four nights a week."

Xander heaves a rather aggressive sigh, mulling over my proposition until countering. "Four evenings of the week, from six till nine, and your Sunday mornings."

I avoid his eyes. "And is there a time limit for Sunday mornings as well?"

"Hmm..." His smirk returns. "Eight until eleven? Surely that's fair." He tosses the last word at me with a hint of a smile.

"Eight?"

He rolls his eyes. "Fine, nine till noon. What say you to that? Mondays, Tuesdays, Wednesdays, Fridays, and Sundays?"

"For how long?" His gaze turns cold and unwavering, and by his fierce look, I know he will not dignify my question with an answer, not when I already know it. Forever. Even if forever was a dearly long time. "Not Fridays."

"Why not?" he asks tightly, his rigid posture somewhat more relaxed than before.

"Because." My retort sounds childish, even to me, and I cringe internally. I don't have to explain my reasoning to him. He smiles nonetheless.

"Agreed. Now let's talk about physical contact."

REHASHING TERMS
- Chapter 5 -

Somehow, I manage to convince Xander to begin our "friendship" on Monday instead of Sunday. A feat I marvel at, seeing as how our discussion had turned into a tense standoff of compromises and deals. Did I come out with the advantage? I'm not sure. Last night I made decision after decision without hesitation. The behavior was a complete one eighty from my usual timid nature.

It's difficult to recount every aspect of our conversation and dissect it, but the final agreement between Xander and me isn't terrible. I'd written all of the "rules" down.

Meal Deals
Mondays — dinner at home with Gran & aunts
Tuesdays — dinner alone with X
Wednesday — dinner alone with X
Thursday — dinner at X's with family
Saturday — nothing!
Sunday — Breakfast

Physical Contact
   Handholding — only at dinners with family present
   Hugs — maximum ~~2~~ 4/day
   Kissing — ~~NO~~ cheek & hands… okay
   any other physical contact outside of the above can only be initiated by me

Sniff*

I frown at the paper, eyeing the last word on the page. Xander's last request is by far the strangest, in that I allow him to *sniff me*. My skepticism gave way once the aunts made him drink the truth tea and repeat his request, assuring me my scent calmed him. Vowing to keep it to a minimum and perform the act only in the privacy of our homes, I relented.

He left looking far more satisfied than I liked, his lips barely brushing my cheek as he retreated with a soft goodnight. I went straight to bed after the affair, not wanting to talk to dissect the night's exchange with the aunts.

I hardly have my mind wrapped around everything before Monday night rears its ugly head, and with it, one of the worst dinners I have *ever* been party to.

The food I prepare is truly awful. Every bite bitter and tough to chew. The aunts do their best to alleviate the situation—Gran absent once again—but to no avail. The night ends in a slew of harsh comments and barbed words. When the clock finally struck nine, Xander bid his farewell hastily, dragging me from the table to escort him to the door. His hand held mine in a viselike grip before abruptly pulling me into a crushing hug, inhaling deeply, and leaving without another word.

79

Tuesday and Wednesday go a little better, both nights ending in their own heated confrontations.

Xander constantly scolds and lectures me for my unwillingness to cooperate. I growl back how I hadn't wanted any of this in the first place. That the proverbial race between friendship with *him* or slowly going mad is a close one, but my self-preservation continues to prevail. He blanches at my caustic replies and agrees to end each night early. I wonder each night why I put up with the forced charade. Contemplating thoughts of going crazy more seriously, then switching back to self-preservation mode. If I end up continuing the "friendship" with Xander, there is a very large chance I'll still go mad.

It's Thursday night, which means dinner at his family's house. I stand outside his home. His very large home, I might add, hoping beyond hope that tonight will go better than the others. Maybe if nobody talks, it will go smoothly.

I knock only once before an elderly woman dressed in black gestures me inside with a wry, but excited, grin and leads me to a room down a short corridor on the first floor. Irina and Ryatt sit near one another with drinks in their hands speaking casually. When I enter, they each send me their own greetings from afar. Ryatt shoots me a salacious smirk. Irina raises her sculpted brow. I smile uncertainly back.

"Zoelle!" A smooth feminine voice calls from the other side of the room. It is an older woman with long dark hair and fair skin. She must be in her fifties, maybe early sixties, but she wears her years well. Dressed in a figure-hugging A-line dress, she strides toward me with purpose, her eyes alight with unspoken curiosity. "My name is Katerina," she says, her Russian accent a lovely purr as she pulls me in to place a kiss on each cheek.

"Our mother," Ryatt says, watching the exchange before coming over to greet me as well. "Drink? Dinner will be ready soon enough, but there's no need to head into the lion's den without some liquid courage."

"Don't you mean wolf's den?" I say. His low chuckle fills the room. "A drink would be wonderful, thank you." I step out of Katerina's light embrace and force my strained smile to remain.

"What's your poison?"

"Gin and tonic?" I ask hopefully, catching Irina shaking her head out of the corner of my eye.

"I'm afraid there's no lime," Ryatt tells me as he hands me my drink a few minutes later.

I take a tentative sip, holding back a wince at the sharp effervescence. "That's all right. Thank you."

"Zoelle!" I turn half way before I feel Xander's hand on the hollow of my back. His touch, warmer than the average human I've learned, sinks past the fabric of my dress to my skin. I take a sharp breath as he presses his lips firmly onto my cheek and much too close to my lips. They linger unnecessarily, so my elbow gently reminds him to behave. He takes the hint, but as he pulls away his hand drags lightly across my hip, and his eyes run down my body in appreciation. I step away quickly. Not bothering to hide my disapproving stare.

"I've been informed dinner is served. Shall we?" He offers me his arm, eyes bright and warm as I reluctantly place my hand on the crook of his elbow.

As the dining room is on the other side of the house, I am treated to a small tour. Paintings by renowned artists litter the hallway, bringing a stark contrast to the dark walls with their vibrancy.

"You have quite the collection," I comment once I'm seated.

"Indeed, we do. We house a few Chagall and Picasso on the ground floor, and some Monet and various impressionist paintings on the others. My grandfather was a collector you see, and he passed along to me his love of art and most of his collection,"

81

Katerina answers softly, humming in delight as our salad plates are placed before us.

The salad is crisp, with large pieces of nuts scattered heartily throughout it and a light pepper lemon vinaigrette to top it off. At least the food is bound to be good tonight. "Xander tells us you can cook?" Ryatt inquires.

"Oh, wonderful!" Katerina exclaims before I can respond, "I've always been of the belief that a wife should be able to cook for her husband, but, lucky for you, dear Zoelle, we have a chef on staff to fit our needs."

"If you don't mind Mrs. Adolphus, I prefer Zoe." She smiles back at me magnanimously.

"Then I must insist you call me Katerina." I nod and stuff my mouth with a forkful of salad in lieu of responding to her actual comment. I cast a discreet frown at Xander, who clears his throat but does nothing to correct his mother.

"I consider myself a foodie of sorts," comments Ryatt, picking up where his mother left off. "I love a good feast of the senses."

"An amateur cook then? How quaint." Irina chimes in before I can speak. I take another large bite of salad and await my turn. "Mother, I completely agree with you. I'm sure there is no greater joy than cooking for one's family, but it is true. The Adolphus women are held to a certain standard. There will be no slaving away behind a hot stove for any of us."

"No cooking?" I finally say once I've cleared my small salad. A swell of foreboding builds in my stomach.

"We'll need to do something about your overall look of course. Teach you the politics and ways of our world, that sort of thing. There won't be much time for your little cooking hobby I'm afraid."

"Wait, just—hold on a minute." I lean to the side to allow my salad plate to be replaced by a fine piece of halibut. "My cooking isn't a hobby. I've just graduated from the Missoula College Culinary Arts program. I'm a chef, and I certainly don't plan to give up on my dreams or plans to be some... some accessory."

"A wife is hardly an accessory," Katerina replies. "As the wife of the alpha, you must assert your position as the female alpha of the pack, which includes many responsibilities such as the care and well-being of the pack, maintaining our traditions, and being available to your husband."

I turn to Xander hoping he will interject only for Irina to speak once more. Somehow, I hold back my groan. "It will take some work, but mother and I will whip you into shape." Her teasing words are laced with too much condescension for me to bear.

"I think you're under the wrong impression," I say after allowing a small silence to sit at the table. "What exactly did Xander tell you about our conversation last weekend?"

Xander clears his throat, throwing an anxious look my way. "Nothing out of the ordinary, only that we had come to an agreement to see each other."

I ponder his words, frowning down at my plate before meeting his eyes. "An agreement to see each other?"

"I'll admit," Ryatt says with a mischievous glint in his eyes, "we were worried about the outcome of your little discussion. What with the mishandling of the soul binding those years ago no doubt weighing on your conscious. But tell us, how did my dear brother persuade you to be so... accommodating?"

"Ryatt." Xander growls in warning. "Enough."

"Yes, do tell us, brother. How did you manage such a feat?" Irina asks, jumping on the bandwagon. I breathe a sigh of relief as her gaze turns to her brother and off me. Her voice takes on an innocent air that fools no one. "I, for one, am not surprised at all.

You're so good at charming every woman you meet. It's no wonder Zoe, here, succumbed."

"I said enough," Xander barks.

"Leave your brother alone, both of you. What on earth are you two trying to prove?" Katerina scolds, clearly confused by the sibling interaction.

"We only marvel at our brother's newfound emotional depth. You see, Zoe, Xander here has the emotional capacity of a teaspoon, and then you came along—"

"I suppose you would have me pursue love the way that you do, Irina? Wear my heart on my sleeve and pine away at every other woman who crosses my path? Never mind that they might have ulterior motives regarding our family."

Irina stands sharply, her gaze unwaveringly cold. "Don't be cruel, Aleksandr."

"Sit," he commands, his voice hard.

"Yes, sister, be a good girl and sit," Ryatt mutters behind his tumbler. She does so reluctantly, throwing biting glares at her brothers as her lips seal together tightly.

I feel a pang of empathy for the beautiful girl and let my frustration build. "I think," I begin slowly, pushing the halibut around my plate, "that you have misinformed your family about the conversation we had, Xander."

"Oh?" All eyes fall on me. Except for Xander's.

"We did agree to see each other. Five times a week for limited periods of time—with restrictions in regard to physical interactions."

"Oh," Katerina exclaims wide-eyed. Irina and Ryatt share a smile. "We agreed to be friends. Just. Friends. I will not be marrying your son, Katerina. And I'm certainly not going to give up cooking, Irina." Irina shrugs and scoffs at my response, but it doesn't have the same bite.

The table goes silent at my confession. Scanning the table for their reactions, I eat the fish in silence along with the others. Katerina is put out, shooting pointed glances at Xander, a small pout on her lips and a furrow in her brow. Ryatt quietly chuckles under his breath, a large smile on his face. Irina smirks victoriously, and Xander tenses furiously. His eyes bore into the side of my face imperiously as I continue to ignore him.

No more words are spoken as we finish our plates. I glance at my watch: 8:20 p.m. Only forty minutes more and I can get out of this place and go home. *Thank God.* Just as they clear our plates, a loud vibration hums through the room. We eye each other curiously around the table before a flush rises to my cheeks.

"I'm so sorry, would you mind if I...?"

Xander nods stiffly. "Of course, dear," Katerina agrees, shooing me away with a good-natured smile. I answer my phone once I've entered the adjacent room.

"Ben, hey!" I tuck a curl behind my ear. "How are you?"

"I'm good. I miss you!" I smile softly at his enthusiasm.

"I miss you too. When can I see you again?"

"Actually, that's why I was calling. I should be up near you tomorrow, are you free?"

"Yes, and if I'm not, I'll just move around my schedule."

"Perfect. I thought we could go out in the afternoon for a long walk, then grab something greasy for dinner."

"That sounds wonderful. It would sound even better if we could do dinner somewhere decidedly far away from my aunts. Let's work out the details later, all right? I'm out tonight with new... *friends.*"

"Of course, of course! I'll text you. Expect me sometime in the afternoon, all right?"

"Okay."

"I love you," Ben says casually. As if he's done it every day since we've met. My heart does a flip, the words on the tip of my tongue.

"I'll see you tomorrow." I end the call, shoving my phone back into the pocket of my cardigan and slip back into the room that seems somehow even quieter than before. I take my seat, relieved to find dessert set out, a single scoop of shiny pastel green, mint perhaps or pistachio.

"Who called?" Ryatt asks, his mischievous smirk back in action. I hesitate, weighing the options of lying in my head.

I clear my throat. "My boyfriend." I don't dare look beyond the bowl in front of me knowing all eyes are on me once more.

My fingers fumble with the spoon before I take a large scoop of the dessert. I cringe at the frozen treat, cheeks pulling inward as I let out a stream of air. "Wow, that's really cold." I mumble.

"Boyfriend?" Katerina questions a frown marring her beautiful features.

"Yes," I respond once I've swallowed, still avoiding eye contact. "We've been together for some months now."

"Xander, you didn't say anything about another man being in the picture."

"I hardly consider it a problem," he tells his mother easily, a lazy sort of confidence underlying his words.

"Agreed," I snap back. "Seeing as how our agreement is in regard to friendship and not a romantic relationship. As such, I hardly anticipate our arrangement affecting my relationship with my boyfriend." I steel myself to meet his gaze and feel a flush of victory run over me as he stiffens.

"Shall we retire to the drawing room for a nightcap?" Irina drawls, standing with more grace than I could ever possess. Ryatt and Katerina stand as well, but before I have the chance to stand, Xander's hand stretches across the table and fastens around my wrist. I shoot a pathetic look toward his family's backs but receive no help. I yank my arm back toward my side and let out an exaggerated sigh.

"What?"

"Why must you defy me at every turn? Humiliate me in front of my family?" he asks, his voice deadly calm as a storm brews behind his green eyes.

"You're the one who lied to your family—"

"I merely stretched the truth. We have agreed to see each other. Was it so wrong of me to impart on them the same hope I have? That you will one day see that it is I, who is your match and not this boyfriend of yours? That we will be together?"

"You didn't even tell your mother about my boyfriend! How could there possibly be any hope for a romantic relationship between us, when I'm with someone else. Who, I might add, I may just end up marrying." The words spill out in anger and frustration, and a delightful smugness rises in me as his shoulders sag ever so slightly.

Xander takes a deep breath. "You'll see him tomorrow, then? In the afternoon?"

I swallow, glance at my lap, and wipe the imaginary crumbs from it. "Yes. We'll spend—wait, how could you possibly have heard? I was in the other room. I was being quiet."

Xander leans back into his chair and takes a small sip from his tumbler. "Yes, well, I am a lycan. We are entitled to certain, *heightened senses*, above the average person. Haven't you spoken with your grandmother about this yet?"

"We've spoken a bit," I tell him, briefly looking away. "She's just been busy. So, you could really hear me?"

87

"We could all hear you," he informs me, eyes pinning me in place.

"Anything else I should be aware of? Weird shedding habits? Glowing eyes in the dark?"

"There's a wolf inside me," Xander tells me seriously. "All that he is capable of, so am I. I'm stronger and faster than any man you'll ever meet. Doubly so, as I'm an alpha. My senses are tenfold. I can smell your emotions." He pauses, taking in my astonishment and explains further. "Your emotions don't produce a smell on their own, but your body's natural reaction to your emotions does. It produces a recognizable scent from your sweat glands. My sense of smell is sensitive enough to pick up the differences. Fear and shame are similar. They're both bitter and harsh on the nose. Your anger is always so mixed with your increased heartbeat and flush of your skin that it's easy enough to recognize. Your arousal," he pauses, letting his next words sink it, "is by far the easiest thing to scent on you."

"Oh, and what do I smell like now?" I ask tartly, fighting down the blush of my cheeks. Xander sends me a lopsided grin.

"Angry and annoyed. A touch surprised. Your heart is racing as we speak. Perhaps you're a bit afraid as well." I shake my head and his eyes narrow, "Maybe you should be. I am hunting you, after all."

I swallow. My heart skips a beat and begins again with a stutter as his declaration sinks in. His eyes smolder back at me like a forest fire, and his voice, pitched low and refined, continues. "Everything you do, down to the smallest tick of your expression I catalog and analyze. Everything you say, I remember. All of it, Zoelle. There's a reason I said I wasn't concerned about your little boyfriend." He takes a long drag from his glass, a hiss slipping past his lips as the alcohol scorches its path downward. "He's no match for me. I'll have you at my side, Zoelle. It's only a matter of time."

I stare dumbfounded, unable to compose a response, split as I am between outrage and bewilderment. Among other things. "Um."

"Come, they'll be waiting for us." He stands in one fluid motion, hand held out for me to take. I gulp, not liking one bit how I am watched beneath hooded lids. Nor the cunning gleam that slips past them. I stand on my own, scraping the chair backward in my haste. Xander politely ignores my blunder, even as I refuse his outstretched hand and walk toward the door. His hand finds the hollow of my lower back, guiding me to the drawing room.

"We came to an agreement you and I, or have you forgotten?" He breathes against my temple, hand gliding across my back to hook around my hip. I swallow delicately and take a deep breath, willing my heartbeat to stay the course with its steady pace. My soulmark trembles against my flesh acknowledging the nearness of its match.

"I'm well aware of our agreement," I tell him smoothly, congratulating myself on my composed delivery. I remove his hold on my hip and lace my fingers with his. *Handholding.* Stupid agreement. His hand is rough and warm. The product of manual labor. *Or other things*, I think unwittingly, imagining what manual labor his hands might do on my body. I try to wipe the image from my mind as quickly as I can, too aware suddenly of the way my body reacts to my reckless thoughts. Strong hands to pin me down. Or grab my hips. Or keep my legs spread wide open for him to—

I gasp, both ashamed and aroused to be thinking such things. My eyes dart nervously toward Xander's face, praying that he's holding his breath. I certainly am now. Irina's laughter rings down the hallway, and I pick up my pace, locking eyes on what must be the drawing room door, but Xander resists. A throaty groan drags from his mouth as he looks down at me, and then I am pressed between a Picasso and Degas. Xander's hips belay my escape. They fit themselves snugly against my lower stomach as his hand reaches up to cup my neck. The other to lean against the wall. When his head dives in, I let out a whimper that's covered by his heavy inhalation. His head rests on my shoulder, nose and lips fitted against the side of my neck.

"I would give anything to know what you're thinking. To know if the pull between us, is as strong for you as it is for me. I want that more than anything," he tells me roughly, drawing in my scent once more. "Tell me," he pleads. A thousand lies run through my head until I land on one, readying my reply as my hands fly to his chest, pushing him back with little success. He growls, the feeling vibrating through me and raising the hair on my skin.

"We had an agreement." His fingers splay, daring to brush into the hair curled there. "Don't be afraid," he murmurs, nuzzling further until his lips are ghosting over my skin far too frequently. I shiver in response, my traitorous heart racing a mile a minute as I endure his attentions.

The soulmark flares to life inches above my breast, pulsing eagerly at his intimate touch and bringing with it a feeling of intense satisfaction. One that I have never known before. Not even with... my eyes widen, and I push once more against his chest, my body suddenly weak and helpless to his embrace.

"Ben," I breathe.

His hot breath, which drifts past my clavicle, stops sharply.

A wave of self-hatred courses through me as a sudden warmth gathers between my legs at the sensation. I grit myself against the unexpected lust that pours through me when his breath lingers over

90

the soulmark. I have a boyfriend. One I care deeply for, and this—this is wrong. These feelings are wrong, and so are my actions.

I take a deep breath, my thoughts coming back into focus. *It's only a chemical reaction*, I tell myself over and over. Any man could leave me feeling this way. Hugh Jackman, Idris Elba, hell, even Ben if he was to be this... assertive. Xander stiffens, taking a few deep breaths before he pulls back, hands moving to hold my shoulders to keep me in place. His face torn between frustration and remorse.

"Damn your, Ben," he spits. "Why stop? I can smell your arousal. I can feel you come alive at my touch. Even your mark recognizes my touch. It's acknowledging the connection between us, as is mine." I stare steadfastly at the wall behind him, refusing to answer. "Deny it all you want, Baudelaire, but you want this. You want what I can give you, at least at a fundamental level. So, tell me why?" He inhales sharply, his features contorting into a severe scowl, "Ashamed of your feelings? Or is it me you're ashamed of?"

"We had a deal," I tell him weakly. "And I wouldn't read so far into my reactions if I were you. I was thinking of *Ben*, and if you remember, you're only supposed to sniff me. Not grope me." I glare pointedly down at the hand that has found its way under my breast and hips that still press tightly against me. Along with something else. "This wasn't part of the deal. This isn't what friends do." He releases me at my reasoning, shoving his hands into his pockets. Xander levels a scowl at the floor.

"You're right. I over stepped my boundaries," he concedes with a sudden sag of his shoulders. "Please, accept my apology." The air feels trapped in my lungs as he raises his softened gaze my way.

"Your family is waiting for us," I tell him faintly instead of accepting his apology. A part of me is unwilling to allow him forgiveness. He nods as if understanding. It's obvious he wishes nothing more than to anchor a hand to me, guide my body into the room to stay by his side, but his earlier transgression restrains him. I'm thankful. We spend the rest of our time, what little there is, making stilted small talk. It's awful. I can't shake the knot of tension in my stomach. I can't shake the way Xander's presence leaves me unsettled and my overwhelming guilt at my reaction.

Though we barely touch the rest of the night, he makes sure to stay nearby, leaving but an inch between us. I hate the attention. Hate the way it makes me feel and this awful, dreadful night. When the time comes, I leave with clumsy haste.

+++

The next day with Ben is a welcome distraction and comfort. Though thoughts of last night linger in my mind, I keep the details of dinner to a minimum. There's no reason to drag Ben into all this supernatural nonsense. We eat lunch and explore the town. I show him all the places I've applied, but have yet to hear from. We walk the river's path. It's perfect.

There's no pressure with Ben. Everything we do is comfortable and without stress. It reaffirms what I already know that he makes me feel safe. He is safe. There's not an aggressive or wild bone in his all-American-boy body. It makes me appreciate him more, and as a result, I'm far more affectionate with him throughout the day. I can see how pleased it makes him, and he takes advantage of my fair mood, towing the line of what affection is appropriate to display in public. By the time our long day comes to an end, I feel myself already missing him.

"Don't go," I whine, holding tightly onto his hand as we say goodnight and goodbye on the front porch. I admire our entwined fingers, cocoa against creamy ivory.

He smiles down at me benevolently before placing a lingering kiss on my forehead. His fingers wistfully trail over my jaw before they brush my dark curls behind my ear. "I wish I didn't have too, but work is picking up speed. I don't know when I'll be able to come up and visit you again."

"That's okay," I say with a sigh. "Next time I'll just come down to you!"

He laughs, planting a kiss on my lips so sweet I curl myself into his body, wrapping my arms firmly around his neck until he responds in kind and deepens the kiss. I moan in response. His hand moves to my cheek, the cool metal of his numerous rings pressing against my flushed skin before his thumb brushes along my cheekbone. His tongue begs for entrance, running softly along my bottom lip. A warmth spreads out across my body, and I open my mouth shyly in reply, only to fall deeply into the rhythm of our kiss. He pulls back just slightly, hands cradling my face while he catches his breath.

"You are spectacular," he whispers. His hazel eyes stare down at me with reverence.

I smile dumbly at him, releasing another moan as his lips mark a swift path down my neck to my shoulder. With a jolt, I am instantly reminded of my moment with Xander. Flashes of the dark-haired wolf assault me as Ben nibbles at my skin, laves it with his tongue. I hold back a groan, not wanting to remember but unable not too. Behind closed eyes, it is Xander lavishing such thorough care to my skin. Xander pressing his thigh between my legs. Xander's fingers drawing artwork along my spine. I pull away with some effort, eyes opening to stare into Ben's hazel eyes. He grins down at me, swooping in to deliver another kiss. I fight with myself not to present him with my cheek and smile anxiously at him instead.

"It's getting late," I manage to say, putting on a tired face. Ben leans in to kiss me once more, unable to hide his disappointment, but he seems resigned.

"You're right. It's a long drive back, and the night has been coming on earlier with autumn approaching. Let's plan to Skype or FaceTime sometime soon, all right? Texting just isn't the same as being able to see you and hear your voice." I nod and offer him a chaste peck on the cheek.

"All right."

"I love you," he whispers, eyes closed and a soft smile haunting his lips. My throat tightens, the words trapped against the end of my tongue. I kiss him once more, more softly than before, and he leaves after giving me one last kiss and a sizable hug.

I'm inside the house a moment later, leaning my back against the doorframe as I hear the rumble of his truck start before driving off. *I should have said something. Anything. But what?* My head hits the doorframe as my eyes search the ceiling for an answer to my question. *What?* How does one tell their boyfriend they are supernaturally attached at the hip for the rest of their life to another person. The person not being them. So I didn't tell him. I didn't tell him Xander kissed me. My tongue refusing to budge as I valiantly tried to force the words up my throat. Instead, I fed him pleasant stories of making friends with Irina and meeting her family.

God, I'm pathetic.

Tires crunch to a stop in front of the house and derail my thought process. My heart skips a beat, *Ben.* Breath fills my lungs, expanding them to their fullest extent before I release the air in a *whoosh.*

I have to tell him about the kiss.

There is no other recourse. The thought leaves my stomach feeling sour, and it bubbles up my esophagus and throat. I press my ear more soundly to the door to hear the soft sound of feet making their way up the driveway. No doubt Ben forgot something, or he wants one last kiss for the road.

Despite it all, a fond smile curves my lips. Back in school, Ben would say goodbye, drive around the block, then come right back to my door for a kiss for the road. Which is different than a kiss goodbye, of course. It's the sweetest thing. My eyes slip closed the same moment my smile falters. And now I'm about to tell him another man, *my lycan soul mate*, kissed me....

A knock at the door breaks my reverie and causes me to jump forward. With a hand over my thumping heart I compose myself and open the door. A grin is painted over my lips to greet Ben. Except it isn't Ben. My breath releases in a shaky breath.

"What are you doing here?"

"May I come in?"

"No," I reply scandalized, closing the door a fraction more than necessary. He smiles, but it does not meet his eyes in the right way.

"May I come in, please?"

"What are you, like, stalking me now?" I try my best to sound contemptuous, cutting, but my voice carries the slightest vibrato that betrays my slight fear. His smile grows more disarming.

"No, though the thought has crossed my mind. I do, however, have some of my men watching you. All to ensure your safety, I assure you."

"Excuse me!"

He leans casually against the doorframe, eyes narrowing as they rake over me possessively. "Let me in, Zoelle. I'd rather the entire neighborhood not hear our conversation."

My fingers itch to slam the door in his face. "It's Zoe, and for your information, I don't want to talk. Or listen to whatever it is you have to say. I'm tired, and I'm going to bed."

The specks of jade in his eye darken to evergreen. "You're being awfully rude," he purrs. "Invite me in. I won't be made to stand outside. Come now, I'm waiting." He pauses, lips twisting in a way that raises my defenses. His voice *breathes* authority. Clearly, Xander is unused to being denied, though I have certainly made a habit of it. I harden at his imperious tone, indignant anger rising as it so often does when he is around. Without another thought, I shove the door closed. Almost. His hand easily catches the door before it can close and forces his way inside in a single stride. The door closes softly behind him.

"This isn't part of our deal," I tell him, backing away toward the staircase. He scowls in return.

"I'm well aware of the details of our deal," he says, prowling forward.

"Then why won't you stick to it!"

He swears, a fierce growl surging forth, "You know why." And then his mouth descends on mine.

+++

I'm pushed against the stairway railing, my back slamming painfully against the wood driving the air from my lungs. His lips are unforgiving, kissing me hard and gripping me even harder. I should fight back. Should push him away, but he steals my breath; completely dashes away my senses, drowning me in sensory overload.

I tear my lips away with great effort, panting from the exertion. His wild eyes capture mine. They are flecked with gold. Almost glowing. *Oh.*

"What are you doing?"

"Something I should have finished last night," he tells me hoarsely, fingers burying themselves into my curls.

"No," I protest instantly. Stopping, he takes me in with a hunter's eye before drawing himself upward and inward. Almost every inch of his body presses against my own.

"You don't want me?" he asks quietly. I hesitate, mouth falling open in dismay. It's all the permission he needs, for my half-second hesitation is enough to betray me. His eyes gleam, the amber gold flashing brighter against his lush green irises.

His head dips, nudging my face to the side so that he can explore the length of my neck. I shudder a sigh, gripping the banister behind me with taught knuckles. I can feel the curve of his smile against my neck and instantly feel ashamed, but then his teeth rake themselves downward leaving goose bumps in their wake. His fingers tighten in my hair tilting my head further back as he sucks harshly against the abused flesh. His nails scrape against my scalp in delicious friction as he continues to assert his control. When he lets out a moan of his own, I feel myself grow hot and let my thighs tighten around his leg.

It is almost my undoing, for Xander counters with a sinful thrust that leaves us both gasping. His arm crushes me to him, and I marvel at his strength. The power that lies within his bones. His raw strength is both terrifying and electric.

And so tempting.

He lets out a small moan, my name falling reverently from his lips as they recapture my own. Though his lips are soft, his kiss is bruising, volatile. I whimper in response; a picture of Ben breathing my name as we lay together spent in bed crosses my mind. Before I know what I am doing, my hands slam into his chest and shove him away.

He eyes me incredulously and takes an uncertain step forward, hand outstretched. I snatch myself away and stare at the offered hand warily. All too aware of the way it makes my blood sing. Makes my mind go blank as my body succumbs to his persuasion.

"Don't come any closer to me," I tell him breathlessly. "Get out."

"No." He pants harshly, "If you let that *boy* kiss you, then so will I."

"He's my boyfriend!" I shout back incredulously. "He's. My. Boyfriend."

"And what am I?"

I pause. The air between us grows tight and thick with tension. "An inconvenience."

Xander's face pales, but his eyes remain a turbulent storm. "I see."

"Where do you get off coming here, and—and, kissing me!"

He growls, the sound of low thunder, and paces the space between us. "You're my soulmark. Mine."

"I'm nobody's but my own, and you'd do well to remember it." I reprimand him harshly.

"Or what?" he asks, voice deceptively calm.

"Or you can forget our deal." If possible, his face goes even whiter, the storm receding from behind his eyes. "In fact," I say, my mind spinning around images of Ben and me together. "I think it best we take a small break from this little arrangement we have. You seem to have trouble keeping to all that we agreed on. I think you need time to reacquaint yourself with all our rules." *And so I can learn how to control this supernatural desire I have for you and pull my thoughts together.*

He takes a hesitant step toward me. "Don't be rash, Zoelle. You know what it will do to me. To us."

"It's Zoe!" I tell him shrilly. "And I mean it, Xander. I want you out. Gone! Do you understand me?" He freezes in his approach, swallowing with some effort. Outside a car door slams shut, and he cocks an ear.

"Your grandmother has returned," he tells me quietly. "Are you positive this is what you want... more time?"

"Time away from you? Yes." I tell him resolutely though I find myself shaking. *Why am I shaking?* His eyes close, a grimace following the action, but he manages to nod his head.

"Of course. A week then?"

My nose tips higher into the air. "Maybe more."

He exits as Gran and the aunts enter, his head kept low as he passes by them. The women take me in; eyebrows raised comically high. Heat floods my cheeks as I stare right back.

"Good night," I tell them through gritted teeth, darting up the stairs and locking myself in my room. There's no reason to doubt it anymore... I'm a cheater.

COOKIES ARE A GIRL'S BEST FRIEND

- Chapter 6 -

There are several paths that I knew my life would never take me.

I would never be an astronaut, pilot, or professional skydiver, my acrophobia too daunting a fear to overcome.

I would never be an entertainer, my disdain for spotlight clear from an early age.

And I would never be a cheater. Or so I thought.

My fingernails dig into my palm unconsciously, a curl of guilt and shame twisting my stomach. *How did I let this happen*? Especially, after everything that happened with Jamie. Jamie who broke my heart after cheating on me for *months*? The heartache still lingers inside me, touting with doubt and fear.

An angry tear almost slips into my batter. I hastily drag the back of my hand over both eyes, letting out a long, slow breath before taking up my task again. I'm guilt cooking, and it is *not* pretty.

My heart lies in neat little jagged pieces, and my emotions are a steady flow of remorse and anger. I'm drowning in shame, unable to come to terms with the way I succumbed to my body's desires. Even if for just a short amount of time. Even if the magical pull between Xander and I cannot be undone. *I should have done more to end the kiss,* I think, gut clenching painfully once more, *and Xander should have never kissed me in the first place.*

I beat the batter with more force than necessary. The whisk scrapes against the bottom of the bowl with every flick of my wrist.

Who does he think he is?

My kisses, my body, *my love*—they belong to Ben. Reliable, loving, sweet Ben, and while my mind tries to reconcile itself with these thoughts, another emotion continues to rear its ugly head: sadness. A deep, throbbing depression forging its way across my flesh and bones, and it stems from the soulmark. Unfortunately, there's no tea or spell that seems to dull its effects. My only therapy is cooking.

The kitchen becomes a balm to my bruised heart. An outlet for my thoughts and rampant emotions. Thankfully, the aunts and Gran seem to understand and steer clear, when they hear me inside. A fact I appreciate. I need the time alone to figure out how to break the news to Ben.

I slow my whisking, thoughts turning a mile a minute in my head. If Ben leaves me, then nothing will stand in Xander's way from pursuing me full force. For a moment I struggle to breathe.

Full force...? I coerce my traitorous lungs into taking a deep breath. To think he isn't doing so now is... *unnerving.* I quell the shiver rising on the nape of my neck.

My cooking stops altogether as I duck my head, a furrow coming to my brow. How can I possibly explain to Ben the forces that draw Xander and I together?

How can I tell him I'm *trying* to be faithful to him, but oh so slowly, I feel the center of my world edges closer towards a man I've only just met? A man who is half wolf? And that I am a *witch*? I will try harder to keep Xander at arm's length if it means I can keep Ben. I'll just need to learn to deal with the soulmark's negative effects. My teeth sink into my bottom lip. I squeeze my eyes shut as I take in a shaking breath.

God, *what do I do? Can I really ignore the soulmark?*

All of the warnings, everything I have been told and read, pale in comparison to its power. I feel him. His drive, his passion, his hunger—hunger for me. My eyes snap open as my resolve hardens. I need to tell Ben about what happened in person. He deserves that much.

I push my thoughts to the task at hand, when a strange pull at my heart distracts me. It's Xander. The current of his emotions trickle through the soulmark. I do my best to force them away, but they still manage to thrum at the back of my mind. He's angry. Angry because Gran placed a spell on the house, barring him entry.

It's a spell Gran promises to teach me, so that I may take on the burden. But I've only mastered simple spells of levitation and will binding *once*. The former is a novice-level spell but contains elements similar to will binding in that they both require clear direction of power onto inanimate objects.

Gran gives me a small book of enchantments and spells to study, allotting me till week's end to gain some level of control over my magic. The pressure weighs dauntingly on my shoulders, but it can't snuff out my excitement.

The spell book, with its sage words and illuminating enchantments, easily steals my attentions. I feel connected to the family heirloom, and in turn, feel more connected with the magic inside of me. The scrawling script speaks to me. The written words call my magic to attention and leave me breathless time and time again. It's odd, certainly. But somehow, so right.

Simple spells and enchantments are woven between thoughtful verses of lecture on best practices to connect the mind and body with magic. How to clear the soul and think with the heart to better capture a spell or enchantments intent. Because intention is everything; and in knowing yourself, the magic inside you will grow all the more powerful. And with age, it professes you will only learn to know yourself better. Hence, with age, a thoughtful witch gains more power.

How, after twenty-four years with all the things life has thrown at me, am I not wise beyond my years? Yet, this supernatural world leaves me second-guessing everything I know. *How can I possibly know myself when I'm torn in so many directions*? I desperately wish for an easy solution, but know all too well, time can't be rushed.

Though the book calms and excites me, it's also a thoroughly frustrating affair. My progress is nonexistent, and nothing I do seems to help. Of course, my frustration bleeds into my guilt cooking.

+++

Sunday

It's difficult to "think with my heart" when it is flooded with guilt, let alone "clear my soul."

Everything seems inconsequential compared to the bruising pain I feel when my thoughts wander to Ben instead of focusing on the levitation spell, *resurgemus*. Gran has tasked me with learning the spell as a precursor to the barring spell I must take over from her, adding another burden on my mind. An ominous presence lurks around my shoulders, leaving me rattled and second guessing myself. I can't stand it.

I lean back in my chair, eyes narrowing with contempt at the chopsticks resting on my dinner plate. Dinner had been a beautiful balsamic chicken pizza with caramelized sweet onion and crispy bacon. A tried and true favorite of mine to make when my head is muddled with too many thoughts. The methodical treatment of each ingredient always managed to aid in sorting my thoughts.

Unfortunately, it hadn't worked, despite the ease with which I executed the meal.

With one bite I knew it to be rotten. The entire pizza felt disjointed, none of the elements complementing each other as they normally did. The balsamic tang tasted sour and spoiled. The chicken chewed like tough rubber. And the bacon left a bitter taste on the back my tongue.

Dinner turned into an order of Thai food, with the chopsticks now acting as the test subject for my spell.

"Resurgemus." The word is gently spoken. Barely audible. My palms face upward, identifying the direction in which the chopsticks should move. Nothing. "*Resurgemus*," I attempt once more with feeling.

Nothing. "*Dammit.*"

+++

Monday

Monday lives up to its reputation and proves to be a tiresome day. Nothing goes right. I find a stain on my favorite white blouse. I don't have enough money for the ingredients at the grocery store—*why hadn't I just brought my debit card?* And I receive seven text messages and two missed calls from Xander, but nothing from Ben.

My nails dig into the soft flesh of my palm as I recount the other mindless incidents of the day that have somehow made it even worse.

A mess of laundry scattered around my room.

The paper cuts on my index and middle fingers.

The near empty bottle of orange juice left in the fridge instead of being finished and put in the trash.

I put my fist to good use and smash it into my dough, kneading it ruthlessly. I've pushed past my guilt from yesterday, tucking it away to a dark corner of my heart, and I grasp hold of *anger*.

Anger at Xander.

Anger at magic.

Anger at myself.

The sticky dough takes my beating with good grace, slowly transforming into something smooth and malleable. I wipe my brow with my forearm, surprised to find a light pant falling past my lips. *Why can't life be as straightforward as baking?*

I didn't want magic in my life, or the complications it brought.

Liar, a soft chime rings in my head. I swallow convulsively for a long moment before regaining my grasp on my anger.

Magic is the source of all my problems. It brought Xander into my life. It looms like an angry cloud over my relationship with Ben as a secret I know I can never tell. Yet, even as magic burrows itself deeper into my life, somehow it remains elusive to *me*. The resurgemus spell continues to lie beyond my reach, *unbearably so*, and it shakes me to my core. *Why can't I do it? What am I missing?* I am unbalanced, where I was once sure footed. And magic is wholly to blame.

Shoulders sinking, I carefully place my dough in a well-oiled bowl, covering it with plastic wrap and once more wiping at my forehead. The churning of anger turns to spite, before sifting to sadness. The flesh around my soulmark tingles in response, a distant echo of anger and sadness that only solidifies my own.

I spin around from the counter and face the sink, my heart beating twice its normal pace. *Don't focus on him*, I tell myself sternly, *focus on the spell—for Gran.*

I raise my hand, palm outward and eyes fixated on the dishrag hanging off the sink's faucet.

"*Resurgemus.*" My eyes close in defeat as my hand falls to my side.

+++

Wednesday

My anger, so potent at the beginning of the week, turns to stout disappointment. Dozens of cookies litter the kitchen island in a pathetic attempt to appease the constant ache in my heart. Another chocolate chip pretzel cookie disappears inside my mouth and I release a leaden sigh. It does little to help, except in expanding my waistline.

I thought anger had been the answer. It burned clear through me after all. But I was wrong.

Anger doesn't solve my problems, most certainly *not* those of the magical variety.

I swallow past the hard lump in my throat, clearing my throat of delicious cookie crumbs, and reach blindly for another. My magic isn't working, no matter how hard I try. No matter how much I concentrate or attempt to clear my heart. Nothing works.

In the middle of my baking frenzy lies a torn piece of paper, dotted with several grease spots and a smear of chocolate. I stare at it somewhat contemptuously as I chew, my nose scrunched and brows pinching slightly together. It's a list the aunts and Gran have made for me to help me clear my soul.

The list is short—very short—with only one piece of advice from each woman.

Emotion is never weakness. Feel. — *Maureen*

Always fill your own cup first; self-care isn't selfish. — *Lydia*

Be free. Embrace who you are. — *Gran*

The advice is all well and good, and I'm certainly grateful for it, but how can I implement it? Can it be that easy? My eyes slip closed. *Can it?* For a moment I enjoy the stillness of the house and once more feel a surge of gratitude to the aunts and Gran, who have left me be to sort out my issues. The house smells of my freshly baked cookies, but also of sage and basil and mint. The living plant wall was recently trimmed and treated by Aunt Mo, and the freshly ruffled plants share their wonderful aroma with the kitchen as well. The scents combine, bringing memories of cooking with my mother to mind.

What would she say to me now? What advice would she have?

I open my heart to thoughts of her, letting her all-knowing words come to mind. *Acceptance. Breathe it all in, honey.*

My head bows in reflection. *Acceptance.* My teeth find my bottom lip to chew as I mull over the thought. Accept what though?

I know I'm in the wrong with Ben. I do. I also know that I will do right by him and tell him, face-to-face, about what happened because he deserves more than a text message or phone call. As for the soulmark...it's a harder pill to swallow. I don't *want* to be tied to this volatile alpha male who makes me feel things I've never felt before—a feeling of yearning so strong it's unstoppable.

But the sealing of the soulmark isn't something that can be undone. It just can't.

It's another painful truth to accept, and yet, somehow, I feel a heavy weight fall from my shoulders.

107

I can't go back in time and fix these things, but I do have a say in how I tackle my future.

Slowly I straighten, my hands resting gently on the island's cool surface as my shoulders gently roll back and my chin lifts. *Accepting magic, and all the crazy that goes hand and hand with it?* I laugh, shaking my head from side to side, my curls swaying with the motion. I can't give up on magic, even with all the crazy that accompanies it. I'm not going to let Gran down.

"*Resurgemus.*"

My eyes flutter open as an unexpected wave of heat tingles through my body. All around me chocolate chip pretzel cookies hover precariously in the air. Another laugh erupts from my mouth, my feet tapping the ground in excitement as I snatch one of the treats out of the air.

"Finally!" I chomp down on the cookie with glee, my careful concentration wavering as I do. In an instant, the floating cookies fall as one onto the counter top, breaking and crumbling upon impact.

"Shit."

+++

Friday

I'm multitasking. As a chef, this comes naturally to me. I'm used to keeping watch over many things at once, all while keeping my hands busy chopping or dicing another ingredient. What I'm not used to is the magical strain of maintaining a spell *while* cooking. Given Wednesday's success in casting, Gran opts to teach me the barring spell on Thursday evening.

The sensation is…odd. My magic pulls lightly from all parts of my body. My spine. My toes. My gut. It's exhausting, to be frank, which is why I'm baking a batch of chocolate hazelnut biscotti to pair with our massive tea collection.

Though my heart feels lighter, and my magic is coming along, one issue remains. The soulmark. Despite the fact that I had restored my calm and made a plan to see Ben as soon as possible, a pit of depression builds inside me due to Xander's absence.

My hand gives a noticeable twitch and I pause my actions to settle my nerves. With a long, drawn breath, I pivot my thoughts to the task at hand. I place the biscotti logs into the oven and begin to straighten up the kitchen. Halfway through cleaning, the front door opens and closes, and raucous laughter immediately fills the house. The aunts are home.

"Zoe?"

"In here," I call back. *Where else would I be?*

Aunt Lydia and Mo come strolling in, their gazes resting knowingly on the half-cleaned kitchen island and my soapy hands. They begin to help silently until the task is complete and only a few minutes remain on the clock.

"What are you cooking?" Aunt Lydia asks as I set out a clean cutting board, serrated knife, and two cooling racks.

"Biscotti. I thought they might go nicely with some of the tea we have." Both aunts hum their appreciation, sitting down on the stools on the other side of the island. "Where were you two?"

"Oh, just at the Wellington's for some coven business."

"I hope it all went well."

"It did. Your gran is still finishing some discussions, so we thought we might come home early and see what you were making. Check on how you were doing," Aunt Mo says. "You seem like you're doing better, honey, are you? Some say the soulmark can be intrusive."

109

My lips pinch together as I stew over her question. The soulmark *does* feel intrusive. I don't want to feel Xander's emotion, but it's an unavoidable consequence of the bond. And I feel him more than ever now that my mind and heart are cleared. "I'm doing better, I think. It's not… *easy*, but I'm learning to deal with it. I feel—*a lot*. And not just my own emotions." My eyes flicker toward their calm expressions, "That's what's been hardest."

"Well, you've done a fine job of keeping your head on your shoulders through all this nonsense," Aunt Lydia commends, fingering her jewelry. Her cat-like eyes narrow. "Just know you're doing the right thing. The truce that has resulted from your willingness to cultivate a relationship with the Adolphus boy certainly has its benefits for the coven."

"Friendship, Lydia," Aunt Mo corrects, not minding the way Aunt Lydia rolls her eyes in response.

"Friendship is a type of relationship, Maureen. Now, Zoe, is Ben aware of your arrangement?"

I shake my head firmly, eyes comically wide as I respond, "No. Definitely not. Witches and lycans? He would try to commit me to a psych ward." What did they expect me to say to Ben?

Oh, don't mind him, Ben! I just have to stay within ten feet of Xander at all times in order to maintain my sanity. Want to grab a coffee?

I flinch at the thought, the action covering the twitch in my hand that follows. The soulmark shivers against my skin in a wholly unpleasant way. *Damn.* The aunts give wary nods in unison at my passionate declaration.

"It's best to keep supernatural revelations to a minimum, dear," Aunt Mo advises delicately. "But I'd mind how affectionate you are in public with your Ben when you next see him. I've been told that the

Adolphus's have their dogs out watching you and reporting back to their alpha on your movements."

"*Seriously?*" I mutter, feeling myself running cold, then steaming mad at the news. "This is ridiculous! Whatever happened to privacy? Isn't being magically tethered together for the rest of our lives enough?"

Aunt Lydia cackles, her laughter almost covering the sound of the oven timer going off. "Zoe, your life is tied to that man, whether you like it or not. Though you may not have completed the process, Xander is an alpha. Your bond is naturally stronger than others. Say for some reason you were injured, it would affect him, and in turn the pack."

"What she's trying to say is it's in the best interest of the entire pack to keep you safe." Aunt Mo interrupts her.

"Which is why my every move is being watched," I finish. "Because they think it will keep him safe. Them safe." My correction takes on a bitter note. My nose scrunches in distaste as I pull the biscotti out of the oven to cool. "Maybe if I were a caster and could wield my magic better, I wouldn't come off as so helpless." A slow fire builds in the pit of my stomach. "I'm a *witch* for goodness sake! And an independent woman to boot! I can take care of myself, no adult supervision necessary."

My rant leaves me breathless, and the aunts mildly stunned, but mostly amused.

"You'll come into your magic just fine," Aunt Lydia reassures me. Aunt Mo nods her agreement, her wavy white hair swaying. "In fact, I dare say you have a better handle on it than you think. You're focusing on magic that isn't your forte. Of course it will be challenging, but you've been brewing up a storm all week. Remember what we told you before? You transfer your emotions by way of magic into your cooking. You can make people feel what you want them to feel. You can give your creations purpose."

111

"But I want to be able to do the things all of you can do," I whine giving into my self-pity, "Like lighting a candle without a match? I could start the stove and set a potion to brew like that!" My fingers snap sharply together. "But can I? Nope. Not me."

Aunt Mo gives me a dry look, "Don't complain, child, it's hardly becoming." My shoulders sag. "If you're finding it difficult to call upon your magic, it's because you're still holding back something inside of you. Let it go, Zoe. Let yourself feel. You can only grow by knowing yourself inside and out, and to do that, you need to accept all the feelings running inside of you, good and bad."

"I know," I tell them, the words rekindling hope inside me. "So, what had Gran staying later at the Wellington's?" The aunts exchange a measured glance.

"Your grandmother is working on obtaining safe passage for an item of interest for the coven," Aunt Lydia finally says. "It's important that it goes smoothly, and there is nobody who can negotiate like your grandmother."

"Is that why she came back? To broker some deal for the coven?" My fingers press gently into the biscotti to test how warm they are. Not too bad, I decide and begin cutting them lengthwise into half-inch thick slices. Once I finish arranging them cut-side down, they go back into the oven to firm up.

"How much has your Gran told you about the Trinity Coven?" Aunt Mo asks, watching my methodical movements.

"Not too much," I say, chewing at my bottom lip, "mostly just about mom and the talents that run in our family."

"I see," she murmurs. "Well, there's much more to it than that. You see, our families, the Clybournes and Steins, along with the Baudelaires, moved here from the east around the same time. Our families have been connected for a long time, dear, and when the

Steins decided to move west, we all followed. This land was flush with ingredients both magical and natural we were needed. I, along with your grandmother and Lydia, form the Elder Triad of our coven. We're the matriarchs, and together we lead and provide protection and counsel to the witches under our wing. We made do with your grandmother away for so long, but it's been a relief to have her back. Our coven is meant to be led by three, not two."

The door sounds again, opening and closing swiftly. Gran enters a moment later, shrugging off her knitted shawl over one of the kitchen chairs. She comes over and gives me a kiss on the cheek, wordlessly putting on the kettle before diving into the tea cabinet in search of something specific.

"Where is the tea for cephalalgia? I feel like a bullet's trying to split its way through my head." Aunt Lydia eyes the tea cabinet, her expression relaxed yet thoughtful. With her gaze intently focused on the cabinet, its door swings lightly open. A tinkling of movement among the glass jar rings throughout the kitchen before a short and stout jar boasting purple and black tea leaves floats out of the cabinet to the kitchen island. Aunt Lydia casually waves her hand and the door to the tea cabinet closes. Gran's shoulders fall with relief from their tensely held position. "Thank you, Lydia." Aunt Lydia nods, twisting the cap off the jar and working sans-magic on fixing gran her tea.

"Not feeling well, Gran?" I ask tentatively.

"It's been a tiring week, even with you taking over the barring spell." My heart gives a pang of sadness as I nod weakly in response. Gran gives me a small smile in return. "Don't go worrying about me, honey. We Baudelaire women are strong, and don't you forget it." I nod once more, startling at the beep that sounds from the stove a moment later.

113

"How about a chocolate hazelnut biscotti to go with your tea? That will definitely make you feel better," I tell her as I pull the baking trays out of the oven. "They're still pretty hot, but they should cool down in no time." I move the biscotti onto the cooling rack once more, waving a spare plate over them to aid in the cooling process.

"That sounds wonderful," she tells me with a soft smile, cradling the steaming cup of tea Aunt Lydia hands her. When her tea has steeped long enough, she picks a biscotti up delicately between her fingers, nibbling on the end with a satisfied expression.

"Delicious and they pack a bit of punch," she proclaims. The aunts and I take one each, following suit with tentative bites as the heat engulfs our mouths. "Hmm, you're right. I think this is helping my headache already." She lets out a small sigh of gratitude, and I can't help but grin.

"I told you." "And we told you," Aunt Mo chimes in, "Your intentions are coming through your baking. A brewer through and through." My eyes widen in short surprise before a happy smile finds its way onto my lips. Perhaps I'm not so hopeless after all.

+++

The tricky thing about making a soufflé is that so many things can go wrong and when it does there's no hiding it. It's about getting the soufflé to rise and not fall afterward. Having the oven temperature just right and not overworking the eggs.

Despite the precision and detail a soufflé dish requires, I enjoy the challenge of making them. It makes me feel like a *real* chef and a proud reminder of all the things I've accomplished. Plus, they are the perfect treat to have straight out of the oven. The *absolute* perfect late-night dessert on a Saturday night, drenched in strawberry sauce that will leave you feeling pleasantly full till morning.

My mind is happily free of its normal worry, thanks to time spent with Gran today. We had talked magic, meditated, and she had me performing more spells by the end of the day. Even a few potions and tea concoctions to help restore my magical energy. Maintaining the barrier felt easier after drinking the tea. My confidence restored, I decide to reward myself with a strawberry soufflé.

Just as I am placing the soufflé into the oven, I feel a stir of anticipation in my stomach. I straighten. Gran told me to expect the feeling anytime someone approaches the house with the intention of entering. I glance at the clock on the microwave. The aunts and Gran had left twenty minutes ago to meet with the Reynolds and won't be back for at least another half hour or so. I take a hesitant step toward the front door as the feeling swells until finally, a knock sounds hard and heavy at the door. I take a large breath, walking forward with purpose and peeking through the eyehole.

It's Xander.

Fuck.

"Go away," I tell him through the door, ready to turn back to wait out the soufflé.

"I just want to talk. To see you. It's been a week, Zoelle, please." I feel frozen at his hoarse words. Swallowing down the lump in my throat, I take my time to think of a response. "You can't just shut me out like this."

"It's late, Xander, and I really don't want to deal with you right now. Especially if you haven't learned how to respect other people's boundaries. So my answer is still going to have to be a firm *no.*" My parting words give me a rush of adrenaline as I watch him glower through the peephole.

115

"I only want to talk. Face-to-face, and apologize for my actions last week."

"Yeah, well, I don't particularly want to listen." He cocks his head to hear my softly spoken words. His eyes flash a sudden amber gold as he leans in toward the door.

"Come now, Zoelle, don't make me play the big, bad wolf. I know the barrier has shifted control from your grandmother to you. Your magic is hardly strong enough to keep me out on your own. Why don't you come outside and talk to me before I tear this door down? I'd hate to make a scene and create such a mess, but if that's what it takes…"

I swallow. Hard. "You wouldn't," I hiss, fear and doubt unmistakably tainting my voice. Another flash of gold, and this time accompanied by a truly devious smirk. Xander flashes me his canines before his rasping voice drops low and dangerous.

"Do you really want to test me? Your strength against mine? Do recall what happened last time you attempted to keep me out. How easily I gained… access."

My fingers unlock the door with disdain before I inch my way outside onto the porch. There is no way he's coming inside. I glare at his satisfied smile, choosing to ignore how well-groomed he looks. Fitted shirt, sleeves rolled to reveal tan skin and toned forearms. His hair falls in loose pieces around his face, which has an easy smile in place.

"Is this our thing?" he asks teasingly. I give him my best incredulous look. How he can switch between two emotions so quickly is completely beyond my comprehension.

"We don't have a *thing*."

"If you insist, but I'm becoming quite familiar with this particular entryway." His eyes gleam mischievously. It instantly brings to mind his brother.

116

"What do you want?" My voice holds no room for nonsense and his manner changes. Again.

"I wanted to give you these," he holds out before him a small bouquet of flowers and a long, thin box with a dainty white ribbon wrapped around it.

"Pass," I respond tersely. Xander's jaw ticks, and I shift uncomfortably. I fight the instinct to cross my arms over my chest, and instead force my shoulders back to stand straighter. Xander's hands stay outstretched.

"No need to be rude. These gifts are a gesture to accompany my apology. I behaved... irrationally last week. I'm not usually so careless with my emotions, and my jealousy and anger got the best of me. Please accept my apology." He presses the wild flowers into my hands before slipping off the ribbon on the jewelry box and opening it with a small flourish. A rose gold bracelet lays inside. It's one of the most delicate pieces of jewelry I have ever seen. The rose gold is woven tightly together to form small sections of braids.

"I can't accept that," I say softly with a shake of my head. He frowns down at me, fingers brushing against the sensitive skin on the inside of my wrist before he fastens the bracelet there. *So much for my refusal.* My lips draw a tight line. "Happy?" I bite out, valiantly pushing aside the sudden kindling of warmth running through my veins at his caress.

"Very," he responds, "I saw it while in Helena and thought of you."

"I hope you don't think this will change my feelings about you. I've never been particularly fond of people trying to buy me off," I tell him tartly, eyeing the jewelry with forced lackluster. His silence unsettles me, not that I let it show. I straighten and take a step back toward the door. "Is this it, then? I have a soufflé in the oven, and they're quite temperamental when left unwatched."

117

The silence collects between us until the air is thick and charged with all that is left unspoken between us. "How can I acquit myself?" he asks earnestly.

My eyes snap to his.

There is no hiding my consternation at his sincerity. My lips part and my breath catches. I choose to ignore the strange sensation that wraps around my heart at his laden words and direct my gaze elsewhere. *Focus, Zoelle*, I tell myself sternly. Xander only wants to complete the soulmark. Completing the soulmark means strengthening his pack, and that kind of power can, in turn, be used against the witches—the coven. My coven. I take a deep breath. He isn't going to fool me. His trinkets and pretty smile won't make me forget his wild and possessive nature. The one that overrides all others, when I come into view. I let my silence stand for my answer.

"You really don't trust me, do you?" his voice sounds oddly hollow. Again, I fight the urge to believe him, to comfort and reassure him. It comes on so strongly I almost careen forward. *No.* I tell myself harshly. *These feelings aren't real. It's just the soulmark.*

"How could I? You've hardly kept to the agreement. You lied to your family about what we agreed. You take liberties with me whenever you can—don't think I haven't noticed the way you always find a reason to get your hands on me. Brushing things off my shoulder. Fixing my hair. Steadying me before I can even stumble." I level him with a pointed glare, ticking off the offenses on my fingers. "Let's not forget that you blatantly ignore the fact that I have a boyfriend and have the audacity to kiss me." I shudder in indignation. "I've been sick with guilt all week because of you! I am not a cheater, Aleksandr Adolphus. That isn't who I am. That's not the person I want to be."

My teeth chomp down on my tongue to keep from saying more. Feelings of inadequacies long since buried rise to the surface. Jamie's months of infidelity left me feeling not good enough for anyone, and although Xander and I had only shared a kiss, I don't want Ben to feel the way I had. My head bows as I stare resolutely at the floor. I needed to see Ben. The sooner, the better. "You should leave."

"Is that what you really want?" Xander ducks his head as well, trying to catch my eyes, but to no avail.

"What I want is to turn back time. I wish I never went into that hellish forest and met you, but since time travel apparently isn't in my bag of tricks, I'll settle with you leaving me alone."

He takes a step forward, crowding me in that oh-so-familiar way. The scent of pine and sandalwood waft around me at his nearness. When I finally deign to return his stare, I find his eyes hard like emeralds.

"I didn't exactly want this to happen either," he tells me coldly. "I grew used to the idea of never finding you. I made plans for my pack. I was forming an alliance and preparing a proposal to the Wselfwulf's, and then you come out of nowhere. And now all I can think about is you. All I want is you. Everything I've been working for, everything I so carefully planned... I've spurned it all in my longing for you. And there's nothing I can do about it." He lets out an irate laugh and passes a hand roughly over his jaw. "You are my future, Baudelaire. I can't fight it. And if I'm honest, I don't want to. I won't. You may deny me now, but we both know on some level you want me just as badly as I want you. You need what I have to offer you. Safety. Security. Strength. A way to sate that hunger of yours.

"I can give you the world if you would just say the word. Admit it. Admit to me and to yourself that there's something there beyond the soulmark. Temptation. Curiosity. Even if it's just a crumb. Tell

119

me you feel nothing for me, honestly, that the soulmark has no effect on you other than to enhance what you already feel. I'm sure they have you drinking their potions and rot to keep the feelings at bay, but there must be something. Anything." I stutter a breath at his impassioned speech, and he is quick to take advantage. His fingers dart forward to brush against my lips. Linger at their crease.

"No touching," I tell him hoarsely, jerking my head to the side a fraction too late.

"You didn't seem to mind before," he reminds me, satisfaction carrying through his tone. "Set yourself at ease, sweetheart, we're more alike than you might concede. The soulmark is the embodiment of the soul's match. They are the perfect complement to your being. A mirror image of one another. You're passionate, full of drive, and loyal to your family above all else. You think things through and bide your time, yet you crave something more. Something to overwhelm your senses. Electrify you. Something that will fill that missing piece inside of you. Isn't that right, sweetheart?"

My head shakes resolutely side to side. "You're wrong."

He smirks. It's a devilish thing filled with dark satisfaction. "I'm right," he purrs, shuffling closer still. The flowers that stand between us press against our chests. The plastic crinkling its protest. "And do you know how I know I'm right?" His hand moves slowly to my collarbone. Wrist, to elbow, to shoulder, then down—

"Don't. Don't touch it," I tell him sternly, my hand snapping up to cover the soulmark. It throbs against my palm.

"Fine," he snarls, snatching up my wrist and shoving it past his parted shirt, and up and around his shoulder. I curl my fingers inward, but it's no use, the temptation of the soulmark is too much to ignore.

Xander's sharp intake of breath is nothing compared to my own.

The air pulls straight from my lungs with pure ruthlessness. Stars explode behind my eyes and feeling floods my being. Feelings that burn and blaze from head to toe. It blooms and bends inside of me. Our eyes meet and hidden in the forest of his eyes live a thousand suns. They scorch as they seek their treasure, and there is only him. He shines like some golden god. Brilliant and slipping under my skin like a coat of arms. I have never felt so safe and secure. So loved.

My legs shake unsteadily, the traitorous things, and I stumble forward breaking the connection. Every nerve in my body stands at attention, as a piteous whine slips past my lips at the loss of sensation. Of him. Someone breathes harshly, but I can hardly tell who with the blood beating so hotly in my veins. Xander rests his head atop my own. His arms crush me to him.

Not again.

I feel a sob building inside of me. The turbulent emotions of the soulmark are almost too much to bear. How can this sliver of flesh anchor me so to him? What hope do I have to resist, when at the slightest touch I lose all sense? I take a shuddering breath. It's so easy to lose myself in the sensation it evokes. The dizzying ecstasy it brings both enchants and terrifies me. I sink unwittingly into Xander's embrace, taking comfort in his strength as I attempt to regain my breath.

Every time we seem to meet, I lose a little bit more of myself to this man, and I had only just put me all back together and learned to live this half-life. My heart locked away, never to be broken again. A tear slips down my cheek.

I want Xander out of my life. I want him gone.
I want—

Oh no. The soulmark quivers, my body following suit. *I want.*

"What's wrong," Xander whispers, pulling back with wide eyes as he surveys the river of tears now falling down my face.

"I'm awful," I whisper back, squeezing my eyes tightly shut.

"You're perfect," he tells me harshly, "you're—"

"A liar. A cheater. I'm awful. Please, please leave," I beg as I remove myself fitfully from his embrace and rush inside the house. A furtive glance over my shoulder and I catch the flash of disappointment and dread that pulls the color from his face. I clutch the crushed flowers to my chest as I slam the door shut behind me, my sobs shaking my entire body. *What have I done?*

CHANCE MEETINGS

- Chapter 7 -

"I don't know what to do," Xander mumbles under his breath, his scotch glass hanging loosely in his grip as he stares into the flames of the fire. Ryatt snorts from his seated position in the lounge, his own glass almost empty.

"Well, obviously not what you're doing now." The brothers glare at one another, and Irina's snort breaks their standoff.

"First, you need to get rid of the boyfriend. You're making her feel like some kind of trollop."

Xander frowns. "I'm working on it."

"Well, work on it faster," Irina snarls, sinking back into the divan with a pout. "The Wselfwulfs are bound to have heard of your soulmarking by now. They'll demand to meet her at the dinner and see who is set to rule at your side. She needs to be prepared. She needs to be strong, and she needs to be pack. We can't afford a war."

"We could if Xander at least marked her. Xander would receive a considerable boost in power and then

123

that power would trickle its way through the pack lines and strengthen us as a whole. But if he could complete the bond... *well*, the Wselfwulf's wouldn't dare near us with that kind of power behind our alpha. Irina is right, brother. You need to move things along more quickly. An alpha soulmark is not something the Wselfwulfs will take lightly. She's in danger whether she knows it or not. They'll want her dead to weaken you. To weaken us."

Xander's brows draw together, a sneer pulling at his top lip. "An alpha soulmark...." His scoff finishes his sentence.

"Yes," Irina snaps, her own features pinching together to form a beautiful scowl. "Come now Xander, you know our rank highly dictates not only our strength, but the potency of the soulmark." Irina rolls her eyes at Xander's gentle scoff, before narrowing at the slight.

"And what of the she-wolf's soulmark bond?" Xander asks, his sudden about-face blasé tone and demeanor setting the she-wolf's shoulders back.

"What of it?" Irina asks her shoulders still stiff.

Ryatt crows as he watches his siblings with amusement twinkling in his eyes. "You need only remember how our sister wears her heart on her sleeve so freely, brother."

Irina's chin lifts, her green eyes narrowing on her brother. "She-wolves are known for their passion, and I won't be mocked for it."

Xander releases a small sigh, eyes turning to deliver a pensive gaze to the fire. "You're right, Irina. A she-wolf's passion should be admired and cherished by the pack, not mocked." Two sets of green eyes turn towards the remaining Adolphus sibling, whose hands rise defensively in front of him.

"I was merely teasing."

"And what of Ryatt's soulmark bond? What will it be like?"

Irina's eyes widen, a devious smile curving her full pink lips as she continues to stare down her brother. Ryatt's own smirk falters and he quickly speaks before his siblings can edge in another word. "It will be chaos, I assure you," he says. In the next instant he knocks back the rest of his drink. "The wolf inside me is far different than the others of this pack. It strays often to the forefront of my mind. I'm sure if I find my soulmark both the wolf and I will enjoy the hunt."

The siblings remain quiet for a time, before Irina looks toward Xander. Softly she speaks, "This dinner is a ploy—a distraction. I fear what might happen at home while we're away. If the mark is at least in place, then the binding will be quick to follow. Then the witches will have no choice but to fully align with us and create a barrier around the town to prevent any planned attacks. They're out for blood—our blood. I know it."

"The dinner is in celebration of Marius's coming of age. Nothing more. It will be his first run with his family. The entire Wselfwulf pack will be there. I highly doubt an attack. After all, Marius is Rollins's nephew. He favors him almost above his own son."

The room grows silent with the sibling's contemplation. "Irina is right about one thing. You need to get rid of her boyfriend. I might be of some help with that," Ryatt says with a wicked grin. "I'm quite good with a hammer."

"No," Xander growls. "I won't hurt the boy. She'd despise me even more."

"Surely, she doesn't despise you," Irina says with exasperation. "Very much dislike you, yes, but I doubt she is indifferent to you. The soulmark will have made sure of that. She doesn't still deny it, does she?" Xander shakes his head, his face a mixture of frustration and sadness.

"It's all she's capable of doing, though her actions would say otherwise."

"She'll come around, brother. Just wear her down. You know the game," Ryatt tells him.

"No." Irina's lips form a firm line, before inhaling calmly through her nose, gathering her patience. "Xander, it's clear that you need to spend a little more time listening to Zoe rather than taking every opportunity to try to stick your tongue down her throat. Surely this is the reason why she wanted to be friends in the first place. To cultivate a relationship with you that wasn't based on sex or the soulmark. You must use this friendship as an opportunity to build the foundation of an actual relationship. Give her more. She deserves it." Xander sighs his consent. "Why don't I go out with her? Have a little chat, girl-to-girl, hmm?"

Xander mulls over the idea, the furrow in his brow lessening as his taut body relaxes inch by inch. He casts a hopeful look toward Irina. "I think that would be good. Thank you. Anything at this point would help. I can feel myself growing more restless the longer the bond stays unfinished, and I don't want to force myself on her. And I don't want to go mad. I just... want her." His voice is full of pain. Irina and Ryatt's share a look of quiet concern with one another, silently communicating a promise to help Xander at whatever cost.

"I'll speak with her. Don't worry about a thing."

+++

"I can't afford any of this," I tell Irina petulantly, shifting my weight from foot to foot as I endure her scrutiny. She holds the lilac-colored dress up to me.

"Yes, you've said so," she murmurs, eyes squinting as she pulls the dress back and holds a lovely emerald dress up to me instead, "several times in fact."

I'm not quite sure how I end up shopping with the youngest Adolphus. She showed up on our front doorstep with a large bouquet of flowers from her mother and managed to garner an invitation from Aunt Lydia inside. She promptly informed me that we were set to have a girls' day. Too baffled to object, I let myself be herded from the house and to a slew of stores. Our objective, she explains to me, is to find a sophisticated cocktail dress with just the right amount of cleavage to ensure lingering gazes and no wandering hands.

"Try on the green. The lilac doesn't suit you. And stop stalling on the red dress. Embrace it." She waves me back into the dressing room, resuming her seat on the plush, embroidered chair situated in the private room. We are in *Belle Creations*. A high-end boutique that Irina enjoys because of the accommodating staff and selection.

I love the dress with its rich color, much like its gemstone counterpart. It's a fit and flare style, billowing out pleasantly just an inch or so above the knee and hugging my top tightly. A V cuts down both front and back, displaying ample side boob. Something I'm sure Irina will give high marks.

"Come on then. We don't have all day. If you can't find something here, then we'll have to move onto the next," Irina calls from her throne. I depart the fitting room with an exaggerated sigh, my response garnering an eye roll from the raven-haired beauty. "Well, that one certainly has potential," she drawls, a calculating gleam in her eye. "With the right accessories… yes, that one is excellent. Now try on the red." She snaps her fingers. A woman in black quickly appears to refill her glass of Prosecco.

"Why do I need a dress exactly?" I call from the dressing room, slipping out of the silky material. "I have plenty at home."

"Because you'll need a very nice dress to impress the Wselfwulfs. They think themselves very highbrow."

I still at her words and give a sharp inhalation. The Wselfwulfs, the rival wolf pack of the Adolphus pack, why on earth would I need to impress them?

"Breathe, Zoelle," Irina commands softly, her voice barely carrying to my ears, "you'll be safe with our family by your side." I take in another shuttering breath, unnerved by my own reaction and Irina's perception.

"I'm fine." *Liar.*

She snorts. It reverberates through her glass. "I can hear you, you know? Enhanced hearing is one of our abilities."

"Right," I mutter, pulling on the maroon bodycon dress. Her cerulean eyes zero in on me as I exit my sanctuary.

"They're having a dinner party in two weeks to celebrate the coming of age of one of their boys," she tells me coolly, her finger spinning idly in a circle. I obey her silent command, going on tiptoe to as I spin in place. The dress has cutout sides and an off-the-shoulder top. Though the material is thicker than the green, I somehow feel barer in it. "Our family has grown in the past few years." She captures my eyes meaningfully as I turn back to face her. "And we find ourselves at a tipping point—we are on the cusp of overwhelming the Wselfwulf family with our numbers. Many families are expecting, and more are join our ranks every day. I do not believe the Wselfwulf family ever imagined that within a decade we would have found ourselves to be in such good fortune. They could never fathom the idea that our modern ways might appeal to other members of the pack. And yet, here we are."

"What do you mean 'modern ways'? What was the Wselfwulf pack like?"

"It was a tightly run patriarchal hierarchy within the Wselfwulf pack. Roles were very gender specific. Women stayed indoors and tended the children. Men did all the work and made all the money. Men held all the power. A woman could never be her own. She was either her father's, brother's, or husband's. Of course, there were also the routine punishments to keep everyone in order and the practice of our traditions in place. No matter how barbaric they might seem." She sips daintily from her glass. "I like the emerald better."

I nod, minding the frown I wear at the pieces of information she lets slip. "Xander said he was negotiating some sort of deal with them." Irina casts her gaze toward the storefront and puts on a charming smile. A moment later an attendant enters.

"Can I get you, ladies, anything else? A drink for the Miss perhaps, or another dress?"

"We're fine for the moment, thank you." The attendant leaves as swiftly as she enters. "There was a deal in works," she finally says, eyes narrowing just barely, "I'm surprised he told you that."

I blush. "He only mentioned something about having a deal of some kind, and then, not," I say lamely.

"Why don't you change back into your clothes," she suggests, continuing to speak as I follow her command. "Aleksandr was trying to hash out an arrangement. He was planning to marry the daughter of Rollins who, I might add, is a vile creature. The Wselfwulf's, for all their sweet words and promises to leave us alone, have failed on several attempts to do so. Xander thought it best to bind our families once more, in hopes of lessening the attacks on our land or stopping them altogether. But in the past year, we've had such an influx of pack—family," she corrects, "and several new... markings occur that we can now defend ourselves without such an arrangement in place."

"Well, that's good. Isn't it?" As I exit, she hands me my glass of Prosecco. I drink it gratefully.

"Yes, it is," she murmurs, eyeing me closely. "Zoe, I do not think you realize the profound effect you have had on our family. Or on our pack. The mere fact that you have been sealed has sparked a newfound resilience among us and a peace of mind to our family. Most soulmarks are never found let alone an alpha soulmark. I don't believe Xander has the faintest clue how to proceed or act. For that, I must apologize on his behalf. He's behaved atrociously. Though he has been more bite than bark lately, I assure you he's usually only bark. Not to worry though, I've severely reprimanded him for the way he has been treating you. It would seem that in being an alpha, the soulmark affects him more. I hope you can find it in your heart to forgive his abysmal manners."

"I understand," I murmur around the edge of my glass. "It's been pretty confusing. The soulmark seems to have a mind of its own. While my head and heart are telling me to do one thing, the soulmark is screaming at me to do another."

"I knew you would be the reasonable one out of the relationship." Irina smiles so brightly it startles me, her laughter, a graceful chime, following soon after. "You must tell me something," she asks, suddenly serious. She takes a step forward, tightening the space between us. "You say the soulmark is telling you to do something entirely different from your head... and your heart. Is it truly at odds with the latter? Are you quite indifferent toward my brother? You have absolutely no feelings for him, other than hatred?"

My heart stutters as her question finds its target. I gulp, feeling feverish. "Not entirely, I suppose." I finally manage to say knowing that to lie is pointless. She levels me with another potent smile, triumphant and knowing.

"I, for one am ecstatic that one of my brothers has finally found his match. You have no idea how difficult it's been for me growing up without a sister. Now I'll finally have someone to take my side. I swear, even though they've reformed our customs and laws, they refuse to release their overbearing brother act."

She finishes her drink, slipping into the dressing room I occupied and grabbing the green dress with its hefty price tag. "That's just what older siblings do," I respond smoothly, tenderly reminiscing about how Clara once treated me, and I her.

"I suppose, but now I must ask a favor of you." I nod my head reluctantly. "I think this dinner party is a ruse. The Wselfwulf's have invited my family along with several other higher-ranking wolves to attend the event, leaving the act of patrolling our borders to some of our lower ranking members. It would be an insult not to go, but I cannot with good conscious leave our pack behind without more senior members of our pack to aid in our defense."

"What do you want me to do?"

"Just... talk with Xander. Make him see that I'm not being sensational. The Wselfwulf's do not like us, Zoe. They hate that we left and that we are no longer under their thumb. And they delight in our suffering." She squeezes her eyes tightly shut as if the memory her words bring on is too much to bear. "There are too many families expecting and too many pups not to be cautious. Will you talk to him?"

I avoid her gaze, feeling a building anxiety wrestle in my stomach. *See Xander?* I hate the thought of what might happen if we were to meet, but I can't ignore Irina's plea. "I'll see if he wants to grab a coffee tomorrow. When is the dinner party?"

"Two weeks from this coming Thursday," she squeals excitedly, hands clapping together briefly before smothering me in a hug. "Oh, you're wonderful. I just knew I could count on you. Come on, let's buy this"—she wiggles the green dress enticingly in the air—"and then go grab a glass of wine at Armond's Lounge."

131

"Irina, I really, really can't afford to be spending my money on that when I don't even have a job."

"Not to worry. We'll not be paying for it." She fishes out a black card from her purse. "Xander, on the other hand, will be. And if you need a job, darling, you only need say the word. Plenty of families in the pack own local businesses here. I'm sure an opening could be created somewhere." And with that, she saunters off toward the checkout desk, leaving me both bemused and astounded.

+++

Toes freshly painted, I stretch out on my bed, contemplating my day with Irina. I'm not pleased with myself for agreeing to get coffee with Xander, but I doubt I'll be able to get out of it now. A sigh falls from my lips at the thought.

Bzzz bzzzt; bzzz bzzzt; bzzz bzzzt; bzzz bzzzt. A snag my phone from my pocket, eyeing the unknown number with a frown before answering.

"Hello?"

"Zoelle?"

"Yes? Who is this?"

"Katerina." My eyes widen in response. "I found your phone number on Xander's phone, and wanted to see how your time with Irina was today. She had nothing but nice things to say, but my daughter has an uncanny way of bending the truth to paint a lovely picture."

A chuckle escapes me at the whimsical yet irritated note to Katerina's voice. "It went well. Better than I expected." I scoot my body into a sitting position on my bed, resting more fully against the mountain of pillows behind me.

"I'm happy to hear that," she says. "She also mentioned you would be seeing Xander tomorrow for coffee?"

132

I chew at my bottom lip, gently cursing Irina for sharing the news. "Yes."

Katerina acknowledges my hesitant answer by softening her voice and slowing the cadence of her words. "I know the situation you find yourself in with my son is not entirely desirable to you, and I understand. It is not everyday a lycan and witch find themselves brought together by fate, but I'm so happy you'll allow my son this second chance. You need not worry about any untoward behavior from him, as *I've* spoken with him."

I don't fight the grin that steals across my lips. I imagine Xander being dressed down by his mother, his shoulders slumped and arms crossed. His lips folded in a full pout as Katerina lectures him about how to treat a woman.

"I hope things go more smoothly this time around. I'd love to see you back at the manor." Her voice still holds a current of hope to it that makes it hard to swallow for one painful second.

"Maybe I can send you a text message after our coffee tomorrow?" I offer before I can stop myself. *What am I doing?*

"Oh?"

I rub my face quickly with the palm of my hand, stifling a groan as I sink further into the pillows. *Oh hell...*

"Yeah," I continue with forced nonchalance. "Why not? Besides, I think Xander has the same tendency to bend the truth as his sister."

Katerina's laugh fills the phone line and eases the flash of regret I feel at my suggestion. "He does," she agrees pleasantly. "Well then, I'll await your text anxiously. Perhaps, if it's not too inconvenient, we could chat like this more often?"

I let a beat of silence pass before answering. "Sure." *Why not?* Maybe I could even wrangle Katerina to my side.

"Excellent! I'll leave you to your night then. Goodnight, Zoelle."

"Goodnight, Katerina."

+++

There are rocks in my stomach the size of my fist as I approach Luna Café for my coffee with Xander. He is already there, his shaggy hair styled back while his eyes scan the steady stream of pedestrians with disinterest. Though to any passerby he may look the picture of relaxed, his nervousness beats alongside mine through the soulmark. When his eyes spot me I give a small smile. He stands as I approach, pulling out my chair and waiting for me to sit before he does as well.

"Can I get you anything?"

I lick my lips, eyes skimming the small menu in front of me. "A vanilla latte would be great."

Xander nods, his body thrumming with unsettled energy as he flags down a waitress and repeats my order. "Thank you for seeing me today." My shoulders rise and fall quickly.

"I'm here at Irina's request," I confess.

Xander nods, lips pursing. "Still, I'd like to apologize for my behavior. All of my behavior, from the very start. I've been one-minded and acting without consideration to your feelings. If you'd allow it, I'd very much like to try being friends again. Properly this time."

He leans his body toward mine, keeping his body language open and vulnerable with his head slightly bowed and forearms resting on the arms of his chair. The seconds pass by like minutes as I contemplate my answer, finding myself somewhat mesmerized by his ivy green eyes.

"Properly?" He gives a sharp nod, and I watch as he holds himself impossibly still while waiting for my

134

response. "All right," I acquiesce. Xander's taut frame relaxes with a deep exhale, and he sends me a wide smile. I find my body mirroring his reaction, sinking back into my seat with ease just as my latte is set in front of me.

He remains on his best behavior as I attempt to explain and validate his sister's concerns. Xander nods along accordingly at all the right parts, his foot and fingers tapping out a disjointed yet excited rhythm all the while. A hint of a smile tugs at Xander's mouth through much of our conversation, and I'm loath to admit I find myself doing the same. For though we take opposing sides in our conversation, there is subtle pleasure thrumming through our bond.

"We'll see," he says finally, his eyes alight with satisfaction. Then he launches into question after question about my job hunt, and how I spent my time away from him.

He pays such close attention to my words and slight movements that I can't help the blush that remains on my cheeks for most of our conversation.

"Have you been to the public zoo near Helena?" he asks out of the blue. My coffee mug halts halfway to my lips. My head shakes from side to side carefully. "Would you like to go tomorrow? Atticus, my beta, has business there."

"He has business...at the zoo?"

Xander's eyes crinkle around the edges with the force of his smile. "Yes," he says, "he's a prominent donor. There's a new exhibit, and he wants to see for himself how it turned out."

"I should really be job hunting."

A flash of disappointment courses through the bond, and Xander quickly averts his gaze toward the street. "Of course. I understand."

"Maybe the next day?"

Xander snaps his attention back to me. His forest green eyes effortlessly pin me in place with their intensity. "Yes," he says, voice mildly breathless.

"But as friends." Xander nods.

"Of course." My heart gives a strange flutter as Xander beams at me.

When we finally depart, he pulls me into a giant hug, his face burying itself between my neck and shoulder. Xander pulls back abruptly, eyes dilated and cheeks flushed, before leaving with a short inclination of his head. It leaves me oddly...unsatisfied. And now I can't stop thinking about him and our "not date" with Atticus in a couple of days. On my walk home I overanalyze every word that passed between us.

It seems to be a reoccurring problem in my life now, thinking of that man.

+++

"Don't worry, man. I won't tell anyone you like *The Notebook*," Atticus says.

I bite my lip to keep from laughing as Xander heaves a heavy sigh and rolls his eyes upward. He doesn't fight back. He hasn't for the past hour, choosing instead to endure Atticus' ceaseless comments and comebacks as we tour the zoo.

The friendly ribbing does wonders in wearing down Xander's tightly wound personality. By the time we reach the wolf enclosure I feel I hardly recognize him.

He walks with an easy gait, exuding confidence effortlessly with a smile and laugh that draw stares from the women we pass. It certainly draws my attention. *Where is the domineering alpha I've encountered these past few weeks? And who is this charming and refined man who has replaced him?* Xander catches my stare and shoots me a sly wink, laughing at the punch line of Atticus' joke.

I direct my smile toward the ground, and find a laugh bubbling up my throat as well. Never did I imagine myself in *this* scenario.

"So, Zoe, want to hear some embarrassing stories about our fearless alpha?" Atticus leans against the enclosure railing, an easy smile on his face that makes his crystal blue eyes twinkle merrily.

"Yes."

"No."

A large smile splits my lips at Xander's quick rebuttal, and our trio gives in to another bout of laughter. Xander comes to stand on my other side, leaving me sandwiched between the two impressive men as we stand in front of the wolf enclosure. Warmth radiates from their bodies, a characteristic common in all lycans as their body temperatures run a few degrees higher than the average human. Or so Atticus says. It's a pleasant feeling nonetheless on this rather cool, sunny day.

"I don't see any wolves," I murmur. My eyes flit from left to right across the grassy enclosure to no avail.

"Back left, near the boulder." My eyes follow the direction, and I let out a soft hum of appreciation. When I glance to my right at Atticus, he is staring out into the pathway. My eyes narrow on him, and, as if sensing my gaze, he passes me a lazy smile. His expression is entirely too smug as he stares me down with his cerulean eyes.

"How did you know without looking?" His smile grows larger.

"Wolves," Xander comments, "always know where other wolves are." Atticus wiggles his eyes brows at me and I scoff in return, turning slowly to face Xander, who wears an entirely too pleased smile as well.

"Any other fun wolf facts I should know?"

A pleasant sensation whirls in my stomach at his pleased look. His smile softens from its smug lift to one of genuine pride. I note the way his chest broadens on an inhalation while he rolls his shoulders back. The bulging muscles of his pectorals and biceps strain momentarily against his polo.

"A few things," he says, voice lowering an octave. The hair on the back of my neck comes to attention as I hold back my blush.

"The females and males have separate ranking order," Atticus says.

"Separate ranking order?"

I take a step back from the railing to form our grouping into a triangle instead of a straight line, and wait for Atticus to continue.

"Alpha, beta, the in between, and omega. When soulmarks are involved, lycan or otherwise, they inherit the rank of the higher placed wolf. You," Atticus explains smoothly, "are an alpha."

I take time to process Atticus' words, but find my thoughts slipping to memories of Xander's first impassioned speech to me.

Jewels for your body, silks for your skin...

You would be an alpha...

My alpha...A queen...

Heat simmers behind Xander's regard, his eyelids held at half mast as he watches me react. I do my best to keep my heartbeat under control and give Atticus a short smile.

"And your soulmark would be a beta?" He nods, his eyes widening and his smile becoming brighter.

"She will."

Xander chortles. "Don't get him started. You'll never hear the end of it. Why don't you ask another question?"

"I don't know...I think I understand the lycan culture fairly well." Both men stand a bit taller at my enunciation, and I bite back a grin. Folding my arms

138

behind my back I step back toward the railing, eyeing the lone wolf in the enclosure with a thoughtful furrow to my brow. "Lycans are both man and wolf. Originally free to shift from one form to the other, until a *wicked* witch—" both wolves snort in unison "—placed a curse upon your kind. Said curse suppresses your ability to shift, meaning you may only do so at the full moon. The alpha is only as strong as his pack, and that doesn't just refer to the size of a pack. It's a variety of things. Love and loyalty. Soulmarks and children born into the pack."

"Don't forget she-wolves," Atticus chimes in. "She-wolves are rare among our kind and for some reason have always bolstered the pack's and alpha's strength." *Of course, how could I forget?*

"How do you know all this?" Xander asks, curiosity tainting his voice.

I pass him a coy look over my shoulder. "Your sister, of course." Xander barks out a laugh, leaning in toward me with a happy grin, but stops infinitesimally short of reaching me. A light breeze catches my curls, sending them skirting in front of my face. My hand reaches to brush them back, knocking into Xander's knuckles in the process. Our eyes meet and I feel my throat tighten. The moment between us holds entirely too long. Slowly he retreats, his eyes still warm, but somewhat guarded, as his hand falls to his side.

"So," he says, "what shall we see next?"

+++

We meet again a few days later for another "not date." This time around there is no Atticus to buffer the underlying tension between us, but a handful of witches milling about us in the forest. We forage for magical herbs and plants, wearing funny violet-lensed goggles to spot them and their magical "glow." Well, Xander and I are wearing funny goggles. The other

139

witches have no need for them, as they are already well versed in each plant's identity.

"My mother said she spoke to you the other night," Xander says. My head bobs in agreement as I snip a pale pink flower from a tangle of thorny vines. With the goggles I can see the glittering particles that emit from the flower. Like catching dust in the sunlight, the particles are faint but stand out through the violet lens.

"Uh huh."

"So it went well?" There is an unusual hesitance to his voice, and I cast a look over my shoulder to better look at him. Xander looks calm and collected, despite looking completely ridiculous with his goggles and the basket he carries with our bounty. A closer look reveals the stiffness in his posture and the subtle creases lining his forehead.

"Uh huh." The lines on his forehead deepen, and a smirk curves my lips as I rise. "Worried?"

Xander pushes up his goggles and shoots me a plaintive glare. "You're not going to tell me either I suppose."

"It's really none of your business," I respond, brushing off my knees after placing the delicate flower near a few others of its kind in the basket. Xander's chest puffs up, and his scowl turns a touch icier. I raise an eyebrow in response, or try to at least through the large goggles, and he deflates.

"I...suppose." My smirk remains. Several times this outing he has subdued his more domineering nature in favor of something more approachable. Pushing my own goggles upward, I soften my smirk into a smile.

"We don't just talk about *you*, you know?" Xander shakes his head. "We talk about her day and mine. And yes, sometimes you're mentioned, but not as much as you think."

It's as though I've lifted a weight off his shoulders.
His posture relaxes with a quick sigh, his shoulders
sinking from their rigid position as he shuffles
forward, inhaling deeply. A delicate breeze rustles
through the air not a second later, and I blush seeing
the way Xander's eyes dilate.

"No talk of magic?" My dark curls bounce as I turn
my head side to side.

"We try to keep the conversation neutral."

"Well," he states softly, "maybe you should. I've
certainly enjoyed today's lesson." I swallow and avert
my gaze.

"Does magic really make you feel itchy?" I ask
after a moment. Xander smirks when I peek back at
him.

"Somewhat, yes. My skin feels tighter when I'm
around it. I can't help but be more alert."

"Does that mean I make you feel...itchy?"
Amusement colors my tone as I hold back a laugh, but
Xander's eyes only darken in response.

"You're most certainly an itch I'd like to scratch."
The amusement drains at the low pitch of his voice,
and I'm positive a rosy flush covers my neck and
cheeks. A shiver crawls lazily up my spine as I
continue to stare into Xander's eyes. Something cracks
in the distance, and a shout of laughter from a pair of
witches breaks the spell we are under.

I clear my throat and avert my eyes, spotting
immediately to my left a cluster of bright purple-pink
flowers, sporting four petals each. My feet propel me
toward it without hesitation, and Xander slowly
follows. I know this magical flower without the aid of
the goggles.

"That's lunaria."

"Ah." Xander's eyes flash knowingly. The small
crease in between his eyebrows is the only tell of his
displeasure. "The *truth* plant."

"Yes."

141

When the moment turns too long I begin to fidget, my fingers fussing with the hem of my tunic top. I chance a glance at Xander as he remains mute. He stares at the flowers with a carefully blank expression on his face, though I note the turn of his full lips is slightly down.

"Sorry about, you know, the whole making you drink lunaria—"

"Don't apologize," he interrupts with a quick shake of his head. "You were completely within your rights to do so." Another dreaded silence hangs between us as his lush green eyes pin me to the spot. I feel a tightness squeeze my chest, drawing the air painfully from my lungs as I hold his gaze.

"I think it's a habit of theirs." The words come out of my mouth before I can stop them, and I internally cringe.

Xander's eyes narrow a fraction, and his head tilts to the side. "Who has what habit?"

"The aunts. They gave Ben lunaria too." This time my cringe is visible. *Don't I know how to hold my tongue?*

"I see," he murmurs, watching me far too intently. "And did he face the same inquisition as I?" I snort before I can help myself.

"At least *you knew* what was happening. Poor Ben had no idea why he was saying the things he did. Neither did I. I just thought he was overly nervous. I couldn't fathom a better reason for him to say the things he did."

My sneakers idly kick a small stone near my side. I pensively watch it skid away, ignoring how the soulmark tingles against my skin and Xander's ever vigilant gaze.

"What exactly did he say?"

I shake my head, risking a peek at Xander's intent regard. "Nothing important." *Just casual chauvinism.* Xander chuckles at my sudden, yet severe frown.

142

"That bad, huh?" I let out a chuckle of my own. I drive my gaze back toward the grouping of flowers, lest I stare too attentively at the dark patches of hair spotting his jaw line.

"Something about women being in the kitchen," I offer with forced nonchalance, though swallowing past the sudden lump in my throat proves more difficult than I thought.

"I'm sure he didn't mean any harm by it," Xander says. My gaze darts toward him once more, not quite believing what I've heard. Xander reads my expression neatly and shrugs. "I'm trying, all right?" Another chuckle pushes past my lips, and we fall into a more comfortable silence.

"Thank you for that." Xander ducks his head. The soulmark pulses against my skin, and with it comes an almost bashful excitement. It makes my heart skip a beat. "We should head back," I say a bit breathlessly. Xander nods wordlessly, and we walk back toward Gran's.

Although we share no more words on the journey back, it's hard to ignore the looks we pass between us: furrowed brows or wide-eyed glances. Our lips pouted or thinned to a harsh line. My heartbeat increases with each step as I ponder what to say, or if there is anything left to say at all.

"I'll leave you with this then." Xander passes me the basket filled with greenery and stands closer than necessary at the back door of Gran's house. "You wouldn't happen to have any lemon and ginger tea inside, would you?"

I swallow sharply at his hope-filled eyes. "Ye—"

Bzzz bzzzt; bzzz bzzzt; bzzz bzzzt; bzzz bzzzt

I fish my phone from my pocket, the color on my face draining as I stare at the caller ID. Xander's stunted growl tells me he sees the name as well.

"Another time perhaps," he tells me stiffly, walking off before I can get in a word. Leaning against

143

the back door, I answer the phone, watching Xander stride off with a frown tugging at my features.

"Hi Ben."

+++

I'm once more a patron at Luna Café. Shredding to bits my paper napkin, as I await Ben's arrival. Since talking the other day, we arranged to meet for a few short hours while Ben had the time.

I shift in my oversized sweater, relishing the early autumn sun and the cool breeze that carries over the river. Although my love life is about to mimic the state of my napkin, at least Ben will know the truth.

"Hey, gorgeous."

"Ben!" I stand and am immediately swallowed into his arms and lifted off my feet. I giggle girlishly as he twirls me around, only setting me down once my laughter has faded.

He places a kiss eagerly to my lips, "Zoey!" Ben's excitement is contagious, but it can't quite quell the guilt I feel for what I'm about to do.

"How are you? Here, take a seat. Eat something!"

"Thanks!" He picks at the food off my plate, enjoying the house-made chips the best. "I can't stay long. We're working on a project about an hour out of Branson Falls, and I just got the call I'll need to be in earlier than expected to work on it."

"Ah, that would explain the time change and why I had to order food," I reply, taking a decisive bite of my deli sandwich. It's probably for the best that this lunch date is going to run short. I can't imagine Ben wanting to hang around a second longer than necessary after I tell him about Xander.

"Yeah."

"Listen, Ben...." My heart pounds painfully against my ribs as I summon the words. "I—"

144

"Well, well, well, if it isn't Zoe Baudelaire," I tense at the voice, my head whipping around to see the smirking face of Ryatt. *Oh no.*

"Hi."

He swaggers over to our table, a paper bag in hand bearing the local bookstore's logo. "And who is this?" He outstretches a hand, which Ben takes enthusiastically.

"Ben, I'm Zoey's—"

"Boyfriend," I interject swiftly. "He's my boyfriend, and we don't actually have a lot of time together so if you wouldn't mind...."

"Zoey," Ben's voice carries a low warning to it, eyes darting back and forth between Ryatt and me as he attempts to assess the situation. He's not used to me being so rude, but the Adolphus family seems to bring out my brasher side.

"Ah, the infamous Ben. Truth be told, I've been dying to meet you. Tell me, what exactly are your thoughts on carpentry? Would you say you're more of a claw hammer man or a ball peen? I quite like the feel and swing of a sledgehammer." His smile cuts like a razor, eyes twinkling with malicious intent.

"How do you know him?" Ben asks me, his voice somewhat strained.

"I know his sister. She's nice," I tell him, surprised at my honest words.

"And my other brother," Ryatt interjects. "I'd say he's just a few years older than our Zoelle here. Instant connection those two—I mean with my sister, of course. Why, I would go as far to say that we think of Zoe as family already."

"Well, I suppose if you really thought of her as family you would know that she prefers Zoey to Zoe." Ben retorts.

"Does she? Is that right, *Zoey?*"

"I like them both, but... I do prefer Zoe," I admit abashedly.

145

"Hmmm," Ryatt exhales thoughtfully. "Well, I saw you and just wanted to come by and thank you, Zoe."

I wrinkle my brow. "For what?"

"Why, I haven't seen my brother this happy in ages! Whatever you did or said to him the other day has put him in a right, good mood."

He sends me a saucy wink and salutes Ben before walking off, hands shoved into his pockets, bag bumping up against his side. The most annoying whistle on his lips. I feel the color drain from my face, and the familiar knot of anxiety twist my insides apart. *This isn't how today was supposed to happen*.

"Do you see his brother a lot?" Ben asks uncertainly.

"No!" I reply more sharply than intended. I earn a raised eyebrow in return. "It's just that I see his family a lot. More than I would like, to be honest. They... they deal with Gran's business and the aunts on a regular basis. So, we always seem to be bumping into each other. His sister really is quite kind though." A ton of rocks drops to the pit of my stomach, anchoring me to my seat as the lies slip forth. *What am I doing?*

"Right." There is a tightness to his voice that shames me. "And you all of a sudden prefer to be called Zoe?"

"I like that you call me Zoey. I'm *your* Zoey." My conscious screams at me to confess my sins, but Ryatt's appearance has clearly ruined the moment.

We finish the rest of my meal in awkward silence and conversation, the tension between us growing, but unwilling to bend or break. Something in my heart cracks at my cowardice, when he leaves. Ben only gives me a quick peck on the cheek before racing off even earlier than he originally said. Our farewell lacks its usual spark and affection, with both our hearts stretched thin. *And*, I note grimly, *Ben's kiss is nothing in comparison to Xander's lightest of touches*.

A NEW DEAL
- Chapter 8 -

After the lunch date ordeal, Xander and I
renegotiate our agreement. I can't quite remember the
details of how I'm convinced to do so, but one late
night call from Katerina Adolphus is apparently all it
takes. She pleads passionately on her son's behalf for
more than an hour until I find myself agreeing to her
new terms. Daily texting and/or calls. Visits down to
three times a week, and physical contact limited to
hugs or casual touches.

I can't deny the rush of anxiety I feel after I end
the call with Katerina. The days spent with Xander
earlier this week had been nice. Without the pressure
of an arrangement hanging over our heads, we
actually got along.

Granted, we had pseudo chaperons for those
encounters, but I hadn't minded their presence one
bit.

If I'm honest, I'm worried Xander will revert back
to his old ways now that the new deal has been struck.
But my worries are unwarranted. *Mostly.*

147

For our first few face-to-face meetings I feel much like Little Red Riding Hood, with Xander taking the part of the Big Bad Wolf. But the Big Bad Wolf dressed up in slim-cut suits and Gucci cologne. He always brings flowers and makes sure to flash his dimples whenever possible. He's charming. Downright fucking *pleasant*. To make matters worse, he actively listens to me. Asks questions. Engages me in conversations outside my comfort zone.

Once again I'm confronted with a new side of Xander: the seducer. And he's not just after my body, but my heart and mind as well.

Though my head cautions me still, knowing Xander plays nice only to get closer to me, the pros seem to outweigh the cons. The soulmark is tempered by his nearness, and as such, so is my sanity. I'll endure Xander's unwavering attention if it means I can focus on my life outside of coven and pack affairs. Like the issue of my crumbling relationship with Ben.

I should have told him at lunch, I think for the thousandth time. There's no doubt about it. My relationship with Ben is falling to pieces right in front of my eyes. And I have no one to blame but myself.

As if Xander can smell the end coming, he begins to circle, painting words left to entice, then feigning innocence at my incredulous looks with wide eyes and a coy smile.

"*What can I say, Miss Baudelaire? I aim to misbehave.*" Said while stealing a bite of my chocolate torte.

"*Some of the best moments in life are the ones you can't talk about.*" Said while partially licking honey off his bottom lip.

"*Open wide.*" Said just before offering me a bite of his dessert.

Standing far too near without ever touching at all. Pulling out my chair and reading over my shoulder. The soft pant of his breath hovering closely to my ear.

Showing off his strength in clever ways. Cleaning the front gutters of the house at the request of Aunt Lydia. He does so without a shirt. The taut lines of his abdominals teasing me from my bedroom window. It is a *highly* unnecessary action, yet no less effective in completely stealing my attention. Sneaky bastard.

For every show of strength, he speaks openly with me about some insecurity of his.

For every call I leave unanswered from Ben, he gazes at me with knowing, understanding eyes.

For every bold suggestion comes a swift apology. But the damage is already done.

Images of the two of us plague my mind, both waking and asleep. To date, I had never met a man so keen on seducing me. Nor more adept with his techniques. Thankfully most of our in-person encounters occur in settings flush with a multitude of scents to busy the senses. Lest Xander detect my scent of arousal. By some of his less restrained heated looks, I know we careen toward the end of our game of chase.

I can't decide if I'm relieved or terrified. Both, if my food has anything to say about it.

"This just isn't working," I mutter to myself. Skin prickling in sudden anticipation. I raise my eyes to the front door. It's Xander. I can feel his aura approaching my barrier: an array of deep and clear bright reds that shouts his strength and prowess for all to see. I'm home alone, and I would bet my savings that he knows it. He always manages to get me alone for our time together. Pausing in my work as a knock sounds at the door, I concentrate on lowering the barrier and opening the door with my mind. It takes a long moment, but the telltale click of the lock retreating into its chamber sounds and the door creaks open.

"Zoelle?"

I take a deep breath, stealing my nerves against what is to come. "In the kitchen!"

He walks in, surveying the scene with a casual eye before approaching me from behind. The length of his arm curls around my middle, chest fitting itself snug against my back as he gives me a one-armed hug.

"How are you?" he asks, his voice low and near my ear.

"Fine," I respond with a shrug, disengaging him easily. Glancing over my shoulder, I watch as he prepares a vase for the flowers he has brought.

"What are you making?"

"Apple cinnamon rolls, but a bit differently. I want them to look like one of those blooming apple tarts at the bakery, but I'm not cutting the dough right."

"Maybe I can help," he offers, rolling up the sleeves of his button-down and tossing me a smile.

"I'm afraid Adolphus men aren't allowed to slave away in the kitchen."

His eyes narrow playfully as he mimics the way I place the cinnamon rolls in their ramekins. "I don't mind breaking the rules if you don't," he tells me in confidence leaning toward me. I send him a disapproving glare, but it lacks its usual sting. That has been happening a lot recently. So have my ill attempts at getting him to call me Zoe. Or even Zoey.

"I can manage on my own," I insist halfheartedly.

"You don't have to though," he murmurs. "I'm here." Our eyes briefly catch.

"I know." I duck my head and continue working, letting Xander keep up the conversation until the mood has lightened. He teases and taunts until keeping a smile off my face becomes an odious task.

"Are you always this domineering in the kitchen? Geez."

I laugh and swat at the hand that reaches for the empty dough bowl. "No more! You'll get yourself sick if you keep eating that. It has raw egg in it." He smiles charmingly back at me, dimples peeking through.

His hand darts forward once more, carefree smile still in place, as I smack his hand again with the sticky spatula. With a laugh, he licks the remains of cinnamon sugar and dough from his hand. "Harder, Zoelle."

I blush and guffaw, hitting him indeed harder with the spatula. A rumble of his pleased laughter fills the kitchen. "Behave," I scold as I place the ramekins in the oven and begin clearing the island. I rebuff Xander's attempt to help, asking him over my shoulder instead to fix us some tea.

But Xander stands stock-still. Breath bated at my instruction. Then I realize why. My hand is placed without a thought near the bottom of his spine. The touch is casual yet somehow so *intimate*. It is something I am careful never to do. I stare at the offender in horror, before drawing it sharply back against my chest and turning to the sink.

"You know," I say, forging past the obvious electricity crackling between us. "I hope you've taken your sister's concerns to heart. I don't think it's unreasonable to keep a few stronger members of your pack behind, even if it means coming across rude at the dinner party. Don't the Wselfwulf's have a history of going back on their word?"

"They never made a promise not to attack us during the dinner. It needn't be said. The dinner is a celebration the entire Wselfwulf pack will be expected to attend. If anything, I'll need my strongest by my side throughout the dinner if something happens."

"Well...."

"It will be fine, Zoelle. We've run through a number of possibilities about how the night might go. We're well prepared for any outcome." The alpha comes through in his voice. It is full of calming authority that puts my nervousness at ease.

"That's good."

151

He hums in response, handing me dishes instead of grabbing the tea from the cabinet. I'm all too aware of his nearness. The scent of pine and spice assailing my nose with each brush of his arm against mine. I step to the side, allowing him room in front of the sink, which he eagerly takes.

"You don't need to be afraid," Xander tells me reassuringly. "The Wselfwulf pack will do you no harm. I won't let them." A shiver runs its way across my body at the fervor of his promise. "I won't let anyone hurt you, and neither will my mother apparently. She's mentioned you two sometimes talk." I flush and nod. We did. Little text messages here and there. Nothing to0 intrusive. We work in silence. His words drive me to speechlessness.

I'm not sure when his gentle flirting had turned into such neat promises, but they're beginning to take their toll. I shift my weight from foot to foot, hurrying to get the dishes done, so I can grab the tea.

As we put the last of the dishes into the dishwasher and wipe off our hands, I make a beeline for the tea cabinet only to run into Xander's solid chest. He steadies me. His hands deliciously warm against my arms.

"Sorry," I mumble, getting lost in the depths of his eyes. His fingers tighten for one tantalizing second before releasing me and shifting back. Big Bad Wolf letting Little Red get away? How unnerving.

But as I pass, I can hear him suck in a deep, rattling breath. His resounding groan freezes me to the spot as I cast a helpless look toward him. One hand grips the counter tightly, while the other rests in a tightly balled fist at his side. But he does not turn around to face me. I gulp, knowing very well that I should continue with my task. Knowing that if I do, one of us will speak and break the spell laying between us. But I don't.

My heart hammers painfully against my chest and the soulmark quakes in anticipation. I shake my head at my weakness. *I shouldn't.* I tell myself, ready to correct my mistake when his hand falls heavy on my shoulder.

"He'll never know," he tells me hotly.

With great effort, I attempt to summon the indignation I know I ought to possess. "You can't possibly think that I would—"

He turns fully to face me and takes a step closer. "But you already have." The cool confidence in his quiet words leaves me shaking. He stalks closer.

"It wasn't anything," I protest, missing the hardening resolution of his features. "It was the soulmark."

"No," he speaks slowly, his other hand coming to trace the path from rib to hip. "No more excuses. No more talking."

My words fail to reach my tongue. Heart pounding as it is, fierce and hard in my throat. Xander's eyes dilate, flecks of bright gold stealing around his pupil. For a fleeting moment, I imagine the idea of surrender. The onslaught of pleasure it will surely bring. My eyes flick toward Xander's lips, and it is enough to break our standstill. With a snarl, he crushes me to his chest, his lips slanting across my own in a vicious kiss.

I cannot stifle the urgent sound of longing against his mouth. In an instant, I am itching inside my own skin as he deepens the kiss. His tongue goads me into action until my hands find their way around his neck and steal into his hair. My back slams against the cabinet door just as his thigh thrusts itself between my own. My hips rock forward to meet his as we share a groan of pleasure.

Xander draws back enough to look down at me, a starved look in his eyes. I can't imagine how I must look, panting and mindless. A crazed fire runs through my veins, one I can no longer ignore. *One stronger than magic*. My hips tilt forward to relive the delicious friction.

"You are maddening," he breathes fiercely pressing back into me. My eyes slide shut at his heady exclamation, my neck tilting ever so slightly to the side to accept his attentions. He bites and licks. Sucks the skin until it bruises. "You've made me weak like I've never known before." He growls into my skin, reclaiming my lips and swallowing my gasp.

My nails dig into his skin, begging him closer as the weight of his torturous hands glide across my body leaving fire in their wake. We share the longest, most insistent kiss I have ever known. It leaves me delirious. No man should be able to coax such trembling feeling from a body. I can only attempt to keep up, my own hands wandering down the rigid planes of his chest and abs. My teeth nip at his lips. My tongue urges him on. But as soon as I begin to pursue his touch in earnest, he slows. The kiss turns languid and sensual. *Thorough*. His hands caress my sides, slipping down toward my thighs.

"Let me taste you," he moans against my lips. *Wasn't he already?* I think amid the drowning sensations. Before I can ruin the moment with my indecision, I give my assent, gasping when strong hands lift me and set me atop the counter. My hands are momentarily pinned above my head as his lips attack my own with renewed vigor. A sharp thrust of his hips and the feel of his hard length pressing against my center leave me mewling my consent. *Thank God for skirts*. His hips maintain their rhythm, and I sink into their pleasure. Rubbing and rocking until a steady pant falls past my lips.

"Fuck," the explicative bursts forth from my mouth as his hand travels up my thigh and tugs me forward, till my ass sits precariously at the edge of the counter. I wrap my legs around his torso, and his grip tightens to leave bruises. When I begin to roll my hips in measured cadence with his thrusts, we share a look weighed down with our desires.

Even as his other hand begins to trail down my arm to palm my breast, I leave my hands above my head, reveling in his dominance. His lips move boldly down my body and across the top of my breasts, though he carefully stays away from the soulmark. I whine in response, my hips bucking upward only to meet air.

The warmth of his exhalation crosses my thigh, and I stiffen in response. My eyes darting open to gaze down at him on one knee.

"What are you...?"

His wolfish smirk moves against my skin. He nips at my flesh, and I shiver in response. "Tasting you," he murmurs. My mind barely moves fast enough to comprehend his next actions, but instinct tells me to find purchase and hold on.

When his head dips, I stifle a cry with my fist. Not a second later, I am almost shouting in surprise when I feel his grip on my forearm. He eyes me with unadulterated hunger. "Don't. I want to hear you." His tone leaves no room for argument, and my fingers reach down to curl in his hair as he dives back in. He noses along my thigh, taking in deep, shuddering breaths as he nears his goal.

Distantly the logical part of my brain cries out in distress. That I have let it go this far is unfathomable, and for a moment I hesitate, heart skipping an anxious beat. It isn't a matter of telling Ben about my indiscretions anymore. I have to break it off with him. I suck in a sharp breath. *What am I?*

A sharp bite near the apex of my thighs makes me yelp, concentration broken. I look down to stare wide-eyed at Xander. His mouth lies in a grim line as he eyes me. My skirt is pushed up high around my hips, my underwear parted to one side. I can feel my

155

arousal easing its way down. Xander growls. The sound savage and primal. My heart races, a moan tearing its way from my throat as I clench my legs in response. But Xander's grip is unyielding. My legs barely move an inch.

"Xander—"

"Don't," he breathes harshly, holding my eyes captive. Several heartbeats fly by. "Keep your legs open. Do you understand?" I nod pathetically, watching in awe as he leans forward to taste me. Tongue pressing flat against my dripping center. I nearly cry in relief as he licks his way up. Again and again and again. I shift forward, grabbing at his shoulder with my free hand to gain some semblance of control.

He is relentless. Fucking impeccable. My tender flesh trembles and flushes at his persistent touch. Warmth spilling down my legs, as my entire body goes up in flames.

"*Aleksandr.*"

His name falls from my lips like a prayer, and I faintly hear his cursed response. He kisses up and along the apex of my thighs, mumbling nonsense against my skin as his fingers take up the work. My head rolls back as not one, but two fingers enter me simultaneously.

I bend forward, my fingers slipping from his hair to cup the back of his neck, urging him back as unexplainable pain and pleasure build to a crescendo inside of me.

"Please," I beg as my other hand reaches inside his shirt and inches toward his soulmark.

I know nothing in the next instant, only blinding pleasure as his teeth sink into the soft flesh of my thigh with a feral growl. His fingers are unforgiving as they press inside me. My own strain against the crescent moon etched on his bronze skin. I arch upward, my chest and face toward the sky. A ragged moan escapes as my orgasm crashes over me.

I cannot describe the feeling that pulsates between us. Nor the weight of the anchor that wraps us tightly together. Abundant warmth and satisfaction settle over us as we revive.

He stands in one fluid motion. Barely an inch is between us as he straightens my clothes and presses sweet kisses across my face even as my breath continues in short and shallow bursts.

"Xander—"

"You're mine," he snarls. His hand grabs my face, his thumb presses against my jaw, and his forefinger wraps securely under my chin. He presses into me; head against my own, fingers shoving back into my pussy without pause. He swallows my cry, thrusting his tongue inside my mouth in time with his fingers. His thumb plays across my clit, bringing me near the edge once more with no remorse.

Xander pulls away panting, and I almost fall off the counter, barely catching myself as I stare at him, mouth agape. "I—"

"Break up with him before the dinner, Zoelle," he commands, sticking his fingers in his mouth to clean them off. His stare pins me in place until he finishes. "Or else." And then he is gone, and the oven's timer sounds off.

Celebrations

- Chapter 9 -

It's Thursday, and already this morning I've endured a manicure and pedicure, a Swedish massage, and a hair appointment alongside Irina. Though the pampering is meant to be relaxing and rejuvenating for tonight's dinner, it is anything but, for Irina is in constant teacher mode. She educates me on all the important members of the packs who will be in attendance, and how I should behave with each and every one of them. I am exhausted by the time we finish our beauty routine, but at least I look tremendous. My fingernails and toenails are painted a shimmering opal color, and my hair holds a luxurious new bounce to it. The tightly coiled springs falling to frame my face in a beautifully, subtle way while maintaining their volume. And my dark skin glows from the copious amounts of oils rubbed thoroughly into it.

When all is said and done, I have a few precious hours to kill, which is fine by me. My head is filled with Irina's insights and thoughts of Ben.

I left him a voicemail this morning. Asking him to call me back as soon as possible, but I hear nothing from him. No texts. No calls. I don't want to annoy him with a brigade of either, and so I wait anxiously instead for his call. Sensing my nervous energy when I return home, the aunts and Gran convince me to practice my potion making. With their help I brew protective enamel, healing potions, elixirs of fortitude and strength, bottled blind sight and blasts, and tonics meant to give power over the elements. They are advanced potions, a fact that initially had me wary until I started treating them like recipes. Then, everything clicked into place. I shouldn't be surprised at how naturally the art of brewing comes to me, yet I am in the most pleasant sort of way. Most of the potions take only a few attempts to get right (and some end in war wounds), but once I'm able to correctly brew them, making them comes as easy to me as cooking eggs Benedict.

As my free time nears its end Gran gifts me an enchanted bracelet. It works as a truth seeker and will compel anyone I come into direct contact with to speak the truth. I can't help but roll my eyes as she fastens it around my wrist but give her a small smile nonetheless. I can tell Gran is on edge. Her gaze often lingering these past few days on my jade talisman. A thoughtful frown on her face. She will be meeting with the Wellington's while I am at dinner. The strange item intended for passage through our small town scheduled for tonight.

She's nervous. The aunts are nervous. And in turn, so am I. But it's clear our worries run in opposite directions. While the aunts and Gran fret over the magical object, I can't seem to tear my eyes away from my phone.

My fingers reach for my soulmark, feeling the indentation on my skin that seems to have sunken deeper since my... encounter with Xander. The worst

159

of the ache I feel in my bones has retreated. A change most likely resulting from our renewed contact. Except it wasn't like this before. This time I can't force Xander's baser emotions to the back of my mind. He remains always present. And though the soulmark doesn't cause me tremendous pain from being separated from him anymore, it still yearns for him. Much more so than before.

And then there are the dreams.

I swallow thickly. Closing my eyes, the dreams from the past few nights come forth with stunning clarity. Monday night recapped our kitchen escapades, with an emphasis on what would have happened should we have continued. Tuesday night I dreamt of Xander taking me roughly from behind, bent over the desk in his home. Wednesday, we loved each other nonstop, bodies slick and intertwined on silken sheets. I awoke each morning with my hand lost between my thighs, body feverish and unsatisfied. If there is any part of me left to ache, it is becoming quite obvious what it is.

Daydreams further tempt to ensnare my attention throughout the day. Heady thoughts of being trapped between Xander and some ancient tree as we come together beneath a full moon nearly make my croissants inedible. One bite and the strongest sensation of longing strikes a chord inside my belly.

I feel oddly aware of myself during each fantasy. The touch of his skin on mine; pulling, teasing, guiding, and grinding. It's all so real. His breath fans hotly against my chest as he laves my breasts with attention. The erratic thrusts of hips against mine as we climax together time and time again. How his teeth worry the skin of my neck.

"Honey, are you all right?"

I nearly jump out of my skin at Aunt Lydia's quiet inquiry. She takes the kettle off the stove, and its shrill cry recedes.

160

"Yes," I assure her as my hand lingers over my heart. "Sorry, I was just lost in thought."

"Mhmm." Her scrutiny is blissfully short, her attention turning toward the tea cabinet. "You're worried about tonight," she says knowingly.

"To say the least."

"I would give you some kava tea, but it's really quite strong, and if you plan to drink tonight you shouldn't mix the two. Passionflower will do you better." She readies me a cup silently, fixing herself the same.

"I still have a lot to learn, don't I?" I comment, blowing softly at the steaming liquid she places in front of me a few minutes later.

Aunt Lydia chuckles. "You do, but you've got the best teachers a witch could ask for."

I enjoy the silence between us, for once not charged with stifling energy.

"Is tonight going to be okay?"

"You'll do just fine, honey," Aunt Lydia reassures me. I shake my head.

"I wasn't asking about myself," I explain. "It's obvious Gran is concerned about tonight going well. What exactly is being passed through town tonight? And"—I hurry before she can interrupt—"don't think I don't realize the significance of whatever it is that's happening. All the big bad wolves will be out of town, meaning tonight's handoff can be done more safely. Right?"

Aunt Lydia seems equally perturbed and pleased by my guesses. Several times she opens her mouth to answer only to firmly press her lips together in a stern line. Finally, before I can urge her answer, she snaps her fingers twice. The kitchen door, normally always open, shuts with a bang, and the window curtains close with a clatter.

"If anyone asks," she says, "you didn't hear it from me. Your grandmother has secured a trade with the

161

Stormrow Clan, a large family of sorcerers. In exchange for the Wielding Crystal of Dan Furth, your grandmother is giving the clan the Amethyst of the Aztecs in return. The crystal is an ancient Wiccan artifact used to naturally enhance the products of the land almost tenfold. It is a very powerful crystal that could be very dangerous in the wrong hands."

"And are the Stormrows dangerous?"

"Dangerous isn't the right word to describe the clan. Opportunists. Cunning. Manipulative. They strive for power but believe such an artifact disturbs the natural balance of things. It is not the power they seek, but in knowing its meaning to us, they have the advantage."

"And what about the amethyst? What does it do?"

"The gem is set in a gold ring and provides the wearer the ability to walk in sunlight."

I pause, letting the words sink in but finding no meaning. "What am I missing?"

"Firstly, the stone is obviously not meant for one of the clan members. A power like that can only be useful to one type of creature: a vampire." The blood drains from my face and Aunt Lydia reaches forward to pat my arm reassuringly. "Drink your tea, dear," she reminds me. "Now, second, if the clan is attempting to secure the ring for a vampire that means the vampire has control of the clan. The Stormrows cannot, therefore, be trusted."

"But it sounds like we really want the crystal. Does Gran think the clan won't give it to us?"

"We don't just want the crystal. We need the crystal. We're surrounded by warring wolf packs and the threat of vampire compulsions and interference in our affairs. The crystal can provide this town with the protection we sorely need."

"Right," my head bobs along with her reasoning, mulling over them with mounting distress.

"Third—"

"Third!"

Aunt Lydia scowls. "Third, and final, the ring we are set to exchange in return for the crystal is a forgery."

The mug slides from my grasp as I gasp. "No!"

My fingers splay apart in reaction, and the mug stops midair, tea slopping over the sides momentarily before settling. With shaky hands, I retrieve it and place it on the counter. "You're giving them a fake ring? That doesn't sound like something Gran would do." Aunt Lydia colors. "Why are you giving them a fake?"

"Because we can't trust them with the ring, knowing they're in league with a vampire," comes the overly defensive response.

"And what happens when they find out they've been duped?"

"They won't. We've been working tirelessly to infuse the counterfeit with enough magical ability to act like the actual ring. But it's taken a lot out of us—"

"And that's why Gran and the rest of you have been so tied up and tired. That's why you're having me make all these advanced potions. The coven is preparing for... war?" And that's why the aunts act nicer to Xander. If the coven is preparing for its own war, alliances need to be made, and who better to align ourselves with than a pack of wolves on the rise?

"Just remember," Aunt Lydia says, taking a large gulp from her mug, "you didn't hear it from me."

+++

"Remember, tonight there will be three families to celebrate," Irina restates, "The Wselfwulfs, the Maccons, and the Beldigs. The Beldigs are a very small pack from Juneau. The alpha, beta, and fourth are coming. The fourth with his soulmark. Their names are—"

"Samuel, Dominic, Christopher and Monica."

163

"Yes." Irina's praise comes softly through, "The Maccons will be coming with almost the entirety of their pack, but you need only know the names of the alpha, beta, and the third. They have a few soulmarks within their pack, all bonded"—she gives me a pointed look which I ignore—"and are from Canada. The alpha is older, even older than Marius, and does have a wife. They're Jacob and Lydia. The beta is Carlos. And what are you supposed to remember about Carlos?"

I pause in my pursuit of the sprawling grounds we drive past. "Not to stare at the scar on his face."

"Correct. Now, we're obviously coming to the Lunar Ceremony with a sizable amount of the pack. Which, as you know, has its advantages and pitfalls."

"Are you quite finished with your lesson, sister?" Ryatt asks, sipping on his champagne as he fingers his tie.

"No, I am not," she snaps back, attention never wavering from her task. "You are here tonight to make a polite impression and not offend. We are not here for a show of strength, merely to show that we have great power and choose to be peaceful with it. You should be formal and alert; there is no doubt in my mind that the Wselfwulfs will do their best to bait us. Of course, you should not be overly pleasant or eager to please. The Wselfwulfs will not look kindly on a sycophant."

"Yes, well they have so many already," Ryatt mutters.

"Indeed." Irina can't help but agree as she takes a breath. "Though you should not be overly eager to please, you should not strive to be too reserved. Lest you come across as standoffish. Don't be overly meek and try not to let your pride respond for you. Lord knows how many battles have been started because of that little sin."

"None of that makes sense! It's completely contradictory."

Irina colors. "I'm only trying to—"

164

Xander squeezes my hand. "You'll be fine. Just stay by my side tonight."

"And if your date has to ditch you tonight, it'll be best to put yourself on my arm," Atticus chimes from the other end of the limo we ride in. His chestnut hair is combed back stylishly, and the dark suit he wears fits his frame well. *Extremely well.* The beta is a large man standing at six four with the build of a tight end and an inviting smile almost constantly on his lips. He sends me a quick wink as I continue to stare.

My lip twitches upward in response. "I'll most certainly remember that." Xander growls playfully at his beta, but Atticus laughs it off. Leaning back in his seat he continues to speak with Katerina.

"He's right," Xander tells me softly, tucking a wayward curl behind my ear. I keep my eyes on my lap at the intimate touch. "You may need to stay near Atticus's side at some point tonight. No doubt Marius will wish to speak with me and the other alphas at some point privately. I plan to depart before the night's run commences, but I cannot guarantee I won't be stolen away. Besides," he tells me, voice still low and soft against my ear, "I'd rather you not face Marius, or any other member of his pack, unattended."

The limo stops. One by one we exit just as the others pull up and the rest of the Adolphus pack unloads. *I can do this.*

"Have you spoken with Ben?" Xander asks casually. Too casually as he pulls on the cuffs of his suit sleeve. My mouth dries instantly, and my head moves calmly from side to side. *He still hasn't returned my call.* The space between us becomes cold. I can feel the sharp stab of anger radiate from him, and the soulmark pinches in pain. "I expect it done before the end of this week," he tells me harshly beneath his breath, holding out an arm.

I feel my own sharp anger rise at his commanding tone, but choose not to answer. Rather stiffly, I place my hand at the crook of his elbow, and we walk toward the opening doors. It's now or never.

+++

"You're doing fantastic," Katerina says as she comes up to Xander and me. "Everyone seems to be playing nice tonight. A feat I am marveling at."

"Dinner has yet to be served, but I'm sure someone will begin to bite soon enough," he remarks.

"Thanks for the vote of confidence," I say to ease the sting of Xander's words. He's unusually tense and gruff. Of course, in part because of my news, but mostly I think it has to do with the amount of testosterone in the room. Four alphas overfill a room. All claiming the position of strongest and most dominant. A clash of wills ending in teeth and blood seems inevitable, of that I am certain.

Much like the way my magic pulls at my core as I perform and hold complex spells, Xander uses the bond between us to attempt to calm his nerves. I'm not just a prize to be shown off on his arm tonight. I'm there to keep Xander in check. I act as a buffer, and for that reason, the Adolphus pack holds an advantage. Our wolves will hold their tempers better if their alpha does and—

My thoughts stop so suddenly I almost stumble into Xander as he guides me to the dinner table. He casts a worried glance my way, but I shake my head discreetly to call off his attention.

Our wolves?

Shit.

"Aleksandr, how good it is to see you," chimes a lovely voice from behind. Xander bristles and stops, slowly turning us to face the new voice. I shoot a quick look Katerina's way and see her face turn pale and drawn, before going neatly blank. The woman is

166

roughly my height, slim, and with deeply tanned skin. It's almost as if...

"Anastasia." Xander gives the woman a curt nod.

"Well," she says after a drawn-out moment, her eyes sweeping over the two of us. "Aren't you going to introduce me to your soulmark?"

"Anastasia, this is Zoelle Baudelaire. Zoelle, this is Anastasia."

She holds out her hand, "His mother," she says. I should be praised for the way I maintain my mask of politeness in place, never hesitating in shaking Anastasia's marble hand.

"Nice to meet you." Her lips tighten around the edges of her mouth. I have clearly not given her the reaction she wanted. *Good.*

"The pleasure is all mine, dear. I feel as though I haven't seen my boy in ages, and now here he is, with his soulmark no less. My how time has passed. It seems like only yesterday he was my young little man." I maintain my easy smile. "You know, dear, if you hadn't come along my Carrie over there would have no doubt been on Xander's arm tonight." She lets out a shrill little laugh, pointing out a woman in a tight red midi dress across the room.

She is surrounded by a large group of men, but she only has eyes for Xander. As if sensing my regard, she turns her icy blue eyes my way and shares with me a wicked smile. She is stunning, and she knows it. Owns it, wearing her confidence like some badge of honor. And that smile... it's a little too knowing for my liking. I feel as if I've been knocked in the stomach, my breath sweeping from my body in a singular *whoosh*. The eyes in the room begin to look our way.

"Oh," I finally remark, swallowing thickly. The rapid beat of my heart sounds in my ears, but I know that I am not the only one who can hear it. Every single person in this room can. I somehow catch Atticus's eyes at the back of the room. He gives me a wink and takes in a deep breath. I do the same and straighten, returning my gaze to Anastasia. Her eyes gleam in satisfaction at my discomfort. I swallow once more before speaking again. "How quaint."

The words slip past my lips before I can stop them and the room immediately quiets. Anastasia bristles, nose tilting upward. "Quaint indeed," she jeers, eyeing me with distaste before brushing past us.

"Explain please," I whisper to Xander once the room begins to speak in earnest again. The rising voices thankfully hiding my own.

"Anastasia is my birth mother," he explains shortly. "She left my father, when I was six for Rollins. Katerina is my stepmother, and Ryatt and Irina are her biological children."

"You are no less my son," Katerina remarks from the side so quietly I almost miss her whispered words. She passes by us to her seat, her hand brushing against Xander's arm in doing so. "Do not forget."

Xander doesn't acknowledge Katerina's comments. Instead, he wraps his arm around my waist and guides me to my seat.

"And who is Carrie," I ask quickly before I can be engaged in other conversations.

"Anastasia's daughter. My half sister."

Oh. Is this one of the "old traditions" Irina eluded to during our shopping excursion? I try not to cringe outwardly as a server sets pumpkin soup before me.

"She means nothing to me," he murmurs. His fingers reach out to graze my hand but pull back at the last moment. A strange sort of fervor hangs to his words. A cut of vulnerability he does not mean to share. Before I can stop myself, my hand covers his and gives a gentle squeeze. He stares at me in nothing short of amazement and a surge of pleasure scores across my body at our contact. For once, I do not retreat.

"I know," I reply shyly, catching the glint of my bracelet in the light.

"Good evening, everyone!" Rollins booms. He stands chest puffed and arms held out wide before the gathered tables. "It is my deepest pleasure to welcome you here tonight to pay tribute to these fine youths embarking on their first Lunar Ceremony and Full Moon Hunt. This coming of age tradition, which has been passed down through the ages, deserves our utmost respect. Moreover, I am proud that we might all come together on this eve to witness my nephew and godson, Marius, take on the hunt tonight."

I cast a glance toward Irina across the table. She ignores my confused expression and keeps her eyes trained on Rollins. Hunt? I thought tonight is just about the pack running through the woods with the new wolves. At least, that's what Ryatt explained. My gaze shifts toward the other Adolphus brother. His features, though laid smoothly to reflect no emotion are ever so slightly strained.

"But tonight, we not only celebrate our young who come of age. Tonight, we also celebrate the power of the soulmark." Curious and knowing stares come our way at Rollins's obvious pause. "Two of our own, Knox and Avery, have recently completed the binding of their soulmarks to two wonderful wolves. Though they are not here tonight, I assure you it is for a good reason." He gives the crowd a salacious grin. "To all those we honor tonight, let us raise a glass in their favor. To the youth, may your paws always find the earth strong beneath you. To the women, may you bear the pack worthy pups. Long live the days of the pack! Let the moon light our way on even the darkest of nights!"

Glasses raise in the air at his closing remarks, but a disturbing charge lances through the air around the room. I try to keep calm while the meal progresses, busying myself with small talk and counting the

169

members of each pack. I falter as I reach the Maccon pack, my numbers falling short.

"I thought to see more of the Maccons tonight," I comment lightly to Xander as the dinner plates begin to be cleared by staff.

"It would seem as though the Maccons thought better of bringing their entire pack tonight."

"But I thought—"

"Hush," he commands, gaze pinning me in place. "No more talking about the Maccons." A protest sits ready on my lips, but the words are lodged in my throat. It is a disconcerting feeling, made even more so when I try to speak once more but can't. Piercing dread and a spike of fear resonate throughout my body as I realize the familiar bindings of some kind of spell. Xander's hand cups the back of my neck and brings our heads close. "Don't panic, Zoelle. Do not cause a scene. Everything is fine. We'll stay an hour more and return home. There's nothing to get worked up over. *Calm down.*" My body obeys, but my mind still races in horror. How did Xander suddenly possess such control over my body?

"What did you do?" I hiss. I feel at odds with my body. My consciousness rebelling against its treachery, even as my breathing evens out to a placid pace. *I'm calming down*, I think with astonishment, feeling my anger retreat. I sink back in my high-backed chair. This doesn't make sense. How can Xander's simple commands have such hold over me?

"It's the mark, dear," Katerina coos from her place a seat down. "There's nothing to fret over. The second portion of the soul binding—the marking—is always a bit unsettling." I open my mouth to retort, when flashes of memories barrage me.

He kisses up and along the apex of my thighs, mumbling nonsense against my skin as his fingers take up the work...

"Please," I beg as my other hand reaches inside his shirt and inches toward his soulmark...

I cannot describe the feeling that pulsates between us. Nor the weight of the anchor that wraps us tightly together...

My horror and anger return. I tremble in response. The loose sense of calm I am commanded to have crumbling as my heart breaks. Katerina reaches out to pat my knee, leaning over one of the scariest looking members of Xander's pack to reassure me, Justin. Though dressed in a fine black suit, tailored to his stocky form, it only succeeds in making him look like some well-dressed bodyguard. Not a dinner guest.

"Xander really is quite awful at explaining all of the finer details, isn't he? You must forgive him, but know that if you have any questions, you might come to me. I'll explain everything, dear. I do love our short chats and would love to spend more time with you." Katerina straightens and gives Justin a charming smile for putting up with her antics.

Something trails down my neck and back— Xander's hand—I realize faintly. It slips away at his mother's commentary, moving to rest in his lap. Balled in a white-knuckled fist. His gaze anywhere but at me.

I don't speak. Too many thoughts and emotions rage through me to discern which are my own. A soft rage burns in my throat. How could I be so naïve? How could Xander do this to me? My foolish heart has led me astray once more. Among the hurt and confusion, I feel an indignant anger and shame. It must be Xander's. I disregard his shame, the small swell of sorrow I feel aching upward through our bond. That he can possibly find a reason to be angry with me only fuels my own ire.

"Let us allow the women to retire to the drawing room and men to the parlor. Those who will run tonight may prepare themselves in the meantime." I ignore Xander's proffered hand to help me stand, turning and rising from my seat on my own. Shoulders set stiffly back as I stare past him.

"Katerina, walk with me?" I ask, voice deceptively calm.

"Of course, dear. Justin, do follow behind." A pang of hurt jolts my heart, but I refuse to meet Xander's eyes.

"I'd love to know more about the soul binding. Your son isn't always so forthcoming with the details." Katerina reaches my side in a single stride, slipping her arm through mine and giving me a kind smile.

"I would love to tell you." Thank goodness. We wait till most of the people have emptied the room, trailing behind the last of the women to bring up the rear. "What would you like to know exactly?"

Everything. "I know about the soul binding process," I begin after swallowing past several lumps in my throat. "I know there is the sealing, the marking which involves blood, and the binding that requires spellbound words from both Xander and me. What I don't understand is this... *feeling.* Why does Xander have such control over me? I don't understand."

Her steps slow. "It seems my son has done you a grave injustice, if he has yet to explain the added effects an alpha brings to the process." I flush.

A bitter laugh pushes past my lips. "And here I thought we're supposed to be each other's soul mates."

"You are," she tells me adamantly. "Your souls are but two halves of one yet to be complete. The soulmark isn't just about finding your soul mate. It is about becoming whole. Becoming one. As you were always meant to be. Though many face trails during this process, I admit the alpha aspect can be daunting. My son is a powerful alpha. Wise beyond his years, having taken on the pack at such a young age, but he is a good man. He always puts his pack first, but that can be a problem when it comes to matters of the heart."

I lean into Katerina's side, slowing my pace as we walk to our destination. "Why can he control me, Katerina?"

My low-pitched plea softens the older woman. Her brows furrowing as she gazes at me with sympathy. "In completing the marking, your souls are brought closer together. Close enough that you have been drawn into the pack, my dear, sweet girl. *All* members of the pack do as the alpha wishes."

A shaky breath escapes me. "I didn't realize," I say. My shoulders sink as I stare blankly ahead. "No one told me."

"Your family may not have understood that particular nuance, but my son should have." Her voice goes hard, and she squeezes my arm reassuringly. "Make no mistake, Zoelle. I will be having a talk with my son about the way in which he has treated you. It is unacceptable, and he knows better. I fear he is too caught up in the threats that linger too near our pack to act as the man I know him to be. Good. Kind. Respectful. I hope you'll find it in your hear to forgive him. I would hate to find you driven from our lives. I would hate to find you driven from my life. You have such a lovely warmth about you, my girl."

"You don't need to speak with your son, Katerina. *I will.*" Katerina lets out a bark of laughter, covering her mouth with the back of a hand as it continues. A smile graces my lips as the older woman composes herself. "I need to stand my ground with him. Be stronger and stop second guessing myself," I tell her, quiet passion in my words as they ring true from every fiber of my being. An old touch of confidence sparks inside of me. No more hesitating, I think to myself.

"I'm glad to hear it. Your life can only be lived once. One should not do so passively," Katerina agrees as we near the drawing room. "It is about time my son met his match. But never forget, you are my son's happiness, and in time he may be yours as well. Being

173

that, if I can help in any way to make this passage easier, I will. You need only reach out to me, and I will be there."

My throat tightens, thick with emotion. Katerina is much more than the alpha female of the Adolphus pack. She is truly a mother. So much so it brings to mind my own.

"Does the marking do anything besides bring me into the pack?" I ask.

"Only that, my dear. You may feel the undercurrent of the packs' emotional state now that you are part of it. You are now another thread in our giant web, so to speak. And again, there is the will of the alpha that we all feel compelled to follow. Fear not. My son is a good man, Zoelle. He does not abuse his power with the pack. He might bully a person into getting what he wants out of them, but it is done with only love in his heart. My son is a good alpha," she insists, head nodding firmly at the punctuation. "And he will make you a good husband one day."

I duck my head at her presumptions, though if I'm honest, I no longer think them so far off the mark. The heightened emotional connection between us and my body's urge to heed Xander's every word make much more sense now. A flush spreads at the base of my neck, crawling upward as I recall once more when Xander marked me.

Katerina pulls me into the drawing room. We earn several pointed looks, but for the most part are ignored. A fact I am thankful for as I rein in my blush. A short look over my shoulder reveals no Justin. I frown. When the giant man had slipped away I have no idea, but I dislike the thought of him relaying our conversation to Xander. Hopefully the giant man would remain silent.

"As for the binding," Katerina clears her throat, coloring prettily. "It's quite... intimate—"

Crash!

174

Every head turns toward the patio doors at the unexpected noise. Conversations halt as panicked looks are shared. It only takes a moment for the women to rush outdoors toward the scene, heels clicking decisively against the dark cherry flooring in their haste. Katerina and I share a grave look before running after them.

BROKEN

- Chapter 10 -

"I unjust?" Rollins snarls through the thick of the crowd. "You have the nerve to speak to me of injustice? Your father ripped apart this pack with no regard to the aftereffects of his actions. Centuries of tradition abandoned. There are great consequences—"

"He paid for them with his life," Xander growls back. "Him, along with countless others. Enough is enough."

The women push their way through the crowd, inserting themselves closer to the scene, Katerina and I among them. Rollins's laughter echoes in the clear night sky, a smile full of teeth directed at Xander.

"I merely seek to claim retribution for every man and woman of the Wselfwulf pack who died at your father's hand and that of your pack of dogs." The crowd snarls and growls viciously at the insult, but it merely urges Rollins on. "Thirteen dead of mine, and thirteen of yours. These are the laws that rule the pack."

"Your pack," Xander retorts hotly, "not mine. We seek no revenge, only peace to live as we wish."

"And go on so flagrantly disregarding our ways? The laws that bind us all together as one?" The gathering simmers to a quiet, and an uneasy feeling washes over me. Things are about to take a turn for the worse. I know it without a doubt. I begin to move closer to Katerina, navigating my way closer to her side when a hand snatches my upper arm and drags me back.

"Not yet," a female voice hisses into my ear. I turn my head a fraction to see Carrie's mahogany curls. Her sapphire eyes shine with eerie specks of gold. Her nails dig sharply down, and the sharp point of cold metal presses into my side. *Iron.* I think with a shiver as I feel its piercing pressure down to my bones.

"Let me go," I spit through clenched teeth.

"Not yet," she mocks. I can feel my flesh tear beneath her unrelenting grip and bite back a whimper.

"Twelve, Aleksandr. I am owed one more."

"Now." She pants against my ear, using her extraordinary strength to plow us through the crowd and toss me forward into its center. Right into Rollins waiting hands.

"No!" Xander roars. Rollins laughs again. The manic cackle scratches at my ears as I attempt to escape his hold to no avail. Xander's cutting fear and rage rocket through my body.

"She is a pretty young thing," Rollins coos, fingers dragging across my cheek and neck.

"You're disgusting," I say vehemently.

"And what bark!" The Wselfwulf pack laughs, but the others remain stoic. I catch Xander's frantic eyes, feel his mounting panic the longer I remain within Rollins hold. I whimper in response. *I must be strong.*

"Fuck you, asshole," I snarl. "My grandmother will *kill* you for this. Whatever your pathetic reasons are,

177

know that for this slight, my coven will hunt you down like the pack of dogs you are."

The outdoor collection silences at my threat. Certainly not expecting such savage words from such a petite girl—no, not girl—woman. And this woman is filled with righteous anger, and she will no longer stand idly by. I catch the eyes of several pack members, their shining resolve and determination giving me strength.

Rollins cackles. "Oh, my poor little witch, what big words you have. Tonight, is nothing personal. You're merely... collateral damage of the best sort. I only wish to crush the Adolphus pack. See them suffer and regain what I have lost." His words are sickly sweet. *Mad*, I think, *he's mad*. All manner of crazed joy drops from his face. A wicked leer pulling at his features. "No matter what the cost. I will not stop until I have them *begging* for their end."

Heartfelt loathing covers his words, and the pack of wolves around us become restless with nervous energy. Even Rollins seems unsettled by his manic confession. His words are a clear contradiction to his earlier justifications thanks to the bracelets effects.

"You would seek harm to another pack for selfish gains Rollins Wselfwulf?"

Samuel Beldig steps forward, arms folded across his mighty chest. A large man, well over six feet tall and stacked with muscles, his heavy voice laces with displeasure, and much of the crowd shrinks back away from it. From the other side the crowd parts to reveal Jacob Maccon, a dark frown on his face. He nods to Samuel and Xander, shifting toward Xander's side of the makeshift gauntlet.

"What say you Rollins Wselfwulf?" Samuel persists.

I can feel Rollins heart hammering against his breast from behind. He holds me tighter, forces the breath from my lungs in his crushing grip.

"Yes," he cries hoarsely. The crowd gasps in astonishment, followed by a murmur of dissatisfaction.

"Please—" I pant, squirming uncomfortably.

"Let the girl go, Wselfwulf," Jacob commands. But his words only stir a violent reaction. I scream out as Rollins tightens his hold, several of my ribs cracking in protest.

"Let her go!" Xander bellows, taking several steps forward. Xander is nearly foaming at the mouth, his body shaking with terrible tremors.

"I will have my thirteen," Rollins thunders back, sidestepping Xander's advance, but there is nowhere for him to run. Even his own pack stall in confusion at their alpha's crazed will.

"Then take me in her stead," a voice cries from the crowd. Katerina bursts through the crowd, her head held high.

"No!" Xander and I shout at the same time. But our pleas are useless. In a moment, everything comes crashing down.

I am flung to the ground, and the wolves descend. Mutely I watch in horror as Rollins lunges toward Katerina, and she toward him. The other alphas, a hairsbreadth too late to stop their impact as the Wselfwulf pack attack to protect their alpha. Bodies collide into one another with deadly intent, and I am roughly pulled to my feet, an angry fist in my hair. I claw at the hand, panting and heaving as I am dragged backward.

"You slu—" Carrie does not get to finish her taunt. I brace my feet beneath me and surge back into her hold, no longer resisting her forceful pulling. My head butts into the middle of her chest, and she releases me with a grunt. "You're going to regret that," she promises, her eyes going completely golden, her features transforming when a body slams into her own.

179

I clutch my sides as I take in a few ragged breaths, trying to stumble my way out of the fighting packs. My eyes search for Xander and find him easily. He's taken on several members of the Wselfwulf pack, throwing punches and expertly dodging their hits. I lurch toward him, only to run face first into Justin's chest.

"No—"

"I have to get you out of here," he tells me gruffly, lifting me off my feet and into his arms. He barrels through the crowd before I can protest, and then I hear it. *Feel it.* A shattering of something inside me as Irina's scream cuts through the air. Justin swings around and shudders to a stop halfway. "I have to get you out of here." His voice is strained with anguish as his feet continue to move him forward.

"What's wrong? What's hap—" I pull myself up and frantically search over his shoulder into the crowd only to let out my own shrill cry.

Because Katerina isn't moving. *She isn't moving.* I kick and punch at Justin, worming my way out of his hold despite the twisting of my ribcage and the flood of pain that follows. I have to get there. I have to save her. I barely get two steps around Justin before his arms are locked around me once more.

"Stop fighting me, pack mate." His orders fall on deaf ears, for my body is pulsing and shivering with emotion as I stare at Katerina's lifeless body. "There's nothing you can do," he whispers roughly in my ear, his voice clotted with emotion.

But there is. There has to be.

My hands jut out. Ancient words hurtle past my lips. Ones I am unfamiliar with but somehow inexplicably know.

A blinding flash of green light erupts around us, and then there is nothing. Nothing at all.

+++

I sleep through her funeral. It's like a punch to the gut, when I awaken and discover this fact.

They couldn't wait for me to awaken from my spell-induced slumber. The one created from the backlash of my spell.

Yet the shame and pain I feel are nothing in comparison to that of Xander's or the pack. Pack mate. That's what Justin had called me. There are bonds, I learn quickly, that tie us all together. Each pack member's sorrow and mourning pulses through the pack bonds and are only enhanced through my soulmark with Xander.

Xander and Atticus have the audacious task of soothing the pack's heartache. It is a task I do not envy but live through nonetheless. As alpha and beta, they can manipulate the pack's emotions. To feel courage and strength. To give love and take away the pain. Or soothe it. Calm it and put it to rest. They make steady progress, Xander caring for the higher-ranking members of the pack, and Atticus the lesser. Once enough of the higher-ranking wolves come to some semblance of peace, they too begin to help the other members of the pack heal. To accept the great loss and begin to move on.

I wish I hadn't woken up. Stayed in the darkness of my mind and left behind the new world I find myself in. But it's not to be.

I come to weeping, the pack's pain echoing through the bonds and leaving me helpless, afraid, and so terribly heartbroken. For I know her sacrifice had been for naught. The Wselfwulf pack will not be satisfied. They will never be satisfied until Xander and his entire family lie crushed beneath their feet. Until the Adolphus pack is destroyed.

Xander and his siblings hardly know what to do about my ramblings and hysterics. To be honest, I don't either. Emotions overload my senses making me sick with grief. Of course, my downward spiral spills through the soulmark, and soon enough Xander finds himself combating my depression as well. The aunts and Gran are called, but Atticus puts my fears and sorrow at ease. He soothes the wound against my soul as he pours his love onto me through the pack bonds.

I sleep for three more days after that, and when I awake next, all I feel is numb. Gran comes and brings me home, Irina tagging along with a suitcase almost as large as a Newfoundland. They force draught after draught of Essence of Peace and Tranquility down my throat till I wonder if I will ever feel anything again. Irina assures me softly each night that all will be well, and that my distress distracts Xander too greatly. He cannot heal the pack if he is so constantly wrapped up in my despondent state.

"I thought you were supposed to be a cook," Irina bemoans by my side. She tosses her magazine to the floor with a *humph* and rolls on her side to face me.

"A chef," I correct without much vigor.

"What's the difference?" A note of genuine curiosity comes through. I almost smile. Irina has barely left my side all week, and it's clear to me now that her snobbish mask is just that. A mask. She feels with great depth, but her societal airs would have you think otherwise. Now I find them more amusing than anything since I can catch the teasing gleam in her eyes.

"A cook doesn't go through any real schooling or formal training. I went to culinary school. I might not have made my mark yet, but someday." *Someday when my emotions are mine again. When my heart isn't in tattered pieces.*

"Maybe today we just have tea." I hum idly in response. "Zoe." My eyes turn toward the raven-haired beauty. She looks at me thoughtfully, but a particular pain stains her features. "Mother"—her eyes well slightly with tears—"she wouldn't have wanted you to stay this way for so long. She would have wanted you to be strong. For all of us to be strong."

My eyes close softly, and I turn my gaze up to the ceiling. "I'm sorry."

"You don't have anything to be sorry about," she reprimands me harshly, then sighs. The bed shifts with her next movements. Most likely turning on her back the same as I am. "Mother went in there with a plan in her mind. One she didn't share with any of us, knowing how we would respond. She—she left a note. A letter for all of us. Even for you."

This stirs something inside of me. A small symphony of emotions swell in my stomach for just a moment before deflating. Some mix of happiness and sadness. They are at least my own.

"It's on your dresser. You can choose to read it or not." These words come out more steadily. "And we really do need to start bringing you back to the real world again. Agnus and Charlie at the bakery understand the circumstances, but I've only recently learned that you're the one who added the bourbon apples to their blooming sin-a-bon recipe. And they won't make them without you there."

I manage to lift the corners of my lips. "Really?"

"Really." Her disdain and pout come through crystal clear. "Your emotions should be more manageable by now. I know that you were unprepared for what you felt, but Xander and Atticus have allayed most of the pain. By the time you are off all of these nonsensical potions and such, you should find that all of your emotions are your own."

"And Xander's," I add dispassionately.

"He's trying to temper the bond between you. So that you don't have to feel so much."

"Because he thinks I'll go off the deep end again?"

"No." She rebukes me. "It is only that he mourns the loss of a mother once more. I think he does not want you to think lesser of him. To see him as weak."

Irina scoffs. "As if anyone would even think of considering him weak. He only just happens to be one of the few great alphas our pack has ever seen." She sniffs delicately, and the bed dips as she rolls away. "I'm going downstairs to put on the kettle and set out some ingredients. When you come down, we can decide what to make. You can't stay in here forever."

Her feet shuffle softly from the room, down the stairs, and disappear. I lay for a moment longer in the silence. Live in it. I can't stay in here forever; it's true. Katerina would not have wanted that or my own mother. Nor I. I sit upright, the movement causing my head to spin as I try to get my bearings. Time to face the world.

I make my way toward the door but hesitate. My feet take me back toward my dresser where an envelope bears my name in dainty, cursive script. The envelope is light. It shakes in my hand as I stare it down uncertainly. Ripping open the envelope, a single piece of paper with only two words on it falls out.

Love him.

+++

The draughts take time to wear off, almost ten days to be exact. Though my heart feels heavy with sorrow, it is indeed my own. I meet with Xander under the supervision of both our families as we return Irina to the Adolphus estate. Our eyes meet across the large expanse of the entrance hall; my heart catches in my throat at the sight of him.

Hair tousled, eyes lined with dark circles and clothes a mess, his eyes still shine as he stands tall before me. I remember the rush of pride that sweeps through me, and the love. The cascading shower of it pouring through the soulmark and pack bonds. I taste the salt on my lips before I realize I am crying. For once, not tears of sadness.

We collide together. Arms interlocked. Faces pressed tightly to one another. The beat of our hearts sounding as one as I hold him closer, so impossibly closer.

"Zoelle." My name crosses his lips like some kind of prayer. Adorant. Fervent. I tremble. I pull back from our mighty embrace only to lose myself in the forest of his eyes.

"I have to go," I tell him slowly, worrying my lip at his crestfallen expression. I raise my hand to cup his cheek, my thumb sweeping over his coarse beard. Through the soulmark, I pass my intentions. His eyes widen in understanding, then darken in want, a deep growl resonating from within him.

It's far past time I take control of my life. To stop living in indecision and fear. Katerina's words surface in my mind.

Your life can only be lived once. One should not do so passively.

"Go then," he whispers, turning his head to press a kiss to the palm of my hand. His eyes never leave my own. "Then come back to me." I nod. A soaring sense of elation runs rampant through my body as I turn and walk out the door, Gran's car keys in hand.

I drive straight to Missoula, my elation evaporating as I near the city limits. *Oh, Ben,* I think in quiet despair, *I'm sorry. You never deserved this.*

And I don't deserve you.

+++

I sit silently in Gran's Toyota Corolla waiting for Ben to return home from work. The sun dips past the horizon by the time he pulls up in front of his townhouse. But he's not alone. A woman, shorter than I am but with pearly white skin and a handsome smile exits the front passenger seat laughing. In her arms is a box filled with files. Ben hops out and opens the back-seat door to reveal a lanky man with glasses holding a box of his own. He makes a comment, and the trio burst into another round of laughter before heading toward the apartment. I suck in a deep breath and exit the car.

I should have taken something for courage. Or more of the draughts. Anything to stave off my guilt.

"Ben." He has to do a double take when he sees me, a large smile spreading across his face.

"Zoey!" he says something to the other two, and they walk ahead into the house, giving me quick smiles in passing. I meet him halfway, and immediately I'm pulled into a hug. "I didn't know you were coming," he exclaims softly into my hair. "I'm sorry I never got back to you before, I've been crazy busy. To be honest, I'm still pretty busy," he says with a laugh, "but if you don't mind hanging around with a bunch of finance nerds—hey!"

My arms stay tight around him as he tries to release me from our union, and another little laugh bursts forth from him at my display of affection.

"Come on, let's go inside. I'll introduce you to Chella and Dave." I shake my head against his chest, and this time when he pulls away, I allow it.

"I can't," I tell him, eyes cast downward. *Just breathe.* I force my eyes to meet his, just like Gran taught me. They are already filled with tears ready to be released. "I *can't*, Ben."

He swallows. Puts away his smile and folds his arms across his chest. "What do you mean? Why?"

My confession lodges in my throat. Refusing to budge. *I have to do this.* No more running away. "I—"

"Come inside," he pleads, "come inside and stay. Stay with me. Don't go."

"*I can't.*"

"Can't or won't?" he asks as he kicks at the ground. "Why did you come here, Zoey?"

186

"I needed to talk to you about something. Something important." Ben's brows furrow and a pang of sadness hits my heart. *I'm so sorry Ben. About everything.* "But as it happens these past few weeks have been pretty crazy for me too. Xander's mother passed away." Ben's mouth open and closes with dismay. He makes a move to come closer. To hold me once more in his arms, but I shift back.

"I didn't know," he utters. "I'm sorry. Please give my condolences to his family."

"I will."

The air between us feels taut. As if I could pitch off the end and hurtle toward nothingness with one wrong move. I don't know how to continue, but it's clear I must. After all, Ben isn't the one trying to break us apart.

"Ben... Xander and I, we... that is to say—"

"You fucked him?" My eyes widen in shock. I stare at the hard lines across Ben's face in horror.

"What? No!" I cry stepping forward. "No. I didn't. We didn't do that." He looks away, cheeks coloring in embarrassment at his hasty conclusion. "I swear we didn't do that."

"Sorry."

I swallow. Hard. No more running. It's far past time I take responsibility for my actions. My biggest regret now is only having put it off for so long. "Don't be sorry. I'm the one who needs to be sorry—who is sorry. There are things that have developed between him and I, Ben. And it wouldn't be right for me to continue on with you. I'm sorry, Ben. I'm so sorry," I tell him earnestly.

Ben remains quiet, his silence grating my nerves as I search his face for some kind of emotion. Though what I seek I know I will not find.

"Say something, please."

"You've been cheating on me with this guy?" he asks. "Xander? The one from lunch a few weeks ago?" I shake my head slowly, feeling as if someone has grabbed hold of my heart and wrenched it callously from its spot.

"No"—*Just breathe. Just say it.*—"his brother." Tears spill over my cheeks at my whispered confession and the way the color falls from Ben's face. "I'm so sorry, Ben. I didn't plan on—"

He laughs humorously, taking a few steps back as he shakes his head. "Right. I get it. Is that the line Jamie used?"

His words cut. Just as they're intended to. I draw in a sharp breath as I fight for some semblance of composure. "This is completely different—"

"You cheated on me, Zoey. How the hell is it any different?" I have no response. "When?"

I wipe away my tears and release a ragged breath, closing my eyes to think. "A few weeks ago, just before his mother died." A stray wind skates through the street, whipping the fallen leaves around us. The streetlights flicker on. They paint Ben's face in gaunt shadows.

"That day at the cafe... when his brother came around. That's when it started, wasn't it? That's what you wanted to talk about that day?" I nod my head disjointedly, unable to speak as I watch Ben run his hands over his face. "Fuck, Zoelle. Did I mean anything to you? Anything at all?"

"You know you did!"

"Do you love me?"

Another hit. One I take less gracefully as I wrap my arms around myself and stare at the ground. "I tried," I whisper hoarsely, daring to look up. His head bows, shoulders hunched. The perfect picture of misery.

"Great," he says bitterly. The cold word bites, but there is nothing more to be said. "You should go. I'm sure he's waiting for you, probably having a good laugh with his brother over this."

"No, Ben—"

"Don't." He interrupts me harshly, his eyes full of loathing as he takes me in. "Just go. You never even gave us a real chance. I should have known better. Go!" I take a few hesitant steps backward.

"I'm sorry," I whisper brokenly once last time, then turn and go.

Bound

- Chapter 11 -

Everyone is in a flurry of activity. Witches and wolves alike enter and exit our home to pick up supplies. The kitchen is filled. Constantly. By me and other brewers as we concoct potions, tonics, draughts, elixirs, balms, and salves. Someone works solely on divining essences of wolfsbane and amber. Another works with a caster to make some kind of magical grenade. It's a sort of controlled chaos, for although people cram into the space, I never feel like they are in my way. Nothing is out of reach, when I need it, and advice and tips are given without thought. It's a unique and wonderful experience. One I desperately need after my breakup with Ben, but it's also mildly terrifying. Because there is only one reason we stock our supplies: war.

The crystal, I learn, was not given in its entirety. To be exact, only half of the crystal was given in exchange for the counterfeit sunlight ring. Which means the crystal will not be able to boost the products of the land. The coven didn't learn of this deceit until a week after the trade was made. It roused the initial production operation. Around the time I was home in my bedridden depression, the Stormrow's ring began to fail, and the resulting confrontation was messy.

The Stormrow's claimed fault over the arrangement, stating that trading the counterfeit ring was far more deceitful than providing only half the crystal. When Gran and the aunts demanded to know why the crystal was not given in full, then the Stormrow's admitted to only owning one-half of it. When questioned why a counterfeit ring was produced instead of the real thing, Gran revealed her knowledge of their nightwalker benefactor. It had gone downhill after that, and though Gran and Aunt Lydia had made it out of the short battle relatively unscratched, Aunt Mo hadn't fared as well. She spent most of her days at the Axleys in their greenhouse.

I went to visit her the other day and was amazed at how large the greenhouse was inside when compared to its outward dimensions. Aunt Mo laughed gaily at that. Her fingers working on a flower crown stopped to clasp my hands in hers. Patches of red and black littered her skin, but she reassured me, they were receding with the help of the All Mother. I had wanted to bring her some treat, but by that time the kitchen had been well taken over, so instead I regaled her with my night at the Wselfwulfs, my interactions with Xander, and my break up with Ben. It was the first time I had been able to speak about any of the events without turning into a complete mess. Though I still cried.

"It's good to cry, sweetheart. Let it out. Give your body and mind the release they deserve from your worries and troubles, and just *be*," Aunt Mo said to me in earnest.

The problem is I have no idea how to *just be*. What does that mean? I don't have time to dwell, though my

191

mind steadfastly returns to the question when not preoccupied, for we are meeting with the Adolphus pack to discuss the coming full moon. After all, the Stormrows aren't the only family out for blood.

+++

"She's sure there will be an attack on the full moon? Isn't there some kind of margin of error that comes with precognition?"

"Kymberly Moon has yet to make a false prediction in her young thirteen years of life. If the girl says there is to be a fight on the night of the full moon, then there will be," Gran tells me, eyeing me through the rearview mirror with a frown. I slouch in my seat. We are headed to the Adolphus manor to talk strategy for the coming full moon, and it seems nothing can be said to alleviate our collective tension. My lips fasten closed as I stare pensively out the window.

Only a couple of days have passed since the breakup, and I have yet to see Xander. Though we speak to each other over the phone, and his heated kisses and caresses fill my dreams, I am on edge at the thought of having to see him.

Where do we go from here? The soulmark is already sealed and marked. Would we complete the binding tonight? And what exactly would that entail? My heartbeat surges forward at the questions. *I might have an idea or three of what it might entail.*

"We're here," Gran says with a sigh, parking the Toyota in the manor's driveway and pulling out her keys.

"It's going to be all right, Diana. Kymberly said as much. As long as we get the crystal in place along with the reinforcement crystals, it should hold. The barrier can be erected, and we'll be safe." Aunt Lydia says.

"Until the barrier fails," Gran responds stiffly, exiting the car. "The reinforcement crystals will only hold for so long. Once their energy is spent, they'll be useless to us. We need to find the other half of the crystal."

Our car doors slam shut in unison. An ominous touch to an ominous day. "Everything is going to be all right," I repeat, more to myself than anyone else as we make our way to the front doors. They open before we are halfway there. Ryatt stands in the doorway with his phone pressed tightly to his ear. He ends his conversation before we reach him, his once-strained features smoothing out into a charming smile as he greets us.

"Shall we, ladies?" He closes the door behind us and leads us upstairs to an area of the house I have yet to see. We pass by a slew of Chagall's abstract work that my gaze drifts over without much thought until we reach our destination. The room is large and already filled with a dozen people. A dozen wolves. We enter, and the room quiets expectantly. Ryatt guides us to a chesterfield for our seats, but my steps stall as I seek out Xander. He is leaning over a desk with a man at each side, but his face is tilted upward, and his eyes are trained on me. My breath catches in my throat, and he slowly straightens.

He's dressed all in black. Black trousers, black belt, black button down. They fit him like a second skin, outlining without reserve every muscle. Something akin to electricity passes between us, and I am seized by an uncontrollable stab of desire. The soulmark flares to life against my skin.

"Work now, play later, little sister," Ryatt teases as he takes my arm and leads me to my seat. I flush and send him a stern glare, but he merely grins happily in response.

"Let's discuss the timeline again, shall we? Our seer is unable to determine when the Wselfwulf pack will descend upon us. Their plans are too erratic, and they keep changing their intentions," Gran begins.

"Which is unusual for the Wselfwulfs. They like their order. No doubt Rollins is under significant pressure from his pack to deliver some kind of promise. While some of the pack shares Rollins disdain for ours, a fair majority wish for peace. If we can finish this tomorrow tonight, it may prove to end our entire feud," Xander replies.

"In your experience, what is Rollins most likely to do? When do you think he'll attack?" Aunt Lydia inquires. Several from the small crowd answer at once, their answers varying greatly until a grand argument creeps up like the tide on the verge of ruining the entire meeting.

"Silence!" Xander hollers, fist slamming down on the desk. "This fighting will get us nowhere. Let's work together to eliminate what is most illogical." The group falls quiet.

"Well," I say slowly, "when *won't* they come? Surely, they won't attack in the daylight, right? The crystals need to be activated at midnight tomorrow, but we could have our men and women stationed in the forest well before then. I mean, we have the hometown advantage, right? Why not use it? The placement of the crystal is only a couple of miles outside of town in the forest. It's well over a couple of miles for the Wselfwulfs." My ramblings receive a small round of murmured agreements and nods.

"They won't come until after sunset," Irina agrees, "which is set to take place at 6:59 p.m."

"There will be too much chance of civilian casualties so early in the evening. They would not dare risk their true faces being seen," a man says. He looks oddly familiar, his dark hair and dark features jogging my memory.

"Agreed brother," Ryatt interjects. "I believe an attack before nine o'clock is very unlikely." Something about the phrase makes me gasp in recognition at the other man.

194

"There's nothing like a new moon, is there, brother!" Ryatt called out joyously.

"I'm not your, brother," Keenan responded, voice gravelly and harried.

Keenan meets my eyes unexpectedly, and a look of understanding flashes over his face. He bows his head to me, a look of contrition quick to flash my way before he does so. I find myself giving a brief nod, not realizing the others in the room watch our interaction closely.

"You've met?" Aunt Lydia asks. Blood rushes to my cheeks.

"Just once," I mutter, "it's not important."

"Then, let's continue, shall we?" Gran states, eyeing me dubiously from her seat at my side. I blush once more, and the conversation resumes. We discuss the placement of wolves and eldritch witches—our coven's warriors—in great detail with everyone crowding around the map on the table until Gran and Aunt Lydia pull out a magic trick to appease the crowded circle. An almost holographic super-sized mirror of the map is projected into the seating area we just vacated. Xander moves a chess piece representing a team of wolves on the map on the desk, and the magical projection mimics its movement.

Things move along quickly then. We agree upon times. Places of ambush and greater lines of defense negotiated and confirmed. Contingency plans are formed. After three hours of nonstop discussion, all seem satisfied. People linger to deliver their farewells, even Gran and Aunt Lydia. I'm sucked into a salacious retelling of one of Ryatt's recent conquests as I attempt to say goodbye. His saga depicts the lengths he went to secure a supposed necklace from a fiery ex-girlfriend hell-bent on ruining his good name. A remark that precipitates my eyebrows drawing into my hairline.

"And then as I finished her off, for I'm never one to leave a woman wanting, my other hand—"

"Enough, Ryatt! Honestly, must you always be so crude? Zoe doesn't want to hear about your extracurricular activities." Irina comes up to my side and places a quick kiss on my cheek. "You don't have to suffer through his indecent retellings, Zoe. Just tell him no and swat him on the nose like a bad dog." Ryatt's eyes sparkle as he opens his mouth to deliver his retort, but the final Adolphus walks up to our small circle.

"Leave us," he commands.

Ryatt rolls his eyes. "As if we need to be told." Irina and Ryatt walk away, knowing smiles passing between them as they leave us.

"Oh," I remark as I take in the empty room behind us. "I didn't realize everyone had gone." Even Gran and Aunt Lydia.

"Ryatt does have the unique ability to capture people's unwavering attention with his stories I'm afraid. Even if said stories are..."

"About his sex life?" I finish with a laugh.

"And told in far too much detail." Xander smiles and laughs along, but our laughter soon dies. The resounding silence that follows fills the space between us. Xander takes a step forward, and I one back. A flash of frustration flickers behind his hooded eyes. He takes another decisive step forward and I, yet again, one back. "Still? After all this time, you would chance the chase, Zoelle?"

I bite my lip, my own frustrations surfacing as our emotions tunnel toward each other through the soulmark. "Why do you do that?" I ask, summoning ire to prolong the inevitable.

"Do what?" he asks back patiently, though his waning temper thrums through the soulmark.

"Call me that." His head tilts to the side.

"Zoelle?"

196

"Yes, that," I respond stiffly. "Nobody calls me that—"

"Your grandmother calls you by that name. Why shouldn't I?"

"Because"—*just breathe*—"I prefer Zoe. Everyone calls me Zoe."

"Except your grandmother." He points out again, shuffling forward. I take two steps away, placing one of the armchairs between us.

"Gran is family," I snap, surprised at the heat of my emotion. He frowns at that. Stills and mulls over my small admission. Inside a sadness long since stowed away tears forth. Only family called me Zoelle: Mom, Dad, Clara, and Gran. Only family.

"You're my soulmark, Zoelle. You're my whole goddamn universe. I think I've earned the right to call you by your given name."

I find myself shaking my head at his insistence. Old insecurities rear their ugly heads. I've lost my family. Lost my first love to another woman. Lost a good man because I can't control my desires. I can't do this. Can't lose myself to this man and the link between us. And what if… what if I lose him too? Tomorrow night Xander will lead his pack against the Wselfwulfs, and there is no guarantee he will come back.

Every nerve in my body holds taut with heightened emotion. Xander pours love and reassurance through the bond, aiming to placate me. But lurking beneath the presence of his wolf stirs. My eyes meet Xander's.

They're hunting me. Both of them.

Blood rushes through my veins, my fear practically paralyzing. Run or stay? I can feel my breath coming faster and faster as I screw my eyes shut. Maybe I can do this. I just need more time! I open my eyes and stumble back with a short cry. Xander easily crosses the distance between us during my short moment of

197

reflection. He wraps an arm around my waist, pulling me into his body with a growl.

"Dammit, Zoelle, stop doing this. Stop trying to put this distance between us. What are you hoping to achieve? You want me to leave? To go? Never talk or see you again? Ignore the soulmark?" He barks out a harsh laugh. "Well too fucking bad. I'm not going anywhere. I'm always going to be there for you. You're not getting rid of me. You're not. *I'm not leaving.*"

His words crash over me like a tidal wave, and I sink into his hold. "Damn you," I mutter, knowing he can hear each word perfectly clear. My fear and walls crumbling as he leans in closer.

"Just give me a chance, Zoelle," Xander pleads.

"*Love him*," Katrina said. Can the answer be so easy? My hands come to rest tentatively on his chest. They fall over his heart, and I listen for one beat. Two. Three.

Our eyes meet.

"Tell me you're mine," he whispers hotly. He steps forward, every inch of his body suddenly pressed against mine. I let out a shuddering breath and feel his own as I utter my response.

"I'm yours."

He pins me against the nearest wall before he reward my admission with a searing kiss. It's full of tongue and teeth. Biting and sucking. He trails his hands across my body. Leaves me squirming and whining in the pleasure he builds between us. My own hands trail down his lithe muscles. I love the way they strain beneath my touch.

"Say it again," he repeats, pulling back from our kiss to look me in the eye.

"I'm yours," I breathe as I rub my body against his, seeking release I know only he can give. He gives a pleased growl and attacks my neck, his hands winding their way underneath my shirt to unclasp my bra and touch me. I let out a wanton moan as his hands cup my breast, my hips bucking in need against his own as he bites and loves on my neck. God, I haven't felt this worked up in... ever. Never has a man inspired such— *ahh*.

His lips capture mine once more. One hand pinches and twists my nipple, and I open my mouth with a heady moan. He deepens the kiss. I strain to pull him closer. He responds in kind, then coaxes soft, little, desperate noises from me that he swallows with his lips. *Dear God, have mercy*. My hands race down his shirt, furiously undoing each button before ripping it off his body.

He looks down at me in a daze. His lips are swollen. His eyes are amber and gold across a forest of green. "Again," he growls, hands tugging at the bottom of my shirt, up and over my head along with my bra.

"I'm—" *yours*.

He steers me around until the back of my knees hit the end of an armchair. We stumble, but only momentarily. His hands are on my hips and back, steadying me as he leans in. My back arches painfully at his hunger, but with a slight nudge, I am pushed back onto the body of the couch. Xander hovers over me, eyes sweeping over my naked chest and stomach possessively. A liquid heat curls and spreads deep inside me, making me ache with want. I catch his eyes once more. See the longing in them that mirrors my own.

Rough hands capture my thighs and lift up. His hips fall forward into my parted thighs as his lips trail down my neck, then across my breasts, where he teases and worries the tender flesh into almost unbearable sensitivity. My fingers claw at his arms and chest. My hips rise to meet the firm heated part of him, fit so snuggly against my own soaking center. I can feel his roguish smile against my breast as he moves lower still, his hands making quick work of my jeans.

199

I should have worn my black lacy thong. I think desperately as his warm breath fans against my naval. *And shaved.* But Xander does not seem to share my worry. His fingers move aside my blue cotton underwear with care, and he makes a small appreciative noise at the unveiling. I tremble in anticipation. Heavy-lidded eyes meet mine from below, and his tongue slips inside of me.

I let out a coarse cry, something close to a whine that gives him pause, and then he returns to his task. His tongue lays flat across my heated flesh, then flicks upward. Again and again. He gives his own groan of appreciation as one arm locks around a still trembling leg and hikes it over his shoulder before diving in. Xander tastes me like a man who has never known the pleasure of a bourbon chocolate truffle. Or sweet decadence of summer's first picked strawberry. His attention is unwavering, and I shift restlessly in his hold. He nips at my clit in rebuke, almost bringing me over the edge.

Xander pulls back abruptly, and I almost cry out in distress, but then his hands are ripping my underwear off. The tear of the fabric sounds almost too loudly, but it's nothing to dwell on. Not when his hands are moving decisively to his pants. I scoot back, my lip caught between my teeth as I watch in anticipation where the dark trail of hair will lead. He doesn't disappoint. The sudden visage of his cock, hard and thick and long—I swallow, and my eyes dart to him in slight panic. I feel a girlish blush stain my cheeks as I avert my eyes. His pants land on the floor with a soft thud and the leather cushion sinks at his added weight.

"What is it?" he asks, lips running over my jaw.

"Nothing," I respond, hating how breathless I sound. His erection brushes against my clit, drawing the smallest of moans from my lips.

"Tell me," he whispers, nipping at my chin. The
commanding lilt to his words compels me to answer.

"It's not going to fit," I blurt out and Xander
freezes. I freeze too, my hands stilling in their silent
exploration of his chest. Then, his body begins to
shake ever so slightly above my own. My eyes dart
toward his face uneasily, before they are taken over by
a scowl. "It's not funny," I tell him tersely as his low
chuckles reach my ears. His hips gently move forward,
his cock sliding the length of my core as his soft
laughter dies and catches in his throat.

"You're right. Not funny," he responds, his eyes
finding mine as he adjusts us. He places one leg
around his hip and braces an arm on the armrest
behind me. "And yes, it is."

And then he is pressing into me. The pressure and
friction so wonderful I keen in response. We stay like
that a moment. Xander pressed fully inside me, his
hand gripping tightly at the flesh below my hip. He
shudders and inhales deeply, a resonating growl
tearing from his throat as he draws back his hips and
slams forward. We both moan at the sensation, our
eyes meeting once more before all thoughts flee and
we are one.

He thrusts remorselessly. He pounds into me with
almost terrifying force. And I can do nothing but buck
my hips in answer. We are a wild union, and
somewhere in the midst of our coupling, his hand slips
between us to rub at the slippery, wet flesh till my
breathing turns erratic.

"Xander," I pant, my hand clawing around his
shoulder and grazing his soulmark. His hips slam
harder into me than expected, the flash of pleasure
succeeding it so great I almost faint. For one fleeting
moment, he is all I feel. Inside me and around me.
Pulsing with heat and want and desire. I tug him
closer. Hitch my other leg around his waist and urge

201

him on. "More." I breathe desperately, almost sobbing in relief as he grinds down into me.

Fuck.

He growls savagely against my neck, pinning my hips down with his own as he barrels into me. I writhe against the couch, my end in sight as he steals a frantic kiss from my lips.

"Say it," he breathes into my ear. I tilt my head back, my neck bent in an offering. "Say that you are mine and that you bind yourself to me, freely."

"I am yours," I moan. "I bind myself to you, Aleksandr Adolphus." His teeth sink into the flesh of my neck, breaking the skin and growling victoriously. My eyes widen as wave after wave of aching pleasure wracks my body. My back arches. My nails claim purchase in his tense sinew. Xander relinquishes my neck with a low-pitched groan, hips spasming against my own as he rides out his own climax.

"Mine." He almost purrs, lying down against me heavily, nose buried against my abused neck as his cock slips from inside me.

"Yours," I mutter back, sinking into oblivion.

LOVE ME OR LEAVE ME

- Chapter 12 -

I stir awake at the soft kisses pressing across my shoulders, that, and the fingers gently slipping between my thighs. A cross between a moan and a sigh escapes my lips as I lean back into Xander's body, my eyes opening lazily.

"Good morning," comes Xander's husky voice from behind me. He presses a kiss to the side of my head, lingering to inhale my scent. We are no longer in the study but a bedroom. The dark color scheme is familiar, and I realize with a small smile that it is the same room I was originally brought to when Xander sealed our mark.

"Morning," I murmur, parting my legs more to allow him better access. I can feel his answering grin as his hand dips deeper and sinks one finger inside of me.

"Fuck," he hisses, "You're so wet for me already." His hand moves away and grips my thigh, lifting it and shifting his hips so his cock brushes up against me, *just right*. I shiver at the touch. I'm unprepared for his entrance with one fierce stroke. We both cry out.

"Fuck." His coarse curse comes as he shifts his body closer to mine. "Don't you dare think about putting that leg down," he growls into my ear, rocking his hips forward. I can only shake my head in response.

My nails claw at the silken sheets imprisoning us as he begins a gentle rhythm, so different from his initial thrust. Each stroke is meant to inflame. Build us up until we both come crashing down together. It isn't long before we fill the room with our heavy sighs and ragged breaths. Just as the pressure intensifies, Xander's hands are moving me. His cock slips out as he rolls me onto my stomach.

He's quick to move behind me, hands gripping my hips and guiding them up and back till his cock is at my entrance again. I lean back and relish the low growl Xander emits as the head of his cock slips inside of me.

"You are a wicked witch, Zoelle," he groans. He gives my ass a sharp slap in rebuke before sinking into me fully. The movement brings a high-pitched sound from my lips. Something between a groan and a whine that only seems to encourage Xander. He keeps his thrusts slow and deep.

I begin to rock back into his thrusts, hoping my participation will drive him faster. And harder. Though my body feels boneless from our previous lovemaking, I push myself onto my elbows and steal a hand back to finger my wet clit. Yet I am thwarted. His hand quickly snatches my hair just as my fingers find my wet heat.

He growls as he carefully pulls my head back. "No touching, Zoelle." He tells me almost cruelly. "If that's where you want my hand, then you have to ask nicely." I whimper and remove my hand bowing my head as he releases my hair.

"Please." I hardly recognize the throaty voice. "Please touch me."

A hand crawls up my back, his touch guiding me to sink lower until my face presses into the mattress. I twist and shift impatiently raising my ass higher and grinding back, when still he does nothing. He lets out a breathy moan at my movements and lets his nails rake down my back, then brush over my hip and to my clit. We sigh in unison. And then he begins to push into me once more. In no time, our bodies rock together in a violent rhythm. Xander's hands roam my body, each touch lingering to caress and stroke me until the tension in my body builds to a near-numbing breaking point. With each thrust, a groan and throaty exclamation sounds.

As his hand fondles my breast, pinching and massaging the oversensitive skin, I reach my hand back to cover his. Guide his hand lower once more. His growl of appreciation is accompanied by a few rapid thrusts of his hips. They drive me further into the bedding with a lustful keen.

"God, Zoelle, you're so hot. You're so wet for me, aren't you, baby?" he practically whimpers against my back as he leans over me. I mewl in response, words lost to me as my body erupts into shaking bouts of pleasure.

"Xander!" I cry out, feeling my soaking core writhe around his hard cock. Xander takes me like a man without sanity. His hips thrust against me with no control. I moan his name once more, the pleasure and pain of his dominance spurs on my orgasm until he grunts and snarls his own release.

We collapse and intertwine ourselves with one another till neither of us knows where one begins and the other ends. My soulmark pulses blissfully against my skin, a sliver of a beat behind my heart. Xander trails his hand up my stomach and past my breasts till they reach my soulmark and brush lightly against it.

205

My whole body tingles in response. It is the single, most satisfying feeling I have ever had the pleasure of knowing, for as he touches the mark and the link between us is left completely open, his love and admiration come pouring through.

I gaze up at him through half-lidded eyes and am pleased to find his satisfied smile.

"Good morning," I murmur, letting out a hum of gratitude as his lips seek mine for a breath-stealing kiss.

"Good morning," he replies, his voice a dusky timber. He brushes the hair from my face tenderly, eyeing the errant curls with quiet amusement.

"Tell me something."

"Anything."

I smile broadly at his lack of hesitation. "It feels... different. Before whenever you touched the soulmark, I felt like I was being pulled under by its power. Like I was drowning in its vastness. But just now when you touched it..."

"It calmed you?"

I bite my lip and gently shake my head, mulling over the right word to use. "It was nice." I laugh at his slightly put out expression. "It was! I just mean that it was almost perfect. It wasn't too much, but it was just enough. It wasn't that I was getting lost in its depths. It was that we were together. It was—"

"Us," he finishes with a smile. I nod. "That's because the soulmark has been completed. We are bound, and in doing so, our souls are finally complete, having found and bound themselves to their other half."

I blush like a schoolgirl at his rather romantic explanation and earn myself another kiss. "That's nice," I tell him, ignoring his short *humph* and letting out a small laugh.

"You're happy, aren't you?" he asks after a moment of silence. His voice shadowed by doubt, and though I wish to respond with an immediate yes, I give myself time to think over my answer. Am I happy? I certainly feel freer than I have in ages. As if our union lifts some strange weight and responsibility off my shoulders and now I can... live. Not just go on day-to-day trying to be normal, doing exactly as others expect of me. Though there have been so many reasons to be sad as of late, I find that I am. Happy, that is.

"Yes," I whisper somewhat shyly leaning into him. "I'm happy." His body relaxes, and his arms wrap around me tighter. "But," I start, another thought coming to me, "I won't be happy if you don't come back from this fight tonight alive."

Xander pulls back and looks down at me, then rolls over me and props himself up on his arms. "I'm coming back tonight, Zoelle. Don't worry about me. Just make sure you follow your part of the plan tonight." I scowl up at him.

"How can you ask me that? Not to worry?" I scoff. "I feel you. I feel your fear and your concerns about tonight. What if you get hurt? Will I hurt? This bond between us is strong, Xander. And what if... what if you—"

He silences me with a harsh kiss till I'm breathless and whimpering against him. "Don't," he pants, pulling back a hair's breath away. "Nothing will happen to me tonight, and I'll be damned if I let anything hurt you. We can control the bond between us now that it's complete. Open it up wide. Or constrict it till it's nearly closed." He hikes my leg up around his hip, my other naturally following. I groan at the feel of his hot length, hard and ready to go again against my heated flesh. "I won't let anyone hurt you," he promises, sliding into me slowly. And making me feel every inch of his cock as it stretches me. A flood of wetness pools around him, and he takes in a harsh breath. "Not even me," he growls, burrowing himself to the hilt inside of me. We savor

207

our moment together like this, eyes locked onto each other. Bodies one. And then we begin again. And again. And again.

+++

The forest is still.
The birds quiet their songs. The trees hush their leaves. The wind dies down.
Predators are afoot. Lycans.
Tonight, blood will be shed. Both the Adolphus and Wselfwulf packs know this to be true, but it does nothing to stop the coming events. Both packs desire vengeance... for family and friends lost... for pride. The packs are two sides of the same coin, yet one is more prepared than the other.

+++

"I want you to wear this," I tell Xander once he finishes sending off a few pack mates into the forest. We linger near the kitchen table, our lovemaking cut short as the clock nears six.

Xander eyes my necklace curiously, "What does it do?" Another wolf passes by, shaking Xander's hand before jogging out the back door of Gran's kitchen.

"It—" A group of eldritch witches file around us, they laugh together at something someone has said, and I pass Xander a strained smile. "It provides protection. When I was ten, I was in a car accident with my family. Everyone ended up being killed from the crash, except me. And it's because of this." I hold out the jade necklace to him, "I want you to wear it."

+++

The Adolphus pack mates thread through the thick tree line with ease. This forest is their territory.

They fight with the advantage. The Adolphus wolves eagerly take their positions. They canvas the greenery with vigilant eyes and spread themselves across the land.

Their numbers are strong—made stronger with the eldritch witches, who will fight beside them. Lycan and witch fighting side-by-side will be a sight to behold. This moment will shake the supernatural world.

But they do not know this yet.

+++

"I don't think that's a good idea," he says softly. He lets out a soft whine at my crestfallen expression, pulling me off to the side as more and more people peel out of the house to take their stations. "Hey, don't think I don't want to wear this. I do. I'm honored that you would think to give this to me for this fight, but I'll be shifting from man to wolf, I don't know how many times tonight. And I don't want to risk breaking the chain."

"I understand," I tell him lightly. He presses a kiss to my forehead and holds me tight.

+++

They do not know what lies in wait before them.
Fire and fury.
Anger and fear.
Man and beast.
The Wselfwulf pack arrives well prepared. A mixture of man and wolf donned for war. Those on two legs fill their hands with knives and guns. Those on four find purpose stalking the forest floor.

The forest releases its breath, and on the wind, a pack mate smells the threat. The Adolphus pack stills, except for one, Justin. The young man glides forward quietly, his eyes alert. His pack mates ready behind him.

He does not see the trap they've set, nor the dozen others. Not until it is too late.

Justin's cry pierces the air as the bear trap captures his foot. Its metal teeth sinking into his flesh without remorse. Digging to the bone.

+++

"I love—" Xander's voice breaks off in a strangled cry, and he pushes me away, dropping to his knees. The witches who remain inside gasp in shock as he reaches up a hand to hold onto a chair, neatly splintering it in half when he lets out a bellow of rage. "Go!" he commands to the last of the wolves.

"What's happening!" A young witch cries. One of the healers. My knees buckle at the weight of the alphas fury. That, and the pack's sudden fear and rush of anger.

"Go!" I shout at him. He sends me a short look of panic, hesitating as he reads the worry etched across my face. "*Go*," I tell him again, my voice stern but barely steady. He nods curtly and sprints away. The last of the wolves and eldritch witches follow behind him. My legs give out beneath me as the chaos of the pack emotion swells inside of me, and I let out an uncontrollable sob.

"Now, come on, sweetheart. You can't let yourself fall in so deep to the pack bonds. Get up." Gran pulls at my arms, bringing me to my shaking feet.

"They were already there. Waiting," I gasp, forcing myself back together and closing down on the pack bonds so only a trickle of emotion could be felt. Gran rests a cool hand and its comforting presence on the back of my neck as she breathes with me. In and out, in long steady pulls of air. "Why didn't we see this?"

210

Aunt Lydia waves her hand at us, then to the phone pressed tightly between her shoulder and ear. She wears an uneasy frown. "Moon says she still has no idea when they will attack."

"They're attacking now!" I all but growl back.

"Exactly, darling, and Moon had no clue. She's had several premonitions of when the Wselfwulfs will attack, and though one or two of them was early evening, there were several others that showed late in the night."

"That's not good enough," I argue, stepping out of Gran's embrace. "We'll lose this fight before it's even begun." Aunt Lydia ends her phone call.

"Settle down now, Zoelle. We made plans for this. We stick to the plan," Gran tells me. A sick bile rises in my throat as I catch glimpses of fear and sympathy running across the other witches faces. "If Moon is still getting mixed premonitions it can only mean one thing. That there will be multiple attacks tonight. What the pack is facing now may very well just be the first fleet of wolves sent to attack. In the next hour or two more may come."

"That isn't what we planned for," I say dejectedly.

"I know, but it's all right, darling—"

"It's not all right!" I shout, silencing the entire room. "It's not."

"You're wrong, Zoelle," says a new voice. A woman with long brown hair and large blue eyes enters the room, much to the amazement of the others in the room.

"Melissa, by the Goddess. What are you doing here?" Aunt Lydia exclaims. Melissa? I eye the newcomer with trepidation, but the witches surge toward her and embrace her like some long-lost sister.

"Who are you exactly?" I ask, my impatience shining through.

"Melissa Wall." Well, that was helpful. I plaster on a tight smile.

211

"Nice to meet you," she smirks at my obvious distrust and ignorance. "You were saying something about me being wrong?" I prompt, crossing my arms over my chest. I feel a pinprick of discomfort through the soulmark and close my eyes in concentration. They are fighting out there, not knowing what will come next, and we can't do anything to help them, save running out into the forest ourselves to deliver the message. Maybe we could spell a piece of paper to one of our own and get them a message. My eyes snap open at the thought and I note that Melissa has made her way toward me, hand outstretched.

"You are wrong. There's a way to get your message to them."

"I know," I tell her smugly and turn to Gran. "We just need to write this down on a piece of paper and charm it to fly over to them! Someone—"

"There's a faster way," Melissa cuts in.

"Oh really? And what is your grand plan, then?"

"You."

"Me?"

Melissa smiles and grasps my hand to give it a squeeze. I startle at the touch and step back, unsure why I instantly associate it with pack. She takes my hand again and squeezes. "Don't be afraid," she tells me kindly. "What you're feeling is real. I know we've never met, but my soulmark Malcolm was once part of your pack."

Oh.

"You're Melissa." My eyes widen in understanding. The witch from years ago. The one who was involved in the soul binding gone wrong. I'm struck by the way she speaks so fondly.

"Yes," she says, smile brightening. "We need to act quickly now though, Zoelle. You must open up the soulmark bond and communicate to Xander what we've discovered."

"I don't know how," I blurt out. "Xander's the one who's been doing it. He has the bond between us tightly closed now so that I don't—"

"Feel any sort of pain. I know," she says, her own past pain slipping into the narrative. "But you can still communicate with him. When Malcolm went to speak with my father about our sealing. To tell him it wasn't forced and that we wanted to try... he did the same to me. He cut me off as much as he could from our small bond. But you can open it back up, Zoelle. It will hurt, but you can still get the message across."

I process the details quickly, pushing aside my curiosity and focusing back on the task. "How?"

"Just like you close off the pack bonds. Concentrate. Find the light that is his soul in your mind's eye and open it wide enough for you to get your message through," she urges me. "This will be much faster than magic, and once Xander receives your message he can communicate it to the other members of the pack through the pack bonds. Those in human form will tell the eldritch witches. We still have a chance."

"Okay," I breathe and squeeze my eyes tightly shut searching out the little light with my mind. *Where are you?* My search frantic and harried. Doing nothing to aid me.

"Breathe, Zoelle. You can do this, sweetheart," Gran tells me softly. "Calm your heart. Take in what's around you and find your center."

I take a few deep breaths and attempt to rid my mind of its worries. Allow my other senses to clear my mind. The kitchen smells of spices and magic. Like lightning lingering in the air. My skin warmed by the constant flames burning on the stove. The sound of bated breath stands eerily in the background of my own. Like an audience in wait for the show to begin. And then I look again.

213

"I found it," I whisper, following the dulled but brilliant light tucked safely away in my mind. *Out of sight, out of mind.* How appropriate.

"Now just open it wider, Zoelle, and speak to him."

I do so. Willing the soft beam of light to expand until the pain scoring Xander's body assaults me. *Xander,* I call out in my mind, *Xander, they plan to attack in waves. That's why the premonitions were so scattered. They'll attack in waves. Be ready. Always.*

I love you.

I tighten down on the bond and it recedes, the light dimming once more. I am panting by the time I finish, a pain in my side still present. I share a worried glance with Melissa.

"Did you do it?"

I open and close my mouth, before finally admitting the truth, "I don't know."

+++

Casualties begin coming in every half hour or so with news of the fighting. Though most we see to are badly injured, those that bring them in are well enough to rejoin the fight. When Irina comes in with Ryatt under her arms he ghastly white, I almost faint away. His neck is torn open, eyes closed, and his chest is bleeding from multiple lacerations.

"Please," Irina begs, handing him off as he is lifted onto the dining room table with magic.

"He'll be all right," I tell her, urging her back outside with me at her side. She watches anxiously as Melissa and two other witches begin to clean him and cover him in salves, while a different witch begins to chant at his head. "He's in good hands."

Her shoulders sag in relief. "Thank God, it's Melissa. I didn't know if she would come."

"You know her?"

Irina gives me a sharp look, then begins to make her way to the forest. "Of course I know her. She's like a sister to me."

"I—"

"I don't have time to answer your questions, Zoelle. Later. All right?" I nod helplessly as she darts off before I can get in another word. She's out of sight after only a blink.

"Damn," I mutter under my breath as I jog back inside.

"The Abernathys have taken in two more. The Monroes one and the Lestates have about half a dozen resting. They've been giving out their wolfsbane bombs to some of the wolves to use."

"Good," Gran says. "Let me get you some of those before you go, Keenan." The burly man nods, eyes critically passing over Ryatt's still form.

"He'll be all right."

"I know," he responds curtly. I bristle in response.

"Good," I snap back under my breath, sounding all of five years old again. He passes me an apologetic look, neck tilting ever so slightly in deference to me.

"I apologize. I'm not very..."

"Friendly?" I offer. He blushes. Two cute little patches of pink stain his already blood-spattered cheeks.

"Yes."

"It's all right," I suck in a shaky breath. "I shouldn't have snapped."

"Here you are dear, go on now. You best not dawdle." He gives us both a nod, though his gaze lingers on me.

"What is it?" I ask quickly. "Is he all right?"

He looks uneasily at Gran, then back to me. "He is leading aptly."

"He is leading...?" I glower. "What the fuck is that supposed to mean?"

"Zoelle, calm down. Leave the man alone and let him go where he is needed." He flees without another glance, and I shoot Gran a heated glare.

"Something's wrong," I tell her.

"You're still feeling the emotions of the pack slip through as well as Xander's. It's bound to happen with everyone on high alert." But my head shakes at her logical explanation.

"No," I tell her. "You don't understand. I have this feeling in my gut. Something bad is happening. It's like I still can't breathe—"

"I said calm down, Zoelle. I don't want you to have to force any kava tea down your throat just to get your head on straight." My lips tighten into a hard line.

"I'm not a child."

"Then stop acting like one." She reprimands me.

"I know what I'm feeling is real," I say just as sternly back. "Something isn't right."

Gran turns her back to me and walks over to Ryatt, ignoring my remarks and helping the others. I turn away from them and toward the kitchen counter, hiding my trembling lips and watering eyes. If they won't believe me, I'll just find out myself. I ease the bond open but am unprepared for the onslaught of pain that wracks my body. I fall to my knees with a gasp, engulfed in agony.

"Zoelle!" Gran's sharp cry brings me back to reality, and I fight with all my willpower to close the bond back down to its original size. I can't. I only manage it about halfway before my body and mind give up in exhaustion.

Arms shift around my middle to haul me to my feet, but the action leaves me gasping out a curse. I lean against the kitchen counter for support, my legs nearly giving out again as almost insurmountable pain runs across my body. My head feels laden, my legs and arms shot. One arm, I think hazily, must be broken, for it falls so limply at my side. I don't even think I can lift it if I tried. And then pressure pushes against my chest. I cough. Nearly choking as my body convulses with each hacking breath.

"Rita, get the white dittany and cataria bark. Quickly." A girl no more than ten runs about the kitchen collecting the items, bringing them along quickly as Gran moves me to a chair. "What happened?"

I wipe the blood from my chin, hissing as I attempt to breathe. "I had to see what was wrong," I tell her.

"Zoelle," Gran admonishes, but her face is ashen. "Did you close the bond down sweetheart? All the way." I give her a sad grin and shake my head, coughing some more and spewing red.

"Couldn't," I gasp, "too much pain."

Gran brings a steaming cup of tea to my lips, the scolding water burning its way down my throat as I sputter and choke around it. "Drink it, child," Gran insists. "It'll heal what's broken inside of you.

"I need essence of foxglove, now!" shouts Melissa. The table rattles from the other side of the room, as Ryatt's body begins to shake.

"No!"

I turn wide eyes to Xander. Keenan is holding him upright, but Xander only has eyes for his brother.

"Put him on the table," Gran orders.

"Xander!" I stumble upward and into Keenan's path. I insert myself on Xander's other side and help move him.

"You have to help him," Xander says through gritted teeth, eyes rolling back as he is placed on the table. "My fault," he utters, his voice strained.

"No, no," I coo, my hands wiping away the blood that coats half his face. "He's fine. Melissa, tell him he's fine!" I yell across the room.

"He's stable. All bleeding has been stopped. He just needs rest now." Her voice sounds both exhausted and proud. I watch as Xander's body goes limp with relief at her words, and I almost cry, but most certainly not in relief. I can feel the bond between us slowly expanding as our collective control begins to slip. The mounting pain begins to eclipse all rational thought, but before I lose myself to it, my fingers slip the jade talisman from around my neck to his.

He jolts. A silent cry of shock piercing his features as the talisman glows brightly on his chest. I feel my legs give out beneath me, but Keenan is at my side in an instant, righting me and keeping me close to Xander's side. He lets out a hoarse holler as his superficial wounds begin to knit themselves together. My right arm tingles to life. The pain in my body is fading, but only just so.

"You gave him your necklace," Gran says in astonishment, cutting away the ragged strips of clothes left on Xander's body. Rita pushes her way to the table's side and sets down several items. "If you can, sweetheart, apply that blue salve to his ribs."

I nod numbly, forcing myself past the phantom feeling of his body healing, but still coursing with so much pain. Keenan helps, and a minute later Melissa and an older witch come to help.

"Why isn't it working?" I ask, my eyes filling with tears as the pain continues. "I don't understand, why?"

Gran stops her work but does not dare look at me. His body isn't responding anymore to the medicine. Cuts remain open. One particularly nasty gash on his side continues to spill what seems like a quarter of his blood out of him. Bruises bloom across his abdomen, and I suck in a shuddering breath.

"Gran!" She looks at me, her eyes filled with unshed tears.

"I don't know what to do, sweetheart," she says carefully, going back to applying a red paste to his right thigh. "When you put your necklace on him that helped, but...."

"Zoe you need to close the bond between you two completely," Melissa interjects, her voice filled with sudden authority. "If Xander—"

"No—"

"If he dies, you could too," she tells me without remorse. "You have to shut it down."

My head sways from side to side as I stare down at Xander. "No," I tell them stiffly. I knock away Keenan's arms and careen toward the discarded white dittany tea Gran forced on me. A cry breaks from my throat as my body doubles over in pain. Both Keenan and Gran rush to my side at once, but I push them away and force myself past the pain. "I'm not giving up on him," I tell them, shakily pouring more water into the cup. It slouches over the sides unsteadily.

When I reach his side once more, Keenan helps me half onto the table so I can place Xander's head on my leg. "Come on, baby. You have to drink this." I push the cup insistently at his lips, willing them to part, but the pain is surging through both of us now. My hands rattle as I press open his mouth and spill the tea inside. "Aleksandr, you have to drink this," I command him angrily, my tears splashing onto his face and into his tea. "You have to stay alive. You have to stay with me!" I cry.

He coughs, coming to and half swallowing, half spitting up the tea I feed him. He gazes at me with one eye, the other swollen shut.

"Drink," I command, biting viciously into my lip as I tilt the cup to his parted lips. "This will help. I promise."

"It's working!" Melissa exclaims. I shoot her a look of disbelief, and then my eyes dart to Gran.

"It's your tears, Zoelle," she cries in realization.

"What?" The question comes out shaky, and I'm too distracted by Xander's frantic gulps to grasp her meaning. "I need more of the tea." Gran takes the cup from my trembling grasp, filling it part way and then pressing it against my cheek. I jerk back in confusion, but she presses on. "What are you doing?" I ask, attempting to swat her away, or at least wipe away my tears.

"Don't!" Gran warns, but she needn't worry. Keenan snatches my rising wrist gently and places it back on Xander's forehead. "It's your tears, Zoelle. Don't you understand? It's your magic. You're healing him."

"I am?" I whisper roughly, feeling rather acutely the tear that falls haphazardly down my cheek before it is intercepted by the rim of the cup. Gran removes the cup and places it once more at Xander's lips. He drinks from it greedily, the swelling and remaining bruises on his face retreating. "Oh God," I weep in relief. Gran passes the cup back into my hands and I pass it from cheek to cheek, trying to collect as many tears as I can before Gran waves the teapot in front of me and refills it.

"The bruising is fading from his stomach, but you should switch to cataria bark. Rita, start to steep some of the bark with the next pot of boiling water. Angelica, I need you to weave the wound on his side closed. This wound was made with magic. It needs to be closed and sealed with magic."

Everyone works quietly—besides my sniffling— and by a half an hour later, the worst of his wounds are treated.

"He needs rest now, with the way this night has been going I expect at least four wolves and two witches to come through that door bleeding all over my furniture. Let's get him to a bed to rest. Zoelle, he'll stay in your room. No funny business under my roof though, you hear?"

"No more," Xander mumbles, eyes opening weakly.

"Shh," I hush him, brushing his dark hair away from his face. "We're all done for the night. It's time for you to rest."

"You don't understand," he wheezes. "It's finished. We won."

Xander waves an impatient hand at Keenan, and he obeys immediately, coming to his side and helping him sit upright. Xander grimaces but shows no other sign of lingering pain.

"We won?" I ask uncertainly, rising to stand. My body, though sore and abused, is most certainly healed.

"I killed Rollins," he states, eyes going dark. "He went after Ryatt while my back was turned. I didn't expect him to attack Ryatt. I thought he would go after me. He's the kind of man who pulls that sort of move."

"It's really over?"

"Carrie led the retreat. We won't be seeing them for the rest of the night. They'll be too busy licking their wounds. *Ah!*" His breath leaves him in one fell swoop as he hops down from the table, wincing at the impact. Keenan and I come to his side to support him, but he waves the larger man aside in favor of leaning against me.

"I told you I would come back to you," he says softly as we limp along to the front entryway and up the stairs.

"You also told me nothing would hurt me and not to worry." I point out as we make our way slowly up the stairs. Very slowly. "I'd also like to add that thanks to my worry you're alive."

I drop my hold around his waist once we've reached my bed. He groans, flopping back with a sigh and throwing an arm over his black and purple spotted face. I cuddle up next to him, resting my head tentatively against his chest.

"I thought." The words stick against the roof of my mouth. "I thought we were going to lose you. That I was going to lose you." His arm retracts and sweeps around me, pulling me more snuggly against his side.

221

"Never." He promises vehemently making me smile as I press a tender kiss to his lips.

"I love you," I whisper my admission, my heart thumping wildly in my chest. His smile is the like the morning sun.

"I love you, too."

The sentiments echo loudly through the soulmark, and I place my lips tenderly against his own. He responds in kind. His hand comes up to cradle my face as an underlying passion and yearning slips through. I moan gently.

Kissing turns to reverent touches and gentle caresses until the loving contact turns to something more.

I fear I'll hurt him, but I cannot deny this man. His dark hair is a mess with dirt and grime. His beautiful body half covered in bandages and wounds. Xander's grimaces of pain intermix with those of ecstasy. Our gentle rhythm coaxing from us the pleasure we seek and desperately need.

There is no regret when he holds me after. Only the knowledge that *this* is how life is meant to be led, without regrets.

EPILOGUE

9 months later

"Good afternoon, you've reached Baudelaire Patisserie and Café. How can I help you today?" My voice purrs pleasantly against the landline phone installed in the back of *my* café.

"Hmm, can you tell me what you're wearing today?" asks a deep and husky voice. I roll my eyes.

"Seriously? Xander, customers could be calling this very minute, and I wouldn't know because you're calling me." He feigns a sigh and his amusement funnels through the soulmark.

"You're right," he yields easily. "Besides, if I'm being honest I didn't even have to ask what you're wearing. Blue gingham dress, your white sneaker slip-ons, and that matching set of black underwear you look so good in."

"Have you been spying on me again?" I ask, scandalized. A blush creeps up my neck to my cheeks. He chuckles. The sound dark and hypnotizing. "For your information," I tell him pertly, "I'm not wearing my matching set, just the bra today."

The back door at the end of the kitchen slams
open. Xander strides forward snapping his phone shut.
Excitement pools at the juncture of my thighs.

"You're not allowed to be here during work hours,"
I scold lightly, my breath catching as I spot the
roguish look in his eyes.

"You closed ten minutes ago," he notes, stalking
closer as I wind my way around one of the metal
worktables. "Come here," he orders breathlessly. The
familiar desire to heed the alpha's order pulls at me,
but my own will trumps it and I stand my ground.

"Nuh uh," I respond coyly, letting out a squeal as
he speeds around the table's side and sweeps me into
his arms.

"Liar," he says with a knowing smirk as he moves
aside my thong with deft fingers and traces the
wetness that has gathered between my legs. I shudder
a laugh, pushing my hips eagerly into his wandering
hand. I moan as he inserts two fingers that begin to
pump in lazy strokes. He nips at my cheekbone.

"Oops."

The thick, hard outline of his cock presses against
my hip as he inserts a third finger, preparing me for
what is to come. I moan into the bruising kiss he
delivers, shivering in delight as I feel the fabric of my
panties being ripped from my body.

"I'm running out of my last few panties, Xander," I
scold with a laugh as I pull back from our kiss. He
frowns at me in feigned confusion while lifting me onto
the metal table and unbuckling his belt and
unfastening his pants. My hands reach out to stop
him, and his confusion turns to exasperation.

"I told you I would buy you new ones," he tells me,
pressing a hard kiss to my lips, effectively shutting me
up. For the moment. I dive into the kiss. Press my
tongue against his and drink him in.

"You said *that* five weeks ago," I say with a gasp as his lips voyage down my neck. My hand finds his cock, throbbing and warm. Hard and ready.

He smirks and drags me closer to the edge of the table, the head of his dick pressing firmly against my entrance, already slick with want from anticipation. "Oops."

Our shared laughter changes quickly to moans of appreciation. The sound of our coupling reverberates through the small kitchen. Xander sets a slow pace, grinding up and into me with long, measured strokes that drive me wild.

"Faster," I plead against his lips, my hands making quick work of his shirt to rake my nails down his dark-haired chest.

"Whatever you want," he grunts back, his pistoning hips driving faster and harder. "Fuck, Zoelle," he growls into my ear as my hand slips past his shoulder and presses against his soulmark. He bites down on my neck just as I cry out my orgasm. He growls, hips slamming one more time into mine as he reaches his own climax. We take a moment to calm our racing hearts. "Why did you do that?" he asks breathlessly. "We were just getting started."

I smooth his hair back before gently pushing him away, a satisfied smile on my lips. "Because," I announce, slipping off the counter and tucking his softening dick back inside his pants, "work sex has to be quickies only."

He frowns at my response, prepared to argue when the back door slams open once more. Xander presses me behind him as he steps in front of me, a vicious snarl on his lips that stops almost as soon as it came.

"Ryatt? What are you doing here?" I peek around Xander's side to see Ryatt looking particularly out of sorts.

He takes a deep breath. "We have a problem."

REBECCA MAIN

CONTINUE READING FOR A
SNEAK PEEK AT **MIDNIGHT SCOUNDREL**

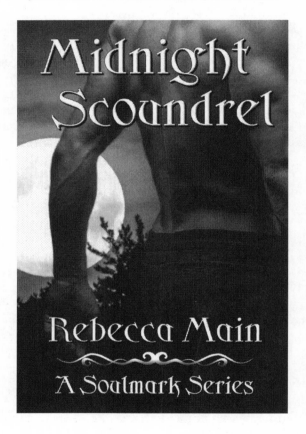

226

CHAPTER ONE

2 days prior

Ryatt

The bar is a dump. A skim of the narrow landscape is all that's needed to confirm the fact. My nose wrinkles at the smell of stale, days-old alcohol. The likes of which seeped into the walls decades ago, along with the patrons. It is not a place to meet new people. Nor to gather with friends and lament your day's end. Here the patrons sit widely apart, each oozing their declarations of "fuck off" with slumped shoulders and threatening scowls.

It suits my needs exactly, for I've no wish to be bothered. I stop midstep when my inspection is interrupted by a golden beauty sulking at the dingy bar.

She's wearing one of those off-the-shoulder dresses that seem to be all the rage this summer. Her hair, half up, sits high atop her head in one of those messy little buns with glimpses of silver dripping from her ears. And then there is her skin. Tan and healthy—*glowing*. She is like an oasis in this desert dump, pining away over several empty shot glasses and a cell phone. The beauty casts a wary glance over her shoulder as the door slams shut behind me. Her blue eyes widen from afar, her lips falling into a gentle "O" before she sends me a determined frown. It's a much gentler "fuck off" than all the others I receive. It's quite adorable really. Certainly not enough to stop me.

I send her a grin that falls somewhere between lascivious and mischievous and saunter forward.

"What's a nice girl like you doing in a bar like this?" I ask, making sure my voice is a pleasant, husky hum as I seat myself next to this golden goddess. The duffle bag I carry is set gingerly underneath the barstool I chose.

"How original," she responds tartly. Disdain evident. Her eyes flicker toward me curiously, to run the length of my body, lingering a tad too long to be respectable. I make sure to keep myself poised under her scrutiny, muscles flexing minutely under it. She scoffs belatedly, a blush rising to her cheeks as if she is aware of her *faux pas*. A pleased smile ventures onto my lips when she turns her attention to the bartender. Fingers fluttering away to signal him. "Another, José."

"I'll have whatever the lady is having, but make it a double." She stiffens slightly, and I watch in interest as she attempts to ignore me. She's certain to have a difficult time of it.

I inhale. She is by far the prettiest thing I've seen in miles, and she smells of a tangle of emotions: fear, adrenaline, and the faintest trace of arousal. All blended between hints of lilac and lavender perfume. Of course, there is a touch of grief mingled in between, but it's the same as every other poor sap in this godforsaken bar. She casts another sidelong glance my way as the tequila is set in front of us. Will she take the bait?

"Cheers," she chirps after a moment's hesitation. Her smile is a brittle thing as she thrusts her shoulders back and swirls her creaking stool toward me. The liquid is down her throat before I can even reach my glass. If I didn't know better, I'd say she was some supernatural creature with her speed and grace, but her scent is completely human. I let out an amused chuckle before knocking back mine.

"Going somewhere, sweetheart?"

I let my eyes flick toward the pale pink suitcase near her feet, but hers do not follow as I expect. A delicate chime trills from her phone and with a sigh, she gives the electronic her attention. Her brow scrunches together, lips pursing as she furiously types a response. By the time she has finished, I have already signaled José for another round. When the drinks are set down, she gives another gentle scoff and flips her hair over her shoulder.

"Gee, thanks." But there is nothing sweet about the way her rosy lips curl into such a saccharine smile. Playing hard to get? No problem.

"Let me guess," I lean closer, a devious and knowing smirk in place. "You just broke up with your boyfriend. This was your first big trip together, and you caught him with someone else. One of those dark-haired beauties around these parts. Now you're making the trek back home, all by your lonesome, pissed off and upset that you wasted your time and money on a vacation that ended in heartbreak. Am I close?"

229

She swallows, her eyes widening and her heartbeat ticking up just a fraction. Her surprise is palpable, so I soften just a tad and reach for the tequila.

"Something like that," she finally mutters.

"I've always preferred the fairer types," I tell her. The scoff I earn is mixed with a furtive laugh, one she is quick to mask behind a cough. *Got you.* "Kyle," I lie, lifting the shot glass in a peace offering. Her icy gaze melts and shifts to the remaining shot glass.

"Fuck it," she mumbles under her breath, snatching up the shot glass and clinking it against mine. We down it as one and politely ignore each other's grimaces as the amber liquor burns its way down. "Mary," she offers. My sights narrow at the way her voice goes a little high at the end, my hearing picking up the way her heart skips a beat. She raises an eyebrow in challenge, but I only chuckle. Why not play this little game of lies and see where it takes us?

"Tell me all about your troubles, sweet Mary," I coo. She rolls her eyes, the hint of a smile gracing her lips.

"I'm not nearly drunk enough," Mary confesses coyly. I'm about to respond when one of her legs drags itself up and across the other. Her dress, already so short, hikes up another perilous inch to reveal more sun-kissed skin. I let my gaze enjoy the newly revealed flesh for a moment before capturing her eyes with mine. I put on a wolfish grin and enjoy the way she replies in kind with her own knowing smirk. Let the games begin.

+++

Mary is a recent graduate from the Art Institute of California in San Francisco. She waxes on about the likes of Friedrich and Turner. How the dark and gloomy Romanticism speaks to her soul.

I am a nomad. Traveling South American with all that's left to my name in the bag at my feet. I tell her how I revel in the nights spent under the stars and my daring treks across the scorched and barren earth, but I'm always hungering for something more.

She has stopped taking her shots in one toss, preferring to sip on the molten elixir instead. Her baby blue eyes turn to steely storms, as the hours tick on. When I tease at her inability to keep up, she reminds me that she has been sitting at this desolate bar much longer than I. And that she is always able to keep up.

Somewhere around shot 11 or 12, I slip and call her beautiful. It brings the most delicious blush to her cheeks. Though she eyes me speculatively from beneath her long lashes, she does not rebuff my compliment. A few more shots taken, and she proclaims she's never been with a real man. One who knows how to take care of a woman, or himself, for that matter. I confess that I've never been in love. That no woman has been able to tame my wild heart. Her eyes widen.

When I return from the bathroom—a literal shit hole—Mary is collecting her things and attempting to finish off a bottle of water she's pulled from her purse. She wiggles it enticingly in front of me, only a quarter of the bottle left. I take it and sit down with a huff, finishing the warm water in two long drags.

"You're leaving?" I mumble. The bathroom mirror has proven my eyes are just as glazed as hers, if not more. They lose their hunter's sharpness, but I know in my gut this night has already been sealed.

"I leave tomorrow on an early flight," she explains clumsily, her heartbeat picking up. "I should really go get some sleep while I can."

I nod knowingly, but reach out and grab her wrist before she can take a step. "Where are you staying?"

"At a motel nearby," she whispers, letting the silence grow between us as she leans her body ever so slightly toward me.

A twinkle sparkles behind my misty blue eyes. "Me too."

+++

Our bags are left carelessly near the door of her motel room as the door slams shut behind us. I let her press my body against the cool metal. I savor the way her luscious curves sink into me as she attacks my mouth. I groan into the kiss, enthused with her eager attentions, and kiss back just as zealously. It has been rough these past few weeks trying to track down the other half of the Crystal of Dan Furth, but I did it. Now our alliance with the Trinity Coven will be cemented, and our lands guaranteed protection. I deserve a reward. One night of wicked splendor spent with this little lost lamb before going home victorious to my pack.

Her nails rake a path down my chest and tug at the belt wrapped around my waist.

"Bed," she whispers hotly against my lips. I nod, driving forward until we land in a heap atop the questionable blanket. The bed lets out a long groan of protest as we work our way toward the middle.

"You. Are. Glorious." I punctuate each word with a searing kiss. She lets out a breathy laugh. "And so fucking soft." I nuzzle the warm flesh of her neck, breathing in the heavy scent of adrenaline and arousal wafting from her skin. It is more obvious to me now that I am in far worse shape than she is, as her deft fingers work magic on my body. She pulls back, out of breath and observes me through lust-filled eyes. A beat later, she reaches toward the nightstand near her head to snatch a water bottle. She downs the small amount of water left in it before tossing it to the ground with a satisfied sigh.

"You should drink more water," she tells me matter-of-factly, tossing a look to the other half-empty bottle still on the nightstand. "I don't want you losing steam halfway because you're dehy—" I roll my eyes but do as she says, seizing the bottle on my second attempt and finishing it off in messy gulps.

"Good boy," she teases before flipping me onto my back. I let out a wry laugh, pushing aside the way my head swims at the motion and placing my hands on her hips to steady myself. If she prefers to take control—scorn that ex-boyfriend of hers—so be it. The view from the bottom is one of my favorites.

233

Mary locks eyes with me and grinds her hips down. Immediately our stunted moans fill the room. She is stunning, her hair mussed and framing her face. Her lips part and eyes darken to a fever pitch. When she rolls her hips again, she lets her fingers fist into the fabric of my Henley, moaning low in her throat at the coarse friction. Then my shirt is being pulled away from my body to explore the expanse of my chest and abs. When her hands tease lower, I watch her through heavy-lidded eyes. She makes her descent slowly, caressing my neck, then chest with her soft lips.

A wave of dizziness stirs in my head at the sensation. An almost purr-like noise escapes as her teeth dare to nip at the taut muscles of my pectorals. I let my hands wander the length of her thighs. Venturing higher and higher until her secret is discovered. I let out a sound of deep longing and look at her with newfound interest.

"You are full of surprises, little lamb," I hiss, fingers meeting only warm skin. There is nothing between her and me, except my jeans. She gives a saucy smile and slaps away my hand. "Tease," I mumble, stretching my arms languidly back and allowing her to do as she pleases. She sinks lower, leaving wet, open-mouth kisses all the way down south of my navel. Nip. Kiss. A swirl of the tongue and down one inch more.

"What's the rush?" she whispers as she undoes my belt and jeans, then jerks them down. I cannot contain my animalistic growl, the wolf inside me howling in anticipation. It is unusually riled, but then again, I have not indulged in skin this sweet in weeks. We are both starved. I attempt to lean up on my elbows but find myself suddenly extremely fatigued. I needed more water.

"Water," I beg, voice hoarse as I look around the nightstand, then to her. My little vixen. She's situated comfortably between my thighs, licking her lips as she stares down my cock.

"Impressive," Mary says, tongue flicking out to trace its head and ignoring my plea. I grit my teeth and inhale deeply through my nose. Screw the water then. My hand reaches down to cup the back of her neck and guide her lips around my aching cock when the most startling sensation overcomes me. With a strangled gasp, my hips lurch upward and I enter the warmth of her mouth. She releases a moan, eyes wide and a bit unsure as they look up at me.

Fuck.

The world around me bends and snaps. It shifts. A monumental movement suddenly centers my whole being around this little slip of a thing sucking so tightly on me now. My fingers tighten and urge her forward. To take me deeper as the passion unfurls inside me like some raging bull. No prior experience can possibly compare to this moment. This revelation.

Without a doubt, hidden behind her luxurious locks is a soulmark to match my own. There is no other explanation for this sudden euphoria, and the wolf inside of me growls its sound agreement. To be sure, my fingers must lie on three lines, stacked neatly atop each other. The matching mark reminiscent of the Greek letter *xi*. She lets out another softer moan, eyes fluttering closed. And then her tongue is moving, a gentle sweeping caress along the underside of my shaft. I must taper back the vicious snarl curling at the rear of my throat as my head falls back from the pure ecstasy of her touch. She draws herself upward slowly. Her lips sealed tightly around me as she drags out the sensation. Just as her lips seek to release me, my hips chase after her of their own accord. A flex of my fingers, and she stalls to accommodate my pursuit. I bow forward, trembling to keep from thrusting too deeply and hitting the back of her throat.

"*Christ.*" A heavy pant falls from my lips as stars erupt behind closed eyes. Around me. Inside me. There is nothing but Mary and her warm embrace.

She grabs my wrist, urging my hand to release its hold. I relax my grip, fingers lingering as I pull back my hips. Her hand becomes more insistent. Then a sudden striking fear takes hold of my heart. I cannot miss what will most likely be my only opportunity to seal the soulmark. My fingers tighten for a fleeting second.

"Let it be known that thee are found," comes my ragged whisper, "and my soul awakened. The stars incline us, my love, and so we are sealed." I gasp at the sudden all-encompassing glory that hits me. Reveling in the sound of her muffled moans around my cock. The vibrations entice my hips to press onward once more in short jerking movements to fuck her mouth.

"Fucking hell," I grunt as my load spills unexpectedly inside her. She pulls away, much to my dismay, somehow finding the strength to push away my hand and remove those succulent lips.

"What the fuck," she hisses, eyes wide and fully dilated. She wipes away the vestiges of my release from her face, an angry scowl marring her beautiful features. "What the fuck was that?" Her hand races to the back of her neck as she slips off the bed. Away from me.

"I can explain," I mutter, trying and failing to roll onto my side and go after her. My limbs lack their usual strength and dexterity.

"Listen," she calls from the bathroom. "I know guys get into the whole, 'choke on this, bitch' stuff, but I need a little warning before getting into that kind of shit, okay? You can't just... do that and not fucking warn a girl. Not cool." The sink turns on full blast, and I hear rather than see her splashing water over her face.

"What's your name?" I ask, unperturbed by her anger. I'll make up for it later, but first I need to know her real name.

"Mary," she snaps, walking up to the bed with her hands on her hips. "Asshole."

"Not Mary," I correct, words slurring. "Your real name."

The smile she shares with me is tight. Her eyes sparkling vindictively down at me. A slow comprehension fills me with dread. She is most

237

certainly not as drunk as I am. I suddenly wonder if
she ever was.

"Guilty as charged," she says with a smirk. "How
are you feeling, champ?"

I swallow, my eyes narrowing even though wave
after wave of paralyzing weightlessness hits me.
"What have you done?" Comes my rasping plea.

"Don't worry, *Kyle*. This will all be over in three...
two..."

My eyes fall closed against my will as the strength
in my body leaves me completely. I succumb to
darkness. Her radiant figure a fixture in my mind's
eye as I drift away into the sea of shadows that is my
mind.

+++

Present Day

"And when I woke up, she was gone. Along with
the crystal," I tell them with a lamenting cringe,
waiting for the outburst that is sure to come. Xander
stands stock still, the little vein near his left temple
jutting out. And dear little Zoelle is both flushed and
flustered. Perhaps I went a tad too much into detail. I
shoot her a knowing smirk, and her blush deepens.

"The crystal is gone?" Xander asks once more.

I swallow, feeling the weight of disappointment
heavy in his words, and hold back another cringe.
Soon enough my feigned composure crumbles under it,
leaving a swell of regret and shame to rise as I am

forced to acknowledge my failure. To know I have let down my alpha and caused him displeasure curls my stomach. Except, I didn't just let down my alpha with my dalliance, but my pack and our allies as well. My head tips to the side with a whine as his displeasure continues to relay itself through the pack bonds.

"It's all right, Ryatt," Zoelle assures me, her hand coming to rest on my shoulder. "We'll figure something out. Right, Xander?"

There is a tense pause. I dare not look my brother in the eye, remaining in my submissive stance and exposing my neck further to appease him. Finally— finally—he lets out a long-suffering sigh and that pressure in my heart, the one cinching it shut like an iron fist, lessens and releases. Another warm hand finds my shoulder. This one larger. Stronger. Better.

"We'll figure something out, brother," he reassures me. I nod and take a deep breath. Then another.

"On the upside," I say, slipping back into a more relaxed stance, eyes lifting meekly to meet theirs. "I found my soulmark." My lips twitch upward, a feeling of unmistakable joy spiriting through me. Zoelle peeks a quick glance at her fiancé, dazzling him with a brilliant smile and burst of gleeful laughter. He melts. His shoulders fall back and eyes light up for his soulmark. The dolt.

"But you don't even know her real name," Zoelle cries in distress, effectively ruining the moment. I roll my eyes at her dramatics.

"*Au contraire*, soon-to-be-sister. I do."

Their eyebrows rise in unison. "You do?"

239

"But of course. I've been hard at work the past day or so getting my fingers into this and that. Her real name is Quinn Montgomery."

"How did you find out so fast?" Zoelle asks, her head tipping curiously to the side. Xander merely rolls his eyes.

"I have a multitude of talents," I inform her graciously, "as you well know, and one of them just so happens to be 'hacker extraordinaire.' Anything can be found on the internet these days if you know how to look."

"What else do you know?" Xander asks. The continued retreat of his hostility allows me room to breathe without that strange pressure around my heart.

"She's twenty-two."

"Young, even for you," Zoelle chimes in cheekily.

"An orphan. No family to speak of: mother dead, father out of the picture. From ages eleven to fifteen, she was in the state system until, seemingly, falling off the grid," I tell them without pause. My mind fills in the blanks I leave out. Father *never* in the picture. The mother died of an overdose only to be found by little Quinn after she returned from school one chilly autumn day. Subsequently, she was tossed from foster home to group home time after time until the therapy she found in painting and sketching just wasn't cutting it anymore. She turned to crime, using her artistic abilities to dabble in forgeries and other petty thefts until one day she found herself playing in the big leagues. Too bad she had yet to learn how to cover her tracks. It's not easy to hide from a wolf, but hiding from an Adolphus is a different matter altogether.

"Sounds like you've been busy," Xander says.

"I have."

"I assume you have a plan," he continues, the corner of his lip ticking upward as I give him a somewhat bashful smile. A chuckle escapes my lips. The one that has been fine-tuned to give my audience pause. Xander raises a brow. Zoelle sends me an unsure smile.

"I have something in mind."

Did you enjoy Coven?

If you have a moment, please leave a review for Coven. Help other paranormal romance readers find a new story and tell them what you enjoyed most about Coven!

Ready for the next installment in A Soulmark Series?

Midnight Scoundrel (Book 2) — *Out Now*
Wardens of Starlight (Book 3) — *Out Now*
Mr. Vrana (Book 4) — *Out Now*
Lycan Legacy (Book 5) — *February 21, 2019*
Lunaria (Book 6) — *TBA 2019*

Let's Connect!

Want to stay in the know on updates and bonus content?

Join Rebecca's Readers
rebeccamain.com

Like me on Facebook
https://www.facebook.com/AuthorRebeccaMain/

Follow me on Instagram
https://www.instagram.com/mrs_rebeccamain/

Follow me on Pinterest
https://www.pinterest.com/authorrebeccamain/

Acknowledgements

To my marvelous husband who has been there every step of the way—*thank you*. Your support and efforts to help me grow this series into something memorable is endlessly appreciated. I'm so excited to keep growing with you and to take this world by storm.

To all my friends and family, thank you for your support and putting up with my writerly ways.

A special thank you to Felicia, Christy, and Kim for being my beta readers!

And, of course, a special thank you to Hot Tree Edits, especially Becky, Peggy, and Kristina, for all of their help and editorial efforts, and generally whipping Coven into shape!

Made in the USA
San Bernardino, CA
26 March 2020